The New Belly Dancer
of the Galaxy

ARAB AMERICAN WRITING

THE NEW

Belly Dancer

of the Galaxy

A Novel

FRANCES KHIRALLAH NOBLE

SYRACUSE UNIVERSITY PRESS

For Ian and Maureen

First Edition 2007
08 09 10 11 12   6 5 4 3 2

Title page: zills courtesy of natashascafe.com

The paper used in this publication meets the minimum requirements
of American National Standard for Information Sciences—Permanence
of Paper for Printed Library Materials, ANSI Z39.48–1984.∞™

For a listing of books published and distributed by Syracuse University Press,
visit our Web site at SyracuseUniversityPress.syr.edu.

ISBN-13: 978-0-8156-0868-4   ISBN-10: 0-8156-0868-3

Library of Congress Cataloging-in-Publication Data

Noble, Frances Khirallah.
  The new belly dancer of the galaxy : a novel / Frances Khirallah Noble. — 1st ed.
    p. cm. — (Arab American writing)
  Includes bibliographical references and index.
  ISBN 978-0-8156-0868-4 (alk. paper)
  1. Syrian Americans—Fiction. 2. Opticians—Fiction. 3. Grandmothers—Fiction.
4. Future life—Fiction. 5. Metaphysics—Fiction. 6. Voyages and travels—Fiction.
I. Title.
PS3564.O236N49 2007
813'.54—dc22   2007022005

Manufactured in the United States of America

The New Belly Dancer
of the Galaxy

1

KAHLIL GIBRAN HOURANI was a dreamer. He'd always had the tendency, but as he approached his fifty-third birthday, he got much worse. In and out of dreams he slipped without warning to himself or others.

"Kali, Kali," his wife, Sophie, pleaded as he slumped heavily on her, his cheek pressing hers into her pillow, his generous sides wrapping over her like warm crust around a ripened fig.

"Wake up. Can you hear me, Kali? Kali?"

He wanted to please her. He tried. It was no use. She sent him to the doctor.

"No, no headaches," Kali answered. "No dizziness. No heart palpitations."

The doctor, a young man, spoke in brusque, confident tones in a single continuous phrase, neither emphasizing one word more than another nor looking into the face of his patient. He scribbled on a little square of white paper, then suspended it in midair: "Your wife says you experience this dysfunction when you're engaged in sexual relations with her. This is nothing to be ashamed of. It happens to men of your age. Here's a prescription."

"Actually," Kali said, "it happens all the time, whoever I'm with, wherever I am." He shivered, naked and exposed, beneath the paper gown with the opening in the back.

"Mr. Hourani," said the doctor a little more respectfully. "You surprise me."

"Oh, yes. It happens everywhere. And all the time. At the Oasis, when I walk in the park, when I'm at church, when I'm having lunch, when I read the paper, when I play cards, when I add sugar to my coffee, in the middle of a conversation, before I start my car, after I . . . "

The young doctor referred him to a psychiatrist, the one who was on the radio whenever someone tried to assassinate the president, the one who'd written all the self-help books and chaired the university department.

The psychiatrist began. "So, it's impotence which has driven you to such distraction?"

"No, it's Situe, my grandmother. Since she came to me in my dream and promised me the answers."

"Answers to what?"

"My questions. Why men have to die; why what you do doesn't change anything in the end; how to keep from being split apart when one foot reaches for youth and the other drags you to old age. And so on."

In their second session, the psychiatrist asked about the dream.

Kali lay on the doctor's couch, eyes closed, his hands folded loosely across his chest. His shoes, unlaced and lightly scuffed, waited close by on the floor.

"I was asleep at home in my bed with my wife when this giant white bird, an eagle with piercing eyes, come down through the ceiling and landed right over me. The eagle's feathers were only a few inches above my nose. 'Do you want to see Situe again?' it asked. 'How is that possible?' I said. 'She died when I was a little boy.' And the eagle said, 'Everything's possible. If you want to see her, come with me.' It started to flap its wings and rise into the air.

It made so much wind the curtains snapped like sails on a ship and some pictures flew off the wall. My wife was snoring gently and wasn't aware of what was going on. I looked at her with tears in my eyes, whispered good-bye, then stood on the bed so I could reach the eagle's talons. And when I grabbed them I saw that my hands had become small and plump again, and dimpled below the knuckles. Like they were when I was a little boy. 'Where are we going?' I asked. 'Why, heaven, of course,' the bird answered in Arabic. "Hold tight."

"This eagle spoke in Arabic?" asked the psychiatrist. "Did you think that was unusual?"

"Not any more unusual than appearing in our bedroom in the first place," Kali sighed and continued.

"We flew through the roof and up into the sky. We flew for a long time. Going higher and higher. All of a sudden, there was Situe sitting on a stool on a cloud. She looked peaceful and calm like all this was routine. Like she'd been expecting me, the way she did on Friday nights when she sat on her front porch and waited for us all to come to visit her."

"'Situe-bitue,'" I called out. I was crying."

"'What brings you here, Kali?' she asked."

"'I can't figure things out anymore. I'm like a fish out of water. I . . .'"

"'Or a goat without a pasture,' she offered."

"'Well, I wouldn't have used that exact phrase,' I said."

"'Why not? It's a nice metaphor.'"

"'How do you know about metaphors? You can't read or write.'"

"'You forget I'm in heaven now. I can do a lot of things I couldn't do before. Now, you were saying?'"

"'I hoped you could answer a few questions.'"

"'Of course. In English? Arabic? French?'"

"'English. I don't speak French and I understand only a little Arabic.'"

"'Pity,' Situe said."

"But before I could ask my questions in any language, I was startled out of my sleep by a terrible noise. It nearly knocked me out of bed. My heart was pounding. I could hardly remember where I was. It was the gardener starting his blower below our bedroom window. And Situe was gone. Since then I've been a tortured person, a man without direction, crippled in my search for truth."

For no matter how hard Kali had tried to retrieve the eagle, he couldn't. No matter how hard he tried again to dream of Situe, he couldn't. He read *How to Control the Content of Your Dreams Through the Power of Suggestion* and, following its direction, hid old photographs of Situe underneath his pillow. He performed relaxing exercises while lying in bed so that the tensions of the day wouldn't block the flow of his dreams at night, starting at the bottom and working his way up, first relaxing his toes, then moving to his feet, his ankles, his calves and so on, but always he fell asleep about the time he reached his hipbone. He asked an old woman at church, known for her insight, to read his future in the coffee grounds, so desperate had he become for relief, but she told him what he already suspected—that he was healthy in body, though not in spirit—and under her breath she dismissed him as foolish and ungrateful. He would have prayed, but he wasn't sure God would approve of what he was asking. Not that he was sure he actually believed in God anymore, Situe's residence in heaven, notwithstanding.

Kali approached despair. He felt like a man with the weight of the world on his shoulders. He became out of sorts, moody. He kept to himself. He could barely tolerate being in his own store. Often, he stood out front on the sidewalk between the parking meters as the cars came and went and people disembarked and returned. Only when a customer came, and sometimes when the phone rang, did he go inside.

"You're there?"

"Of course."

"You going to your meeting tonight, Kali?"

"I'm going to the meeting."

"Directly from the store?"

"Directly."

"Your voice sounds funny. Did you have one of your spells?"

"I wouldn't call them 'spells,' Sophie. I'm thinking."

Neither spoke for a few seconds. It sounded as though Sophie covered the phone at her end. When she spoke again, Kali could hear the interweaving of her sisters' voices in the background. He suspected they were discussing him, commiserating with Sophie over what he had become.

"Try to act normal tonight, will you, Kali?"

With other women, he had more success. They relied on him to gauge the distance between their irises with his mother of pearl measuring stick pressing confidently, yet gently, against the bridges of their noses. They loved the way he warmed the arms of the frames so they'd fit into the indented spaces just behind their ears.

"He reminds me of Omar Sharif, only a little . . . heavier," a customer would tell her friends. Or, "He looks like Rossano Brazzi in that old movie where he tried to steal the Englishman's wife but her children ruined everything and she went back to her husband."

And to them Kali said things like, "The eyes are the windows to the soul." Rapturous words, poetic words. Which, before the dream, he believed.

A woman entered the store.

"You're open?"

"For you . . . of course." Although he'd hoped to close the shop early, hoped for a spare half-hour before his meeting to think quietly about Situe, the dream, everything.

The woman stood before a cabinet examining its contents. Picked up empty frames from the counter and tried them on without looking in any of the mirrors that regularly dotted the surfaces of the store. Kali followed her in his practiced professional manner—discreetly behind, just enough distance between them—ready to assist, to accommodate, to guide. Close enough to notice her tantalizing scent. Close enough to be unable to ignore it. It drew him in at the same time it let him go. It seemed to fill up the room. Pungent. Musky. Distracting. He felt a trifle light-headed.

"Let me slip in some tinted lenses to give you an idea of how they look."

For the first time, she smiled. "It's ginger and citrus," she offered. "I mix it myself."

"Ah," was all he could think of to say.

She handed him her prescription.

"One nearsighted and one farsighted," Kali said simply.

"Yes," she responded and he thought she sounded sad.

"It's nothing to worry about, you know."

"And an astigmatism in the left." There was no doubting it; she suppressed a little sigh as she described her malformed cornea.

"Still nothing to worry about," Kali said. "A small challenge, at best."

From the tall locked cabinet, which contained his most exquisite merchandise, Kali withdrew three frames and laid them arms down in front of her. Tortoise shell, amber, forest green.

"While the elegance of the frame does not actually affect the quality of the lens," Kali said softly, "there is no reason why both shouldn't be perfect."

Kali sat on one side of the counter and motioned her to sit on the elevated velvet stool on the other side. He moved his face closer to hers. He studied the relationship between her eyes and eyebrows. And noticed the proportion of her cheekbones to her cheeks. And the curve of her ears, medium-sized and flat against her head. When he leaned over to finalize his measurements, each could feel the other's breath.

She chose four pairs of glasses. Including two for reading since she always lost them, she said, and one for distance inside and one for distance outside with lenses in the new, dark shade Kali recommended.

"And perhaps next time you'll consider bifocals," he said.

He set the frames in a box.

"Now, all I need are your name, address, and phone number."

Her name was Jane Plain.

"Really?"

"Really."

"What were your parents thinking of?"

"Who can say?"

"Not that it isn't a fine name."

"A fine name."

"Well," Kali said with reestablished conviction, "I shall refrain from making the obvious comment. You must hear it all the time."

"Yes, I do," she conceded. "You can understand why I chose a different name for my work."

"Your work?"

"Entertainment, in a way."

"Are you an actress?"

"A dancer, an actress. Lots of things." She lifted herself from the stool. "I'll need them right away."

The New Belly Dancer of the Galaxy | 7

Kali scribbled "Rush" over the order and handed her a copy.

"Miss Plain, these will be ready in four business days. I'll call you when they're in."

He resolutely refused identification when she paid with an out-of-town check.

2

THE HASHANIAN MUTUAL AID SOCIETY, Southern California chapter, established in 1927, named after the Great Hashani River, which meandered through the old country valley where its original members, including Kali's forebears, had been born, gathered for its monthly meeting in the parish hall of Saints Peter and Paul Syrian Orthodox Church.

Its purpose was threefold: to provide fellowship for male Hashanians of the Orthodox faith; to assist needy Orthodox Hashanians wherever located; and to provide a common burial ground for them (and their families) after they died. Which most Hashanians had already done.

Which is why Father Gregory announced the membership drive from the pulpit at matins every Sunday for a month; why Sophie made Kali join; and why he now sat on a metal folding chair with the other thirteen members, the youngest of whom was twenty years older than he. The only new recruit, he'd been elected to the double position of recording/corresponding secretary, on the assumption that since he was an optician, his eyes were probably the best in the group.

"Kali?" asked President Joseph Saleeby.

"Yes?"

"Are you ready with your report?"

"Yes, yes, of course."

Kali withdrew a folded piece of paper from his pocket—the minutes of the last meeting—and read them in a clear, smooth voice: "And further thanks to Kenny Buttras for providing the styrofoam cups; to Isaac Malouf, who generously brings sugar and milk and artificial cream from his store; to Nick Feres for setting up the chairs even though he has back trouble; and to George Habib for taking them down."

At this point, distracted by a movement in the back of the room, Kali looked up from the text of his speech. And stopped cold. For there in the corner by the window sitting on her stool was Situe, smoking one of her beloved Duke cigarettes.

"Oh, my God, my God. You're back."

The sleeves of Situe's sweater were pushed up to her elbows and her stockings were rolled up to just below her swollen knees. Her short white hair pinned back with combs showed streaks of yellow. Smoke emerged from her mouth in long, strong exhales.

"Please, please, don't leave again until I have a chance to talk to you. Please, please stay."

The members of the society were confused by Kali's words. They strained to understand what he was saying and to whom he was saying it. They waited for him to let them in on the joke. But Kali just stared and spoke in the direction of the corner near the window.

Finally, Isaac Malouf, who had been a friend of Kali's father, asked Kali whether something was the matter; when Kali didn't respond, he stood and said, "Let's take our smoking break now and give Kali a chance to collect his thoughts, God bless him."

Barely aware that they were leaving, Kali made his way to Situe, who had lit a second cigarette and, with obvious pleasure, blew large, loose smoke rings into the air.

"I'm so glad to see you, Situe-bitue. I've been desperate to talk to you." And he lifted the hand without the cigarette and kissed it gently and deferentially. "But you'll get in trouble if you smoke in here. New rule."

"Don't worry about the cigarettes, Kali. They're made in heaven. No ashes, no cough. And only you can see the smoke. Now," she settled into her seat, "what seems to be the problem?"

When Kali returned home after the meeting, he found Sophie upstairs in bed asleep. "Sophie," he patted her shoulder gently, "Sophie."

"What time is it?" she asked.

"Not late."

She turned toward him. "I wish you wouldn't wake me up like this."

"I'm sorry, my dear."

"So, did you have a good turnout?"

"The usual."

"Too bad."

She lay back on her pillow and closed her eyes, pulled the sheet up to her chin. When they were very young, they'd slept naked together. But then Layla learned to climb out of her crib, and she'd come into their room and stand silently next to them, until one of them woke up. Once Layla told her mother, "You forgot your nightgown," and after that they decided to cover up. Now they wore the pajamas that each had given to the other, though Layla and Michel had been out of the house for years.

"Sophie, something wonderful happened tonight."

"What? Joseph Saleeby didn't talk too much?"

"No. Something more important than that."

"Just tell me, so I can go back to sleep."

"Situe came back."

"Oh my God, Kali, no. No more of this."

"Don't you want to hear what Situe said?"

Sophie placed her arm over her face and moaned and turned away from her husband's voice.

"She told me I could have three questions. My first question was, what is the nature of the universe? She said that was one of the ultimate questions. That I should start with something more modest. Also, it wasn't very original. She said that I needed to think more carefully about what I wanted to ask. So we left it that I'm going to work on my questions. Until next time."

"Kali, listen to me. When do you see the doctor again?"

"I'm not going back. He doesn't understand what I'm talking about. Besides, I won't have time. I have to think about my questions. I'll only have a few opportunities to ask them and I can't waste them. They have to be exactly right."

3

"L-E-N-S-E-S!"

Kali, in the backroom, setting aside bills for his bookkeeper to pay the next day, heard the call and emerged in time to see the driver, familiar in brown shorts and brown truck, start his motor and drive off.

A small firmly wrapped package rested on the counter.

Lenses for eleven pairs of glasses, though Kali saw only four: two sets for reading and two sets for distance—one of which was clear, one of which was tinted to protect her eyes (blue, with specks of yellow) from the sun.

He reached for the phone and dialed a number. And received a recorded message, marred by poor reception. He dialed again. Same message, same static. Throughout the day he phoned: in between customers, before and after lunch, and when it otherwise occurred to him. Never actually speaking into the phone; always hanging up at the sound of the beep. It was the first time in weeks that he worked a full day in the store.

At six o'clock he dialed again and spoke. "Miss Plain, your glasses are ready. I assume this is Miss Plain's voice mail, since this is the number Miss Plain gave me and I have dialed it exactly. Actually, I have dialed it a number of times today without leaving any message, hoping to speak to her—you—in person. I hope the

13

hangup calls haven't upset you. There's nothing to worry about; it was only me. Well, thank you. Please contact me so that you can pick up your glasses."

As soon as he hung up, he dialed again. "Did I remember to say that this is Kahlil Gibran Hourani at the Oasis? Although who else would be calling you about your glasses. Well . . . please call."

But she did not call the next day or the next. The box containing her glasses sank, like lead, into the top of the display counter. Their weight was tipping the store. Soon the floor would be at a steep angle and all the cabinets and fixtures and inventory, the velvet stool, and the one potted plant, would slide to one side of the room, pile up, break, spill. There would be a terrible mess.

Kali decided to take matters into his own hands. He wrapped each pair of Miss Plain's new glasses in a tiny tan chamois that bore the words "The Oasis" in the bottom left corner next to his palm tree logo. Enclosed each new pair in the finest cases he had and placed them securely back in the box. He convinced himself that getting these glasses into Miss Plain's immediate possession was a serious medical issue. That, through personal delivery, he was upholding some form of Optometric Hippocratic Oath. He would drive to the address on Miss Plain's invoice; he would put the glasses in her hands and her hands only.

But the distance! It hadn't registered before. He consulted his map book, located the unfamiliar zip code, tracing with his finger the thick, black freeway lines to the suburb where she lived. He wondered why she came to him, to his store, how she found him among all the other opticians in the vastness between them. She may as well live in another world. For the first time in his recent memory he got into his car with a sense of adventure and drove off.

His timing couldn't have been worse. The crush of rush-hour traffic going north; the crawl through the pass; jammed, construction-torn lanes to the far reaches of the valley; an off-ramp he'd never used before, whose name he'd heard only in traffic alerts on the radio.

He passed the time in the car by practicing what he would say as he handed her glasses to her. Bringing his usual professionalism into play—even in this unfamiliar circumstance—he would offer to stay awhile to make sure they fit well and were comfortable and that the lenses improved her vision to the point that her prescription promised. It was no trouble at all, he would insist, and he'd brought his tools with him. (At this point in the conversation, he would hold out the tiny leather case that held the tiny stainless steel implements and its assortment of tiny screws.) His primary concern, he would repeat if necessary, was how well she saw. In spite of the drive and the obscene gestures directed toward him whenever he tried to change lanes, Kali was in a very good, very mellow mood by the time he got off the freeway.

It was dark when he stopped at the side of the road. He took the flashlight from the glove compartment and guided the glow to the street index, which directed him to the numbered and lettered coordinates on the page that depicted the exact point he desired. A few more miles, it said, a few more twists and turns, and he'd be there.

As he got closer to Miss Plain's address, he rehearsed again what he'd say when he saw her. She'd probably be surprised—amazed was more like it—when he handed her the glasses. Would she be pleased as well?

He was startled when he actually found her street. Then dismayed that it had no streetlights, no numbers on the curbs. He barely noticed a woman struggling to push a stroller packed with flattened cardboard boxes over the sidewalk. He drove slowly as near to the curb as the trashcans would allow until he found Miss Plain's address. There was no place to park on her block, so he turned the corner and pulled into the only empty space he could find, at a red curb in front of a fire hydrant. And had second thoughts.

What if the police came by and gave him a ticket? Or had him towed? What if there was a fire and the fire truck couldn't hook up to the hydrant and the building—empty, God willing—burned to the ground?

"Medical delivery! Urgent!" he quickly wrote on the piece of paper, which he crammed under his windshield wiper. Then he smoothed his clothes, and wiped his face with his handkerchief, and smelled his breath with his hand in front of his mouth. The box with Miss Plain's eyeglasses he'd taped up and tied with a brown ribbon and now carried under his arm. Leaving one hand for the flashlight and the other hand free—just in case.Kali determined that Miss Plain lived in one of two L-shaped apartment buildings bearing the same number. The buildings, mirror images of each other, shared a courtyard with a few struggling bushes and a rusted tricycle lying on its side. In the air: leftover dinner smells, at least one argument, a shard of loud music, a barking dog.

There was no directory. He went up the stairs of one building, came to a door that said "Manager," and pushed a doorbell button, which didn't ring. He knocked.

"Who the hell is it and what the hell do you want?"

"I'm an optician and I've come to deliver some glasses," Kali called through the closed door in his most dignified voice.

"I didn't order any glasses," the man said as he opened the door and stood there belligerently, solidly.

"Not for you. For one of your tenants. Miss Jane Plain. My name is Kahlil Gibran Hourani."

"What the hell kind of name is that?"

"Good question. One wonders what her parents had in mind."

"No, yours."

"Ah, yes. Well, it's not original. My mother named me after our most famous poet." When the man looked emptily at him, he continued: "Kahlil Gibran, the famous Lebanese American poet."

"You from Lebanon?"

"No, no."

"Then why'd you say you were?"

The man shifted his weight to his other side, still filling his doorway. "For all I know you could be a terrorist."

"I'm not a terrorist. I'm an optician. Here, look."

Kali removed the wrappings from the box, inadvertently tearing one of its corners, and held it out for the man to examine, silently reminding himself to rearrange the glasses and the package before he handed them to Miss Plain.

"See? Glasses."

The manager stared into one of the open cases.

Kali explained: "Two pairs for reading. One pair for distance inside, untinted; one pair for distance outside. Tinted. For Jane Plain."

"Not here," the manager gestured, turning his back, closing his door. "Over there."

Kali went to the second building. Moving quickly through the courtyard with his flashlight on, adjusting the lens so that it cast a wide, diffuse light that clearly marked his location. Removing, he hoped, any potential fears that he was a prowler or burglar. Letting everyone know that he was there with nothing to hide and no bad intentions. The unwrapped box with the eyeglasses he held firmly under his arm.

Down the ground floor corridor he went, checking the doors for names, at each threshold discovering that he was at least a door away from Miss Plain. What kept his spirits up in the dingy darkness was the thought of how attractive she'd look in her new sunglasses, in all her glasses. He could barely wait to slip them on.

When he didn't find Miss Plain on the first floor, he went upstairs to the second, stepping carefully over the irregular surfaces, dodging patio chairs and small barbecues, children's toys, and items he couldn't identify. Closer to sounds he didn't want to hear; closer to sights he'd rather not see. And surprised that a woman like Miss Plain lived in such a place.

Nevertheless, he listened for her voice as he walked. Would his first awareness of her presence be her voice? Or perhaps he'd track her by the scent of her special perfume. Just when he thought he sensed a whiff of it, just when he breathed deeply to inhale more, the toe of his left shoe caught in a hole in a stretch of green indoor/outdoor carpeting.

It was a swift, hard fall. A fall that seemed to incorporate the weight of his entire day, his entire week, his entire month. A fall that conspired with the force of gravity to inflict as much dull, deep pain as possible. A fall that he stopped with his right knee.

But he dropped neither the eyeglasses nor his flashlight. Instead, he stayed there on that knee. And willed the tears in his eyes to go back to where they came from. When his knee turned numb and the pain stopped, Kali stood, unsteady, but not forlorn. And within seconds, recast himself in his own mind as one of the Knights of the Roundtable: injured, but undeterred. Or as Odysseus, overcoming obstacles in pursuit of his quest. It wasn't necessary for him to get as far as the labors of Hercules.

For there, in front of him, was the reward for his efforts, the salve for his pain. A door with the name and number he had come for: Jane Plain, Apartment 11B.

And tacked on its cracked and flaking surface, a handwritten note:

Gone to

THE NEW BELLY DANCER OF THE GALAXY CONTEST !!!!!

In Santa Vista, Palace of Fine Arts in case anybody needs to get in touch with me

Wish me luck!!!!!

  J. P.

P.S. On the off chance that someone from the Oasis reads this, please send me my glasses.

P.P.S. Also, you can redeposit the check. It should be fine now.

4

"ALL RIGHT, FIRST QUESTION."

"What is the meaning of life?" Kali whispered. Whispered because Situe had insisted on meeting him on the front porch of her first house in East Los Angeles, a white frame cottage barely recognizable now to Kali who, as a small boy, had visited his grandparents there, climbed the fig tree in back, dared to cross the dirt alley and wander down the old sidewalks. The fig tree was gone; the alley, asphalt; the house had succumbed to texture coat. There was a family inside speaking neither Arabic nor English, nor the Italian or Yiddish of earlier decades.

"The answer to that question is beyond me, Kali. Only God himself can explain the meaning of life in any kind of comprehensive fashion. Next question."

"Then there really is a God?"

"That's another question I can't answer."

"Ah, Situe-bitue, what kind of question will you answer? Can you read the future?"

"You mean if you ask me how things will turn out for you, am I able to tell you? I have resources."

"So you can read the future?"

"You have the most simplistic way of saying things, Kali."

"I'm just trying to ask my questions in the . . . best way."

"Just ask them, silly boy, and if I have an answer, I have an answer."

A shadow appeared behind the curtain, a face at the uncovered window.

"I think we'd better keep our voices down," said Kali.

"Nobody can hear me but you, remember? It's your voice that needs keeping down."

"Yes, yes, of course. I'm sorry."

"Well?"

"I'm afraid I'll waste my questions by asking ones you can't answer. Or won't answer. How do I know you'll try to find something out for me just because I ask it?"

"You'll have to trust me, Kali. I am your Situe, you know."

"Well, I remember my mother saying—"

"Ah, yes, her."

"—that Jidue spoiled you—"

"He was a good man."

"—and that you only did what you felt like doing—"

"I did what I did."

"—and that you never let her relax in your house and sometimes you made her cry."

"I didn't realize I was so powerful."

"Now I've offended you and you won't tell me a thing. You'll just disappear again."

"Just settle down and ask a question."

For a few minutes, Kali was quiet, while from inside the small house came sounds of a television, a conversation, a screen door opening and closing.

"All right, Situe, I have one."

"Eh?"

"It's this: how old will I be when I die?"

"Kali, Kali, show some imagination. You ask only the trivial or the impossible."

"But surely when I'm going to die isn't trivial?"

"I don't see how the information is useful. It only satisfies your idle curiosity. What good would it do you to know that you were going to die in twenty minutes—?

"—Oh, no, so soon, oh God, oh God—"

"—or twenty years? Don't you see that the length of a life is only one of its many attributes? Length, depth, happiness, sadness—it's the totality that makes a life. A life is as long as it is. Try again."

"All right," Kali answered. He felt as if he were stumbling blindfolded over an unfamiliar field, each ditch and hole and ridge a frightening surprise. He hesitated before risking another question. "What's heaven like?" he asked, barely daring to look at his grandmother as he spoke.

"It's like every other place. Once you've seen it, it doesn't seem mysterious. Once you're there, you wonder what all the fuss was about."

"The grass is always greener?" Kali asked.

"Exactly."

"Are you going to count that exchange as a question and answer?"

"No. Just background information."

"Thank you."

"You're welcome."

Somewhere down the block a dog howled not in misery but in warning and another dog took up the message and within seconds, Kali heard a siren snaking through the distant neighborhood.

"Don't worry, it's nothing, a false alarm," Situe said. Kali decided not to ask her how she knew and, instead, asked a question he'd been longing to ask all evening. He tried to phrase the question in a way that wouldn't annoy her.

"How does heaven compare with . . . the other place?"

"I know nothing about other places. Only the here and now. I've always been that way."

"But when you say 'here and now' you suggest that you're existing in time and not in eternity. Is there a difference?"

"Are you sure you want to waste one of your questions on the difference, if any, between the finite and the infinite?"

"But my question—"

"—is a futile one. One last chance tonight, Kali, before I have to leave this old porch. Push yourself, expand your horizons."

"How do you expect me to know what to ask? I can barely figure out what's going on around me. I can't judge anymore. What's right? What's wrong? What's good? What isn't? I face the last third of my life and I don't know what to do with myself. Every day I ask, how should I be living now? What should I do with the end in sight? Can I come to terms with it?"

After a long hesitation, during which Kali wondered if he'd failed again, Situe said, "Finally. Questions worthy of answers. Questions worthy of being asked. I was beginning to worry about you. Sit. I'm going to tell you a story."

Doing as he was told, as he'd been told a hundred times before by Situe when he was a little boy, Kali arranged himself to listen. He stretched his legs out straight on one of the porch's wide wooden stairs and leaned back against the wooden column whose acanthus-leaf crown provided a suitably dignified setting for Situe's words. Kali folded his hands in his lap. Situe withdrew a small white china pipe from a pocket in her apron, lit it, puffed silently for a few seconds, and closed her eyes.

Not this century, nor the last one, but in the final decade of the one before, in a small, poor village in the old country, there lived a man named Bashara Ibrahim Bashara.

"Your brother?"

"Shhhh!" Situe said sharply, though her eyes remained closed and her body, still.

Bashara longed to go to America. He thought of nothing else. He'd heard the streets were paved with gold and he wanted to try to make his fortune. But his father, Tofa, and his mother, Tasheeda, didn't want him to go. They were afraid they'd never see him again, or he'd forget them, or something terrible would happen to all of them in his absence. And that they would have to rely on their only other child, a daughter, to take care of them in their old age.

But they were poor, and his urgent promises to send money home, overcame their resistance. He promised not only to help his family, but also his village. He said he'd send money to build a school and a hospital and to install electricity.

As God was his witness, Bashara said, he'd send enough money to wire the whole countryside so that when he returned, it would be to a paradise of blazing light, where people could play backgammon after dark without eyestrain. The sky over their village would be so bright, Bashara said, it would guide lost travelers to safety. It would blot out the stars. Although this last promise was discounted by those at the going away party since it came at the end of the event, when Bashara was so ebullient that he danced the dubke at the beginning of the line and then at the end, his handkerchief spinning above his head, then his prayer beads, then his shirt, before dropping to the floor where he undulated to the music while lying on his back, half-naked.

As his father tried to erase his guilt for wishing he were going to the New World instead of his son and his mother accepted the loss that lay before her. His sister? She set aside her sorrow, for she believed in him.

"Situe, you were the sister, weren't you?" Kali asked quietly. Situe said nothing, but went on with the story.

Yes, his sister believed in him, for Bashara had already done the impossible. He'd learned to read from Father Nicholas; he was on his way to America.

Although it was to Australia, and not America, that he went. Because some sailors he met in a tavern told him that Australia, even more than America, was a land of opportunity where precious stones begged to be plucked from the ground. And because he could save on his passage if he worked on board ship. An important consideration, since all he had in the world was contained in a small leather pouch hanging inside his pantaloons from a rope around his waist.

His family's fortune.

"Then our family was rich in the old country?"

Situe opened her eyes to answer. "Every family had something it considered its fortune, if only an embroidered bedspread or a thriving olive tree. Or a pair of healthy sons." A memory crossed Situe's face like a shadow. "The same value was not always attached to a daughter," she said, "no matter how healthy." She continued.

This pouch contained the only real wealth Tofa and Tasheeda had. They kept it in a chest next to their bed. A beautiful chest. Inlaid with cedar and mother of pearl. It had been Tasheeda's mother's and was given to Tasheeda as a wedding present. It was to go to her daughter on the day of her wedding.

Tofa and Tasheeda had agreed that the chest was never to be opened except to add to its contents. Not when their daughter broke her ankle; not when the olive oil business slowed or one of their lambs escaped and was crushed by a runaway cart. Not even when Bashara planned to leave for the New World. Although Bashara had asked.

"No," Tofa said.

"No," Tasheeda said.

The treasure was their insurance, their promise to God that though they knew He would take care of them, they would do their part to provide for themselves and their family.

Bashara left and sadness filled the house. Tofa, counting his remaining blessings as Father Nicholas instructed, went to the chest to help fill the hole in his heart.

He lifted the lid, expecting to see the small leather pouch nestled safely at the bottom. But the chest was empty except for a note which he could not read. He took the note to the priest.

"Please have faith and forgive me. I will return this with interest beyond your wildest expectations."
Your loyal son,
Bashara

Tofa could not tell his wife. Alone and without comfort, he slipped into despair and illness. Despite Father Nicholas' assurances, he assumed his son's sin as his own. And it festered inside him like a poison. How had this curse come upon him and his family? Why did God punish him so?

Tofa became weaker and sicker, clinging to the shrinking possibility that Bashara would return the treasure before Tasheeda discovered it, before he died of his growing shame. Soon Tofa lay in bed all day and night. Felled, Tasheeda believed, by separation from his only son—a father diminished in body and spirit as he sent parts of himself by prayer over the seas to the New World. Father Nicholas told Tasheeda to prepare for the worst.

After a week's vigil by Tofa's side, Tasheeda reluctantly sought guidance from the husband on whom she had always relied. "Forgive me for asking in your hour of suffering, my love, but what shall I do? How shall we live?"

In his fevered agony, he looked toward the chest. Thinking he wanted her to open it, she removed the oil lamp from its textured surface. She was filled with dread. She expected Tofa to tell her that he was going to die soon, and that this was just the catastrophe for which they had saved the treasure in the pouch.

Tasheeda waited patiently for her husband to tell her to lift the lid, having never opened the chest without his permission. But Tofa merely looked at it and turned his head away, crying out and wailing. He knew he was approaching death and he wanted to tell his wife what to do, how to get along without him. He wished he didn't have to tell her what their son had done, but the time for lies was over. He must tell her the truth. He must say that only God could provide for her now.

All these thoughts struggled to find expression in his fevered voice, as he descended deeper into delirium. He couldn't remember how to get the words out. He couldn't breathe through his overheated lungs. In a last final effort, he faced the chest once again and the anguish which crossed over his face was so horrible for his wife to see that she decided to open it to show him that he needn't worry so much, they'd make out, they'd survive. Slowly, she lifted the top of the chest.

"See, my love, see," she said forcing a smile. "Look here, inside. See our security; see how well you have taken care of us." As she looked inside the chest and saw only bare, polished wood.

"It's empty! Tofa! My God! It's empty! Where are they? Where are the stones? Please, Tofa, where is the treasure?" she asked, pleading, as the double gloom of widowhood and poverty descended on her. She searched his face for an answer. "Please, my love, try to tell me. Where is our fortune?"

Tofa, distracted by a vision of his final passage between this world and the next, could not answer her.

Tasheeda did her best. She worked the olive press with her daughter's help, harvested her vegetables, tended her small and varied flock. Still, the contented resolve that had been Tasheeda's best trait dissolved into resentment and bewilderment. Which rained on her daughter no matter how she tried to take cover. Tasheeda's bitterness was as deep as the sea and, but for the occasional overflowing in her daughter's direction, she herself would have drowned. Her future was clear: work to survive until she did not survive. Her daughter's future was less clear.

Father Nicholas watched over the daughter, seeking to prevent her irretrievable loss. He arranged for the daughter to go to the New World herself, to New York City, to work for a family from Beirut which had gone a generation before and had great success. The hours were long and the work was hard. After her daughter left, Tasheeda contracted a terrible fever and died.

Meanwhile, Bashara became rich. Very rich. As he promised, he sent money back to his village. He paid for electricity. He built a new church. He erected a small medical clinic and paid city doctors to travel there once a month. Because of him, the people of his village had better lives.

"But his fortune was based on a crime!" Kali exclaimed.

"He helped the people in his village."

"But his mother and father died of broken hearts."

"They would have died anyway; does it matter why?"

"His sister endured the bitterness of her mother and worked like a slave."

"His sister would never have gotten to the New World if Bashara hadn't stolen the fortune."

Kali started to respond, but Situe continued without letting him speak.

"Because of Bashara, your grandfather had the means to start the store."

"My father's store?"

"The one that supported all of us."

"Are you saying that nothing is clearly good or clearly bad? That there is no line between good and evil?"

"It's more complicated than you think."

"I still hold him in contempt."

"It was Bashara's money that allowed your grandfather to start the Hashanian Mutual Aid Society, of which you are now, incidentally, corresponding and recording secretary."

"Where is Bashara now?"

"I saw him recently out of the corner of my eye roaming around with some of the others."

"In heaven?"

"So it seems."

"What did you do when you saw him?"

"I vowed that I'd stab him in the heart with our father's dagger if I ever saw him again." Situe stood up and lifted her stool with her strong right hand and began to fade away.

"But I didn't, of course."

"Wait! You'll come back, won't you, Situe?" Kali asked. "I wanted to ask you about one more thing, a new customer I have at the store . . . "

"You've let the genie out of the bottle, Kali. You can't get rid of me now."

After Situe had fully disappeared, Kali tiptoed down the porch steps, down the cement path to the sidewalk, and walked unevenly to his car half a block away. His back was stiff; one of his legs had fallen asleep. The knee in his other leg ached slightly.

It was three o'clock in the morning. He wondered how he'd explain to Sophie where he'd been and what he was doing. Instead of the freeway, he drove down surface streets, usually the only car in sight. The ride home took longer this way, but he needed time to think. He tried to remember every word Situe had said. On one corner against a building, a small fire burned in a garbage can, shielding those around it from the early morning cold.

 **5**

IT WASN'T THAT SOPHIE had always been disenchanted with Kali. Nor in the beginning had Kali sighed deeply whenever Sophie entered his thoughts.

They met at Saints Peter and Paul, the orthodox cathedral that drew Syrians from miles around: Kali and Sophie, growing up on Sunday mornings, bumping into each other on the steps. Part of the tapestry of three generations, sometimes four, sitting together in the pews, even the men doting on the babies, while Byzantine faces gazed down from the walls through a distance of two thousand years.

From the beginning, there was a thinness about Sophie, an angularity. But rounder and fuller wouldn't have made a difference then, for Kali wasn't susceptible. Another girl, not Arab, a girl who glided over campus as though airborne, a girl so free she seemed to skim over the obstacles of daily life, had said to him, "Come with us this summer."

"Me?" Kali responded.

"Of course, you."

"Where?"

"Wherever we end up."

He longed to. He was so full of longing there was no room for air. He tried to imagine what it would be like. He suspected she inhabited a world beyond his current understanding.

Much later when he encountered Sophie on a sidewalk outside a movie theater, she was in the company of her three sisters. At first, Kali couldn't tell which of them she was. When he figured it out, he asked her for coffee and when he went to her house to pick her up and entered her living room and met her parents and greeted four girls who still looked alike to him, he told the wrong girl how pleased he was to see her. Which he partially made up for over time with the sweetness of his nature and his way with words.

Kali and Sophie married. Kali embraced opticianry. They had two children. They bought a house. Their children saw grandparents and great-grandparents nearly as often as they saw their teachers. Usually they went to church. Though, secretly, silently, Kali didn't believe.

After a few years, in spite of reasonably good intentions, Kali and Sophie had worn each other down to about the same degree, so that the score was nearly even, though their methods were different: his—an immersion in unsolvable cosmic problems versus hers—a focus on inner pains partly induced by her failure to capture her husband's attention.

"Kali, not another word about how to survive if you're the last man on earth. Or whether California's going to fall into the ocean. Or whether you should know everything about one thing or a little about a lot of things. . . . You're giving me a headache!"

Or a crick in the neck. Or an upset stomach. For a small persistent ache moved cunningly among her body parts according to some whim of its own, causing little torments, minor plagues. Prompting visits to an assortment of specialists. Thus, if the ache settled in her right big toe for a few days, Sophie visited the foot doctor. If it took up lodgings in her left elbow, she returned to the orthopedic group for the elbow specialist, where she would say hello to the foot doctor as she passed him in the narrow hallway. If the ailment erupted in a rash on her stomach, she made multiple calls: to her gynecologist, her internist, her dermatologist.

On a very, very bad day, Sophie stayed in bed. Though this was rare, for despite her pains, she was a person of regular habits. A very bad day could be brought on by memories of the birth of their first child, their daughter Layla, after—her sisters more than agreed—a difficult pregnancy marked by swoons at the sight of ground lamb and ankles blown up like balloons.

There she was in the delivery room with Kali, her husband and the father of the soon-to-be born baby. While she pushed and pushed until her vision blurred and she thought the blood vessels in her eyes would burst, he spoke ecstatically of the wonders of evolutionary biology. While her insides felt like they were tearing out, he rhapsodized over the prolonged care of offspring, the development of language, natural immunities, and the social organization of primitive man: thrilling over the ability of the human species to reproduce and survive.

Until faced with the emergence of the bloody crown of a specific member of that species, his own daughter, whereupon he crashed to the floor in a dead faint, taking with him the monitors to which Sophie was connected (for it was a high risk birth), the mirror in which she should have seen her moment of triumph, and the small nurse who tried to hold him up.

They stood in the kitchen in the early evening, Sophie thinking of what to serve for dinner; Kali, of what he intended to do.

"Sophie?"

"What?"

"You sound angry before you even know what I'm going to say."

"Tell me, then. I'm listening."

"I need to go out of town on business for a few days."

She didn't respond and for an instant he faltered. He had never before used the phrase "out of town on business" to refer to himself. It didn't quite fit. It sounded false. He wondered if she could tell that he was lying.

"To an opticianry conference," he continued with forced energy. "For opticians, of course."

"I don't understand."

"So I can develop more business."

"You always seem to do well enough with your customers."

"Why, thank you, Sophie. I didn't know you'd given the matter any thought." He felt the blood rush to various parts of his body in response to this unexpected compliment.

Sophie closed the refrigerator door without taking out the left-over *dolmas* she'd decided to serve for dinner.

"Kali," she began deliberately, "has something happened?"

"No, Sophie, nothing. I just thought it might be a good idea."

"You've never gone out of town on business before."

"Haven't I?"

"You know you haven't." In her hand, a yellow sponge wiping again, a clean counter, a clean sink. "Where is this conference taking place?"

"Cincinnati." This was the first city he thought of and he didn't know why. He'd never been there; he wasn't sure he could spell it; it slipped off his tongue like a serpent. He felt like a man establishing an alibi for a murder.

"Isn't there one closer than Cincinnati?"

"Not that I know of."

"Well," she said, setting the sponge down, turning to face him, leaning back against the counter, "maybe this is a good thing." She folded her arms against her chest and appraised him. "You haven't shown an interest in anything for a long time."

The next morning, she called her sisters. "Last night he told me he's going out of town on business. And," her voice softened, "I think he's getting better."

She insisted on helping him pack, of course. Asked whether he'd need a raincoat or maybe an extra sweater, he responded with a five-day weather forecast he'd found on the Internet. And a history of the city, in case she was interested, and a printout from the Chamber of Commerce that described the sights.

She also insisted on driving him to the airport. His notion of slipping away unobtrusively to Santa Vista to find Jane Plain dissolving as the lie grew. He couldn't understand how this had happened, how a short drive south had turned into a flight halfway across the country. Still, his regret that he had not locked the door of the Oasis ahead of Miss Plain competed with his desire to slip the arms of her new glasses, gently yet firmly, over her ears.

They parked at ground level in a short-term lot across from the terminal. Walked over worn pavement to an exit and a crosswalk, where clusters of people on both sides of the street waited for the signal to change. The traffic was dense and fast: shuttles, buses, cars, some marked "official," whose drivers were intent on dropping off, picking up, maintaining position, swerving to meet an invisible timetable—and no one waiting at the curb dared to attempt an unauthorized entry into its flow.

Except for one stout old woman who majestically weaved her way through the middle of it. Emerging on the other side impervious and unscathed. Situe!

Kali gasped. He stole a quick look at Sophie, who hadn't noticed. Nor, it seemed, had anyone else. And inside the terminal, there she was again—merging into crowds, emerging from them, standing in a line, checking the arrivals. It seemed there were Situes everywhere.

Kali's face burst into a thousand beads of sweat. How could she toy with him this way, her own grandson?

"What's the matter, Kali?" Sophie asked.

"Nothing, my dear. Just a little warm."

"You're not getting sick, are you?" and she touched his damp forehead with the back of her hand to see if he had a fever.

The check-in line was long and full, turning at right angles from its beginning to its end like a squared serpent. With Kali as its prey, being worked down its insides to his inevitable suffocating demise. For when he reached the front of the line, he would be found out. Sophie would discover that he had no reservation. That he would get no seat assignment. That he would eat no in-flight meal.

"Sophie, I think you should leave now."

"What?"

"I'm concerned that you might get a parking ticket."

"I have plenty of time."

"You never know. I heard on the news that a man—no, it was a woman—was given a ticket and even though she proved that the meter was broken, the judge said she still had to pay it. A matter of strict liability."

"Our meter's not broken."

"How can you be sure?"

"Kali, you're being ridiculous."

They moved a few feet forward in the line, Kali pushing his suitcase with his foot while carrying his briefcase under his arm.

"Why don't you let me carry your briefcase?" Sophie said, reaching out toward it.

"It's too heavy for you. It might injure your bad shoulder." And he inserted the briefcase—this briefcase that carried Jane Plain's four pairs of prescription glasses, two for distance, one tinted/one not, and two for reading— farther into his armpit, and pinned his elbow more firmly against it.

"For God's sake, Kali, it's silly for me to stand here empty-handed," she said. And she reached for the briefcase a second time.

"NO!"

In a voice so loud it surprised them both. A voice so loud it carried over the immediate commotion of the check-in line to the X-ray machine. Where the security guard took note of the anxious expression on a man's red and perspiring face, the man's excessive hold on a briefcase, and the agitation of the woman who accompanied him.

"Forgive me, Sophie. I didn't mean to raise my voice. I must be nervous about this trip."

Now Kali was the third person in line and sweat poured out of his body and ran down his sides under his shirt. Even the tops of his hands were damp. In a few minutes the clerk behind the counter would ask Kali his name and his destination and require identification. And the clerk would find no record of Kali in the computer. And in an attempt to clear matters up, the clerk would ask, politely of course, to see the credit card with which Kali had paid for his ticket and tell him there was no record of that either.

Suddenly, Sophie announced, "I've thought it over and I'm going to leave now. I don't want anything to get you off on the wrong foot. This trip is the first thing you've shown any interest in in a long time, and I want it to be a success."

And she kissed him on his sopping wet neck just above his collar, which was as high as she could reach in flat shoes. And wove her way through the crowds without looking back since that could bring bad luck. Kali reached the front of the line and the clerk behind the counter motioned him forward.

"Actually," Kali said before the clerk could speak, "I'm not going after all. But thank you anyway. Thank you very, very much." And he turned around and slipped under the same woven barricade as Sophie had, though more clumsily than she, since he carried both the suitcase and his briefcase.

Kali was full of joy. And full of guilt that he did not feel guilty. His equilibrium began to return. The pressure in his ears subsided. He stopped perspiring. He breathed more deeply. He walked lightheartedly, almost giddily, toward the line of rental car agencies. As the security guard from the X-ray machine intently watched and reached for the walkie-talkie that hung from his belt by a yellow and black strap.

At the first desk Kali stopped and said, cheerfully, expectantly, "I'd like a car as quickly as possible, please."

"Haste makes waste," the girl with the nametag responded. Her eyes were dead like a cobra's and her name was Ruchelle. She was a trainee. "Spend a few extra minutes and take advantage of our Spectacular Savings Specials."

"Thank you . . . Ruchelle," Kali answered, focusing on the name tag, having a little trouble with her name, "but I'm in a terrible rush and I'd just like to rent a car as quickly as possible."

"Wouldn't we all." Then, in a lowered, familiar tone: "Even a man of obvious means, such as yourself, should take advantage of a bargain like this."

"Thank you again, Ruchelle. But, for reasons I can't disclose, today, saving money just doesn't matter."

"Of course it matters!"

She glared at him and moved toward her computer.

"Don't you like saving money?"

"I do. Usually. But today I'd just like a car as quickly as possible."

Ruchelle said crisply: "Free mileage, rides to and from, and universally courteous service."

"Undoubtedly a generous offer. Maybe another time."

"If the offer's so generous, why not take it?"

Kali could think of nothing else to say to her. She sensed a drop in his resistance.

"Name please."

"Kahlil Gibran Hourani."

"Spelled?"

He watched her fingers move haltingly over the keyboard as she typed the unfamiliar sequence of letters.

"Business?"

"The Oasis."

"Which is?"

"Opticianry."

"Which is?"

"I sell eyeglasses. Finest lenses. Designer frames," he said proudly.

"Purpose of trip? For our data bank only. Such information shall remain completely confidential."

"Belly dancing contest."

Ruchelle looked up from the keyboard, appraised him, looked down.

"Destination?"

"Santa Vista."

"Accommodations?"

"As yet, unknown."

At the end of her shift, as required of all trainees, Ruchelle reviewed her job manual. In particular the new section on security. In particular the guidelines for determining a "suspicious person."

There seemed to be little doubt: Mr. Kahlil Gibran Hourani was one. She came to this decision somewhat reluctantly, because if he got in trouble or arrested or something like that, he would probably cancel his Spectacular Savings Special membership. And she'd lose the credit for it. And the free trip to Lake Tahoe.

Still, her duty was clear. Her conclusion, inevitable. He'd convicted himself after all: that name; the name of his business; the way he brushed off every good point she made in her sales pitch; the way he got impatient when she asked him a question; saying he didn't know where he'd be staying. But the clincher, the most important evidence against him, was that MONEY WAS NO OBJECT. She underlined and capitalized that part of her report and faxed the whole thing to the head office. In the "Additional Comment" section, she had written: "Forgot to say he says he's going belly dancing, but he didn't look like a belly dancer to me."

6

THE SANTA VISTA EMPIRE MOTOR HOTEL, Conveniently Located One Hundred Yards from the End of the Off-ramp, Available for Catered Parties of Any Size and on Any Budget on One Week's Notice, had three hundred rooms and a giant parking lot. A banner in the lobby read, "Welcome RV'ers." The day clerk assured Kali that he got one of the last, best rooms in town.

This last, best room was stuffy and warm. With a thermostat that couldn't be set lower than seventy-eight degrees because the management figured that no one should want to be any cooler than that. Kali could have opened the sliding window which overlooked the parking lot, but there was traffic coming and going and the noise and exhaust fumes floated up.

He ate the mints on the pillows. Then took off his pants and shirt and folded them neatly over the back of one of two wooden chairs pulled up to a small table. He removed his shoes and, in his new under shorts which matched his new socks—two of several matched sets which Sophie bought him for his trip—lay down on the bed.

He was exhausted. All the lying; Situe at the airport; and Ruchelle, the car rental trainee—had worn him out. As a result, his driving had been more erratic than usual, a string of minor traffic offenses—his normal difficulties with judging distances and speed exacerbated. Such that he drifted in front of a stampeding eighteen wheeler and was herded off the freeway at an unplanned exit. Thereby ending up at the Santa Vista Empire Motor Hotel. Thereby unknowingly shaking off the brown sedan that had been tailing him since he turned the key in the ignition and left the airport.

As the room cooled down, he felt better and turned on the television set using the remote control that was screwed into the nightstand next to the bed. The only light in the room came from the screen. The sound was low, barely audible, and it provided a relaxing background hum. His head dropped back and he closed his eyes.

"Ahem."

A heart-stopping jolt: had he been caught already?

"Who is it?"

"The guilty question of a guilty man."

"Situe?"

"Quite so."

"I've had a terrible day."

"I know."

"Which you didn't help by running around the terminal."

"Some things are irresistible."

"I've betrayed Sophie," he said with a sigh.

"Hmmm."

"And I almost got myself killed getting off the freeway."

She uttered something softly in Arabic, which Kali didn't understand.

"I thought this would be such a simple matter. My God, all I wanted to do was give Jane the glasses."

"So it's 'Jane' now."

"Please don't make fun of me. I can't figure out what's going on."

"As compared to the depth and breadth of your previous understanding?"

The flush under his dark skin would have been invisible to anyone but his grandmother.

"I told Sophie I was going to Cincinnati. I'm glad you found me."

"Finding you is easy," Situe said as she slipped a comb into her thick, white hair. Reminding Kali how, indifferent to its lush beauty, she used to sweep it back from her face, holding the hairpins in her mouth until she was ready to use them.

"We gave those combs to Layla," Kali said gently, "after you . . . died. As a keepsake. Did you know that?"

"Of course."

"By the way, I hope it doesn't offend you when I mention your death."

"It's you who are offended by the word *death*, not me, grandson."

Kali heard the door to the adjacent room open and almost immediately there was laughter, a man's and a woman's. Then the ice machine down the hall spewing cubes, then the door slamming and music turned up loud.

Situe, in the upholstered chair in the corner, appeared not to notice. Kali, on the bed, reached over and turned off the television.

"If only I could be like you were," Kali said. "Solid and sure. You never changed. You never seemed bothered. We always knew where to find you."

"Where would I have gone? I didn't drive. I could barely walk. Every morning I hobbled half a block to Pete's Armenian Market and hobbled home again. Then I sat on the porch and waited for all of you to come."

"But you were the rock, Situe, the foundation."

"I sat there. That was all. But I was lucky. Because sitting, as it turns out, is quite a harmonious act. Quite useful for getting in touch with the universe. It's something I learned recently. My current sitting is very purposeful. You should try it."

"You mean just sitting?"

"Exactly."

"For how long?"

"As long as it takes."

"I don't understand what you're talking about, Situe."

"Ah, well. You can take a horse to water . . . "

"Situe, that's cruel. I'm doing my best."

"One's best can be better."

"No lectures. I'm too tired. Maybe . . . later we'll talk . . . or I'll have more questions. Not now."

"I look at you, Kali, and I know what your questions are before you ask them. You rest and I'll give you some answers."

She began: *Well over a thousand years ago—*

"With all due respect, dear grandmother, how do you know what happened then?" Kali asked in a tired, drowsy voice, lying flat, eyes closed.

"Primary sources, dear grandson. The horse's mouth."

She began again:

Well over a thousand years ago, when our people lived in small settlements along the edges of the desert, they climbed aboard their camels and rode off in huge numbers to raid the caravans.

"Our people lived in the mountains, not the desert."

"I thought you were too tired to talk."

The encounters were bloody; they were murderous. Causing much pain and misery. People cut off each other's heads. And hands. And certain other parts to make sure that their enemies did not proliferate—

"'Our people' couldn't have been involved in something like that," Kali said, rising from the bed. "They believed in God."

"There was a girl. Haleema."

"Why 'Haleema'?"

"It's the prerogative of the storyteller to name the characters. Although, unfortunately, for purposes of this story, it makes no difference whether I call her Haleema or Sarah or Catherine or Carlotta or Cosette or—"

"Call her what you want." He settled back against the pillows.

Somehow Haleema was overlooked in the slaughter; somehow spared the raping and the death. She crawled up through a rubble of bodies, past the faces of her sister and her favorite cousin, and those of a few people she hadn't liked at all. They were frozen in midexpression, these faces: some astonished, some fearless, some terrified, some enraged, some ashamed. When she reached the top of the pile, she was covered with blood and bits of flesh in various stages of drying—

"How morbid."

"The truth, the whole truth, and nothing but the truth . . . "

"What do you mean by that?"

"What do you think I mean?"

"Please, Situe, I try to be a good man. I take care of my family; I give to the church, although I don't believe anymore. I tolerate my wife's sisters; what more do I have to do to have peace?"

Situe sighed. "Where was I?"

"The bits of human flesh."

"Thank you."

Haleema extricated herself from the murderous mound. Her people were dead and the raiders were gone—the dust they'd kicked up had barely begun to settle. They'd taken the animals and anything of value they could carry including the rugs Haleema's family was taking to the bazaar.

She heard moaning. It was coming from a young man lying nearby. A young man she had never seen before. One of the men who had just murdered her tribe. He was so wounded himself he couldn't inflict any injury on her, but she took his sword from his side and flung it away. Crouching beside him, she watched him slip in and out of awareness. He was very near death. He did not speak.

As the sky faded into darkness and the hot, dry winds of night approached, Haleema rose and found a jug of water. Lifting the man's head, she trickled the water over his mouth until he was awake enough to drink. She washed his face. She examined his wounds—

"He helped kill her family and tribe and she helps him?"

"Such things do happen, Kali."

"If someone had killed everyone on my caravan, I wouldn't help them. I'd happily watch them die."

"He was very young—"

"So, it would be a different story if he were old?"

"He had such sorrowful eyes; they remind me a little of yours," Situe said, inclining toward him in a way she hadn't done since her return.

The slight constriction in his chest, the slight choke in his throat—took Kali by surprise. He continued in a softer tone: "He murdered her people; he would have killed her if he'd known she was alive. What about the concept of retribution?"

"You're against rendering aid to a wounded man?"

"I'm against helping the man who killed her family."

"You see no basis for her actions?"

"Only if they were necessary to bring him to justice."

"Do you take this position because he personally held his victims down before slitting their throats?"

"I don't care how he killed them. It's the killing itself that counts."

"Well, at last we're getting somewhere."

With an effort, she reached down to adjust her rolled stockings, then sat back in her chair and took a deep breath. She squeezed her mouth with her right hand like Kali had seen her do a thousand times before—usually when she was sitting on her porch or at family gatherings when she watched and rarely said a word.

Haleema fed the man dried meat. From a goat that had run off terrified during the attack and had found its way back to the ruined caravan, she took milk for him. They watched each other intently.

"Why do you do this?" he asked.

"If you die, I'll be alone," she answered.

Mostly he slept and when he did, Haleema studied the distance for signs that someone was coming for her. Although she didn't know what she would do if her tribe came and saw her with the man. But her view of the desert sands yielded no information—no dust, no shadows, no small figures on the horizon. It was two weeks before the man could stand by himself.

One day as night fell, the young man walked away into the desert. He didn't ask her to come with him. He barely said good-bye. But before he left he reinforced the shelter of blankets and skins and killed the goat so she would have meat. He salvaged as much as he could from the wrecked caravan and put it near her.

"It was the least he could do," Kali said.

Haleema's people had no way of knowing that the caravan had been attacked and that it hadn't arrived at its destination, but when it didn't return home near the appointed day, a search party went into the desert to find what it could find.

They found Haleema, the lone survivor, and praised her extravagantly for her fortitude and toughness. She told them about the attack and the heroic, though futile, defense by her people. She did not tell them about the man.

Months later, in an unguarded moment, she told a female cousin. This cousin told another cousin who was overheard by one of the elders who told their leader. Magnificent in his robes of silk, he called her to him and asked her if she was a traitor.

"How could I be a traitor?" Haleema asked.

"Did you help the man who murdered your family?" he thundered. "Did you feed him and nurse him back to health?"

"Well," said Situe, "you can guess what happened to her."

"Oh, no," said Kali, feeling a little like he'd felt when Isaac Malouf told him Jimmy Hitti's nephew had died. He sank lower in his seat. "And the man?"

"He died in the desert. All by himself. Dried up and blew away. The only thing left behind was his sword."

Situe retrieved her lighter from a pocket in her sweater, lit a cigarette and blew immense smoke rings in the air.

"Is the story true?"

"Ah, Kali," Situe said gently, as she began to dissolve in the clouds of her cigarette smoke.

"What does it have to do with me?"

"You have the same options as everybody else, Kali."

"You leave me more confused than when you arrived."

"Then the story wasn't wasted." She had nearly disappeared and these last words sounded distant and faint.

After she left, Kali took a cool shower and put on fresh clothes. He went to the ice machine where he encountered his next door neighbors, clearly drunk, alternately holding and cursing each other as they negotiated their way down the hall. Meanwhile, a procession of RV's, like elephants on safari, lumbered into the vast parking lot below. Workers set up tables and started fires in portable barbecues. Like palm trees at the edge of an oasis, heat lamps stood—unused—on the perimeter, for the arriving desert winds, the Santa Anas, guaranteed a steady supply of warm evening air. People began to gather. The music that erupted from the loud-speaker system almost obliterated the sounds of the snoring couple in the adjacent room.

Kali realized he was hungry. He also realized that he had never before been so reckless and his old fears of uncontrollable danger descended upon him like a thick, gray cloud. Taking risks: he was bad at that; a terrible gambler, unable to calculate odds, let alone beat them. Some people had that blind wild courage in the face of the unknown. Not him. In family poker games—assuming he could be persuaded to sit at the table with his aunts and uncles and cousins and their shot glasses of whiskey and their lopsided piles of chips—when asked how many cards he wanted, he'd say without looking at his hand, "All" or "None," then fold without making a bet.

In a drawer, Kali discovered a Bible and a phone book, which he went through hoping to locate an Arabic restaurant. *Dolmas, tabbouleh, hummus,* some white Syrian cheese, some white flat-bread—that's the only food he wanted. Greek was as close as he got. There were directions and a map and, even though he was new to the area, he thought it wouldn't be hard to find.

7

LESS GRAND THAN ITS NAME SUGGESTED, the Palace of
Fine Arts showed signs of neglect. Its massive wooden doors,
slightly warped, rasped when opened and the cherubs under the
eaves peeled pastel paint.

Kali had parked in a lot nearby. "Free Belly Dancing Contest Parking," the sign said. But the lot was nearly empty, and he
worried that many belly dancers had not come, and that among
those who had not come was his dear Miss Jane Plain. To reassure
himself, he resorted to certain presumptions: if the sun set, it was
presumed to have risen; if a letter was mailed, it was presumed to
have arrived; if she said she'd be at the New Belly Dancer of the
Galaxy Contest at the Palace of Fine Arts in Santa Vista, California, she would be.

"Is this where the belly dancing contest is?"

"Middle Salon. Fifth floor."

The smiling young man stretched over the mahogany counter
in the lobby, reaching only part way, for it was very wide and he
was very short, and pointed to his left, to an old-fashioned grand
staircase and an elevator a few feet past it.

Kali pushed the elevator button several times.

"Sometimes it works and sometimes it doesn't," the man behind the counter called out cheerfully.

So Kali began to climb, considering as he did, several possible opening statements: "Jane, I've taken the liberty . . . " or, "I hope you don't mind that . . . " or, "As part of my professional responsibility, Jane . . . "—intending to choose the most appropriate one of them when he knew the circumstances of their reintroduction.

During the second flight, Kali almost decided to turn around and go home and simply mail the glasses to her at her last known address. By the third flight his injured knee began to ache, and he was grateful for the cushioned steps.

During the fourth, he tightened his hold on the box that held Miss Plain's glasses—those glasses that the night before in his room at the Empire Motor Hotel, he had repolished and rewrapped in their individual, customized chamois with the palm tree logo, and tucked in their individual cases, like treasured newborns in their cribs. Of the cases, three were genuine leather.

Finally, having arrived on the fifth floor he saw, over an expanse of well-worn carpet, a woman sitting at a card table. The mere sight of another person lifted his spirits, although she didn't seem to be aware of his approach and continued going through index cards in a file box and referring to several pieces of paper taped on the table's surface.

"Good day," Kali said, as graciously as his shortness of breath would allow, "I see I've arrived at my destination." For from the edge of the card table hung a poster of a swirling belly dancer with flying hair. A glorious female who transcended ordinary life, like the ones on the holy cards he'd gotten as a child at church.

The woman looked up at him. "Are you registered?" she asked.

"I wasn't aware of the requirement."

"Then you can't go in."

She looked back down at the work in front of her. "You can't go in unless you're registered, you're a vendor, or you want to shop at the bazaar."

"I'll gladly shop at the bazaar."

"When you finish shopping, you have to come out."

"Then I'll keep on shopping."

She looked at him coldly. "I suppose you'll want a program."

"Yes, thank you."

"The program goes with the ticket." She pointed without looking to a closed double door a few feet behind her. "The New Belly Dancer of the Galaxy Contest tomorrow night in the Middle Salon. Thirty dollars, or twenty-eight if you pay cash."

"A small price to pay," Kali said, aware that he was wasting his charm.

The program announced Amatullah, Amirah, Azizah, Baheera, Hanifa, Jamilah, Kamilah, Muneera, Nabilah, Nasira, Rashida, Safiyyah, Shahrazad, Tahirah, Talibah, Yaminah, Yasirah, Yasmine, Zafirah, Zubaidah.

But not Jane Plain.

"Are these all the dancers?" Kali asked.

"I just put down the names they give me."

As he read over the list again hoping for a sign that one of the names was a pseudonym for Jane Plain, from within the Middle Salon, there came a rhythmic jingling, a sound that registered all over his skin. Stirring and soothing, pulsing, beckoning.

"Break's over," said the woman and she signaled to him to go inside.

He opened the doors, and the jingling crescendoed until it burst around him. A gentle explosion of thousands of ringing coins. Coins bound around a hundred pairs of dancing hips. Coins bouncing as a hundred pairs of dancing feet, bare and in a selection of sizes and states of beauty, obeyed the teacher on the stage.

"The floor is your friend," she called out from the center of the spotlight as she made a quarter turn and then another, while her arms, raised and strong, claimed the air around her. "Use it. Make it serve you."

Kali scanned the floor looking for Jane. But the lowered lights and the continuous movement and the size of the group made her difficult to locate.

"Ratatatatata," the teacher chanted.

"Ratatatatata," the students responded.

"Shout it!" the teacher commanded.

They shouted.

"Raise your arms higher."

They did.

As the lesson progressed, Kali pretended to shop, while scanning the floor to find Jane. He strolled uninterested by the racks of beaded and feathered bras and bottoms, ornate caftans and veils that lined both sides of the auditorium. He stood for decent periods of time near earrings and arm bracelets and candelabra headpieces and jewels and crowns; he picked up swords and pretended to examine trays and finger cymbals. He avoided the aromatics so he wouldn't sneeze. When the woman from the card table came inside and stared at him, he bought two CDs from the only other man in the huge room, then sat down defiantly in a folding chair at the back to watch.

He'd seen belly dancers before, of course. Grew up with them in the background, like the sounds of his parents' voices. Had one at his wedding reception, in fact, though he didn't get into the spirit of it like his cousin, Sabeh, who had his picture taken with his hands on the belly dancer's stomach—a copy of which Sophie ordered for their photograph album and brought out each year on their anniversary for some reason Kali didn't understand.

The dancers on the floor in front of him, though, didn't look like the dancers he remembered. These moved in fits and starts and, heavy or thin, looked angled and pointy and sharp. They had no mystery; they created no magic. Who were these women? Why were they doing this? He had no idea that non-Arabs, non-Mediterraneans (he'd include the Turks, no matter what some of his old relatives thought), knew this type of dance existed. Much less tried to learn it.

Their teacher, on the other hand, was from the old days. She did anything she wanted to up there. She had authority. And no desire to please. She teased her students, danced past the steps they knew. In curves they couldn't follow.

"Western bodies," she lamented as she glided sideways, "there's no cure for them."

The teacher announced a break and the students scattered to different parts of the auditorium. One made her way directly to Kali.

"You made it," she said.

Blue-black hair? Entwined bronze snakes?

Kali wanted to ask if she was Jane, for who else would come up and speak to him, but everything about her was unfamiliar.

"You don't recognize me, do you?"

"Of course," he lied.

"Here." She ran her wrist under his nose, the top of her hand across his cheek, allowing her scent to reacquaint them.

"Jane," he said.

"I'm trying to look authentic."

"I understand."

"People have certain visual expectations for a belly dancer, you know."

"How true."

"So," she stood very still, "do I appear to be genuine?"

He looked at her carefully. "Your eyes are brown."

"Colored lenses. They're quite the thing now, as I'm sure you know."

"Prescription?" he asked, somewhat hurt.

"A mere cosmetic touch."

"Well, that's good," Kali said, relieved. "I brought your glasses."

"I knew you would."

"How did you know? How did you know I'd go to your house and find the note? And that I'd follow you here and bring the glasses with me?"

"Two minutes, ladies," the teacher announced through the microphone.

"I have to go," Jane said.

"But your glasses—"

"Come back at five o'clock."

"Excellent. I'll give you your glasses then. And of course make any necessary adjustments. My tools are right here in my pocket. I never go anywhere, Jane, without the tools of my trade."

After Kali left the auditorium he returned to the parking lot where, for the remainder of the class, he slept in his car. It was the best way he could think of to make the time go by fast and stay close to Jane. The attendant knocked once on the window to see if he was all right.

At five to five, he pulled directly in front of the Palace of Fine Arts and stopped in the no parking zone, for the second time breaking the law in the name of Jane Plain. For he was afraid that he might miss her if she wasn't directly in his line of sight when she came out, and he was afraid that she might change her mind. Which was no excuse, said the policeman who gave him the ticket. Taking an unusually long time, Kali thought, to check the rental car papers and run Kali's license number through the system.

Abruptly, the policeman walked to the back of the car and tapped on the trunk with the end of his flashlight.

"Open it."

It sounded like he was examining the spare tire. As far as Kali knew, there was nothing else in there.

"Is this the usual procedure for a parking ticket?" Kali asked, but before the policeman could answer, Jane arrived and, without hesitation, opened the back door of the car and tossed in her bag and carefully hung up some plastic-covered clothes on the hook by the window. Then got into the front seat next to him.

"So," she asked, "where are we staying?"

He recognized her this time, of course. The car filled with the smell of ginger and citrus and sweat and Kali drove to the Empire Motor Hotel.

Kali insisted that Jane have the first shower. While she was in the bathroom, he rested on the bed and turned the television set on low. As she had done before, Situe appeared in the corner of the room. This time Kali immediately sensed her presence.

"Ah, Situe."

"Ah, Kali."

"Are you mocking me?"

"No, dear grandson, merely answering you—it's a musical convention."

"You shouldn't stay here. She'll see you."

"She'll be in there for hours. Don't worry."

"I don't want a lecture."

"Have I ever lectured you?"

From the shower came singing, several lines from Broadway show tunes, sung extravagantly and drawn out.

"I see she knows how to entertain herself," Situe said.

"Be kind, Situe. She's tired from all the dancing."

"There was only one dancer in that room and she was on the stage." She made a sound halfway between a snort and a spit.

Kali said, "I simply want to give her her glasses."

"Do you think it's that easy? I wish you could hear yourself. Such self-deception. First, know thyself. Socrates says—"

"—Here we go again. You and your philosophical friends."

"Would you begrudge me the benefits of education? Even post-mortem?" She shifted her position in the chair and went on. "Kali, you're running out of time."

"Am I going to die soon?"

"I'm not supposed to give you concrete information; I'm supposed to guide you gently, let you find your own way, draw your own conclusions, seek your own truth. Answer a question with a question. And so forth. But you're such a slow learner . . . "

"Situe. Please. I'll be finished here in a short time. And then I'll go home to Sophie again and everything will be just like it was before. I just need to deliver the glasses."

"Are you lying to both of us or just to me?"

"Please listen. My job is to help people see—"

"That's my job, but go on."

"And, though I'm usually assisted in that regard by an examination by a competent ophthalmologist—"

"Get to the point."

"The point is when you can see the world clearly and without distortion, life is much easier and better."

"Physician, heal thyself."

The singing in the shower stopped.

"Kali, I'll distill it for you. First, open your eyes."

"What am I supposed to see?"

"Whatever you see, you see. There's only so much you can do about that. And second, take your best shot."

"Take my best shot? At what?"

"A vulgar figure of speech, my dear Kali, but it's the best I can do with so little time."

As Situe faded into invisibility, the bathroom door opened and a cloud of fragrance and steam escaped. A tart ambrosia, edgy and agitating.

"It was a wig," Jane laughed, as she removed the towel from her wet hair.

"And look at my eyes now. What do you see?"

Determined to see what was actually before him, to reject his tendency toward extravagant expression, and to take his best shot, as Situe advised, he did not say, "I see heavenly orbs, windows to the soul, paths to eternity," or launch into a discourse on the elegance of the optic nerve. Instead, when he took her face into his hands and, inhaled her delicious fragrance, he said, "Jane, I see irises of blue to blue-green with scattered yellow specks, a slightly sun-damaged cornea, and a hint of dry eye."

He hardly had time to ask how the afternoon's lessons went, before she fell asleep sitting nearly upright next to him on the bed, her arms still pink from the long shower. Every few breaths she made a tiny snore.

"Jane?" he said a few times quietly, but she gave no indication of waking up. He had nothing to read, not even the newspaper, so for awhile he simply let his thoughts wander and held very still so he wouldn't disturb her—this woman whom he'd seen twice, about whom he knew little, who slept next to him in his bed in an overheated motel room.

Moments passed. And her presence created within him a growing tension, a longing that, for obvious reasons he told himself, he could not satisfy with speech or touch. All he could do was look. So he studied her, feature by feature and part by part, letting his eyes rest on those components which were irresistible.

For example, the mole on the left side of her chin. And the most subtle of widow's peaks, composed of fine, fair hair. And the small scar on the left side of her clavicle. He loved how her breasts, when she lay on her back, slid a little to the outside—her nipples barely showing, so she must have been warm.

He delighted in her smoothness, was pleased she wasn't muscular. Unlike him, she had no hair on the second joints of her fingers—a genetic trait he learned about in high school biology. That he would recall such information in this setting made him smile.

In the last instants before darkness, he wiped a silver drop of saliva from the side of her mouth and pulled the spread over her. Much later, having spent the hours in the same position and pursuing the same occupation, he turned out his light. As usual when he first fell asleep, his leg twitched, sending a short, sharp shudder through the bed.

8

"DO YOU ALWAYS LIVE LIKE THIS, JANE?" Kali asked, as he measured his left palm against her right, noting with protective pleasure the disappearance of her hand under his. "You don't seem to worry about anything; you don't make plans."

"I make plans."

"Like what," he said, interlocking their fingers and bending over her to kiss the fading scar on her clavicle.

"Oh," she said, "trust in fate, take what comes along, let life unfold . . ."

"How would it have unfolded if I hadn't come along yesterday? Where would you have stayed?"

"Is my Kali jealous?" she laughed and her hand descended from his chest to his navel to his pubic bone and below.

They'd had the Empire Extravaganza for breakfast.

"Sorry about the slow delivery," the room service waiter had apologized. RV convention slowed us down." He set the food and utensils on the table. "Big strain on the kitchen."

"I can imagine," said Kali.

"Plus the lieutenant governor made a surprise appearance. Security guys everywhere."

"A sign of the times, I'm afraid," Kali said.

"It's because he's a crook."

"Why do you say that?" Kali asked.

"They're all crooks."

"You're quite sure, I see," said Kali, as the waiter stood in the doorway holding the empty tray under his arm.

"And some of the other crooks wanted to take him out."

"Assassinate the lieutenant governor?" asked Kali.

"There's a conspiracy."

"I find that hard to believe."

"I know what I know," the waiter said as he left, closing the door behind him.

Kali had never seen a woman eat so much: pancakes, bacon, eggs, toast, hashed browns, orange juice, coffee. While she bit and chewed in ceaseless motion, he told her of the catalogue of disasters that often plagued his thoughts: from earthquakes to locusts to famine to crashing meteors to local insurrection to terrorist attacks, unresolved personal mysteries and the loss of love.

"Are you going to eat that third piece of toast?" she responded.

What relief he felt! Finally, a woman who didn't roll her eyes when he said what was on his mind. A woman who didn't tell him to change the subject. Who wasn't annoyed when he expressed his real concerns.

"I should add, though," he continued, intent upon giving her a complete and honest picture, "that some of my worries are fading because of the guidance and wisdom of my grandmother."

"You're lucky." Jane said as she reached for a small packet of grape jelly, "mine's dead."

"Mine, too," Kali said sadly.

Jane had awakened before he did.

"Kali," she whispered.

He moaned the way he did every morning in the last minute of sleep. Not necessarily from an excess of anguish, though usually so.

"I want to ask you a question."

Gradually, he remembered where he was and who he was with.

"It's an easy one."

They lay in bed on their backs next to each other. His eyes were dry with sleep; he opened them, looked at the ceiling.

"Do you like me better as myself or as a belly dancer?"

Since Kali never took any question lightly, he thought for a moment before answering.

"I like you both ways."

"That's not a good answer."

"I mean it sincerely."

"You've never actually seen me belly dance. So I think your answer is slightly dishonest." There was a pout in her voice he hadn't heard before.

"I saw you dance during the lesson."

"But you didn't know it was me."

"I looked at you and thought, 'That woman, whoever she is, is far better than most of the others.'"

"Only most?"

"Let me rephrase." he said slowly. "What I meant to say was that the only dancer better than you was the teacher." His usual devotion to absolute truth whatever the consequences—truth with a capital T—dissolving as he became more distracted by how close he was to her. "And that's undoubtedly because she's had more experience. Nothing more."

"Why, what a lovely compliment, Kali. Thank you."

"You're welcome."

She had lain still throughout their conversation but now she began to stir.

"You see, Kali, my future depends on my abilities as a belly dancer."

"Then you should have a bright future ahead."

Deeply, fervently, Kali hoped that Situe was far away, out of earshot, immersed in an activity that commanded her full attention.

"Kali?"

"Yes, Jane?"

"I'm in exactly the same position I was in when I went to sleep."

"We both are," he sighed.

They arose and dressed, Kali deferring to what he assumed was Jane's need for privacy by intently reading the Room Service Menu. Afterwards, as they sat, on opposite sides of the bed, he said, "Now, with your permission, I'd like to ask *you* a question."

"Fair's fair."

"Why did you come to the Oasis?"

"It just happened."

"How can that be when it when it was so far from where you lived?"

"It was just one of those things."

"It must be more than that."

"Sorry to disappoint you."

"Try to remember how you got there, what you were thinking about."

"Well, let's see. I was driving around with my prescriptions in my purse—I drive around a lot when I don't have much to do and I'd just lost my job—"

"—What a shame—"

"—and I was thinking about the belly dancing contest. And hoping that I'd win in my division, which is the Intermediate Celestial Diva. And thinking I probably should have entered as a Novice Aspiring Goddess. Anyway," she paused, still pondering her category, "I stopped at a light. And there was the Oasis. And I thought, you know, 'belly dancing/oasis, oasis/belly dancing.' So I pulled over and parked the car."

"You mean it was a random event? Of all the places in the universe, you just happened upon the Oasis?"

"I guess. Well, I went in," she said as she reached over and touched his arm, "and you know the rest."

This was less than he had hoped for. Either divine intervention or human intention—or their functional equivalents—would have sufficed. Still, the circumstances of their coming together did not, by themselves, determine their present state. He and Jane had just begun; there was more to come.

With renewed expectation, Kali carefully set their dirty dishes on the floor while she gazed absent-mindedly out the window at the decamping RVers—bringing in welcome mats, folding up folding chairs, saying good-bye. He took a towel from the bathroom and wiped the surface of the table, then made sure the drapes were open as wide as they would go—to let in the natural light.

"It's time, Jane."

She returned to the table and, as he did for most of his women customers, if appropriate, he pulled her chair out for her and waited for her to sit down. As he didn't do with most customers, he smoothed her hair back from her face with both his hands and held them there and kissed her on the forehead.

"You have a nice touch," she said.

He set the unsealed box of glasses in the center of the table.

"I didn't have a chance to rewrap it after I got the parking ticket," he explained. Then withdrew the four cases from the box and placed them in a line, left to right, in front of him. And opened each case and, one by one, turned them toward Jane to reveal their contents.

"Palm trees," she said with delight.

"My logo," he said proudly.

Careful not to smudge the lenses with his fingers, he removed the first pair from its protective chamois.

"Lean forward, please."

They were her regular distance glasses. For inside.

"Now, drop your chin a little."

He pushed them up to the top of the bridge of her nose.

"How does that feel?"

"Fine."

"No slipping down?"

"None."

"They look beautiful on you."

With his elegant little measuring stick he made sure they were centered.

"And your vision?"

"I can see a tiny spider in a tiny web in the corner of the ceiling."

"Excellent. Now for the arms."

Reaching behind her ears to determine the arms' angle of repose, and whether they rested gently as intended, and to locate their tips which should be neither too curved nor too long—he found that he could not withdraw his hands. They would not move. They could not leave. They were stuck, struck still. On their own, they'd immersed themselves in the lushness of her hair and filled up the crevices between fingers and wrapped the strands around whatever they could.

"Is this part of your usual service?" she asked.

"No."

He leaned forward and kissed her on the mouth.

"Did you like that?" he asked.

"Yes. And you?"

"Very, very much."

And so it went through the sunglasses and two pairs of reading glasses. When he broached the subject of bifocals, she took matters into her own hands, rising from her chair and going to him and pressing his face against her shirt, then lifting her shirt and placing his lips, his cheek, against her bare, fragrant midriff.

In bed he told her he liked her better as herself. She lay in the crook of his arm, her head resting on his shoulder, her hair brushing against his face.

"I knew it," she answered.

And he confessed that he had not seen her dance.

"I knew that, too."

And he told her that he'd never deposited her check.

"I'm not surprised."

And that he was married.

"I could tell right away."

And she told him she wasn't and never had been.

She uncovered him, stroked him, brushed her face back and forth over his chest. His coarse, dark hair made a crinkling sound in her ear.

"Just a minute," he said and he slid toward the foot of the bed and pulled the covers over his head.

"What are you doing?"

"I like it this way. Come down here with me."

"It'll be too hot. I won't be able to breathe."

"It's nice. You'll be fine."

"I'd rather be up here."

"This way nobody can see us."

"There's nobody here but us, Kali."

"Oh, come on."

"I don't understand why you're doing this. We're the only ones in the room."

"I just want to be sure."

For lunch they ordered room service again. This time, remembering how much she ate, Kali added two sides and an extra dessert.

"I am on intimate terms with the passage of time. I am a man full of sadness," Kali murmured, exhausted, subdued, after making love again, as Jane lay on top of him, her body about one half his width. "Which is the reason, one of the many reasons, that I'm here with you."

"No kidding?"

"Other reasons being," he hastily added, "that you are lovely, beguiling, and talented." He turned on his side. "And you? Why are you here? With me."

Eyes closed, she slid off him, lay beside him, stretched her arm around him.

When it became clear she wasn't going to answer, he continued, resigned, "You see, Jane, I see myself on a path that lies out in front of me all the way to eternity, and Layla and Philip are behind me. Also on the path. Quite a distance back, I'm glad to say. And when I'm gone, they'll carry on after me. After their mother and me, actually."

"What path is this again?"

"The path of life, Jane. The path we're all traveling. Sometimes it all seems so futile."

"Oh."

"And I worry about Philip. More than his sister."

She sighed, eyes still closed.

"I'm afraid he'll never be happy, never fall in love." And it made Kali heartsick, thinking of Philip without the extravagance of feeling, the grand gestures and words of honor and eternal devotion, the noble sentiments that could make one weep.

"Love isn't everything," Jane said. She was almost asleep.

"I strongly disagree. People with passion are the lucky ones. Although Situe would say that passion without vision is worthless. What good is ignorant, blind intensity?"

"Right," Jane mumbled.

"Situe jokes that my passion is asking questions about myself."

"You don't say." Her voice was becoming fainter.

"She said that my imagination runs ahead of my reason and that I should try to equalize their pace."

As Jane's body subsided next to him, Kali became aware of a subtle stillness within himself. He wasn't sure if he was gaining some measure of serenity or if he was just tired from all the exertion. Whatever it was, the perpetual motion of his thoughts slowed down for the moment. The usual pressing demands for philosophical inquiry lifted—set on the shelf for a while, put out of the way. Even the nagging particularities of family life—his marriage to Sophie, his concerns for the future happiness of his son and daughter; the futility of arriving at a truce with his wife's sisters—dimmed. He'd leave it to another day to decide the eternal questions; he'd struggle with them after tomorrow night. After the contest.

9

THE NEXT MORNING, Kali—in bed, surrounded by scattered sections of the Sunday paper, the way he was at home each week with Sophie—cringed.

He knew he should call her, but he also knew he'd stumble over his words as he recounted, falsely, where he was, what he'd been doing. It was the first time he'd thought of Sophie since he encountered Jane in her black wig and brown contact lenses in the dancing class at the Palace of Fine Arts. He pushed Sophie out of his mind.

As Jane, meanwhile, flexed: her spine, her neck, her lower body. Pursuant to the *Pre-Competition Pamphlet,* page seven. Page thirteen explained the Heavenly Belly Sisterhood. And the honor of being Miss Heavenly Belly.

"Which I couldn't care less about," she announced, as she reached toward the ceiling, stretching one arm and then the other higher and higher, while her wig, immobile on a faceless Styrofoam head, waited in readiness on the bureau.

"It's for losers."

"Perhaps."

Now she was down on the carpet on all fours, hands and feet placed at right angles with each other, as nearly as possible.

"A consolation prize."

As she lifted her spine to an inverted U, she inhaled, held for twenty seconds, exhaled, and lined her spine up parallel to the floor.

"Who wants to be Miss Heavenly Belly when you can win the whole contest?"

Ten more times and she rested.

"And after I win, I'll get a new job and see the world."

"You have plans to leave?" asked Kali, jealousy slipping in, burying itself, taking hold.

"I'm not sure," she said, laying flat on her stomach on the carpet. "Maybe on a cruise ship, who knows? I have faith. After all, you found my note and then you found me and now we're here together, aren't we?" she said sweetly.

Kali tried to start another section of the paper, but an image of Jane flexing nude in the middle of the ocean on a cruise ship before a leering captain in a white uniform with brass buttons, distracted him. She lifted herself from the floor and went to him, leaned over and whispered in his ear, "I have a surprise for you, but you have to close your eyes."

He heard the rustle of a plastic bag, the opening of a long zipper.

"You can look now."

He stared silently, dared not say the words that leapt to mind.

"I designed it myself."

It was red, white, and blue. Of beads, sequins, feathers and chiffon. A bra—reinforced, elaborated, adorned, lavish—and see-through harem pants.

"There wasn't enough room on the bra for all the stars and stripes, but I think they'll get the idea, don't you?"

"Without a doubt."

"Do you like the tassels?"

"They're remarkable."

"And these," she said, holding up two long, coiled metal bands, "are my snakes."

"I recognize them from your class."

"They stand for my theme."

"Which is?"

"Don't tread on me."

"Very original."

"That's not Middle Eastern, though."

Kali drank the last half cup of coffee from the room's complementary pot.

"Do you think I have a chance?" Jane asked.

"How could you not?"

"Watch this."

Down she went on her knees. She did a backbend almost to the floor and came up. She went into a sitting position, undulating to a silent rhythm.

"This is floor dancing."

Kali watched intently.

"It's illegal in Egypt, you know. Too sexy."

She descended into a semireclining position.

"They had to dance this way because the tents were so low."

"You're sure about that?"

"Why wouldn't I be?"

Back and forth like a cobra, hypnotic, fluid.

"And when Flaubert (the way she said it rhymed with 'Robert') heard about it, he got the wrong idea. I guess he said some pretty lewd things."

Barely paying attention to her words, Kali, instead, focused on her undulating stomach. The sight of her, the smell of her, the sound of her, the immediacy of her energy and recklessness—filled him up. Leaving no room for criticism or reason. He couldn't see her clearly; he didn't try.

"This is called the 'camel & flutter.' Do you like it?"

"I love it."

"Did you know about Flaubert before I told you?"

"I can't say that I did."

"How can I know more about belly dancing than you do?"

She was flushed and warm as she shimmied, jumped, circled, with arms held high, always high. Beads of sweat collected at her temples.

"And then the hippies started doing it," she said, slightly out of breath, as one part of her body moved, then the other. As she went into another backbend, she said, "Ishtar is the Babylonian goddess of love and fertility. Did you know that?"

"Is or was?"

"And you know what she had to do to be fertile, don't you?"

"I can guess."

A final set of turns and swirls—

"And a 'virgin' was simply a woman who belonged to no man."

—watching Kali's face each time around until she let her head snap to catch up with her body.

"Which makes me a virgin."

Next came the Pre-Competition Bath, taken in the company of a burning candle, preferably scented. As described on page nine. After which Jane creamed the surfaces of her body, and dotted oils of ginger and citrus in strategic places. And glued an occasional sequin. Lined her eyes with blue and silver, covered her mouth in red, changed her green eyes to brown, and her blonde hair to a blue-black mane. While Kali marveled at the obliteration of most of her natural coloring.

She caused quite a stir in the parking lot of the Empire Motor Hotel, her tassels swaying like pendulums, Kali behind her carrying their bags.

❧ 10 ❧

ALREADY, SEATS WERE SAVED: tipped forward or marked with coats and programs. People browsed the bazaar, fingering the fine fabrics. Or marveled over the props—the candelabra, the swords, the trays. A few children, unchecked, slid across the polished wooden floor. The dancers, including Jane, were backstage for a final meeting. Kali had not touched her since she put on her costume; bad karma, she said. They parted awkwardly when he dropped her at the curb in front of the Palace of Fine Arts.

On the way from the parking lot, now full and busy, a man came from nowhere to walk by Kali's side.

"Change your mind?" he asked.

"About what?" Kali responded, startled, before the man drifted into the stream of other pedestrians.

Kali sat in an unclaimed chair at the end of a row, about half way back, waiting for whatever came next. Which, he was pleased to note, was traditional Lebanese *mezza: dolmas, tabbouleh, hummus,* olives, bread and cheese, and more, spread out below the stage on long, portable, rectangular tables.

A man in a brown suit sat next to him.

"So, are you here for the dancing or the food?" the man asked.

"Both, I guess," Kali answered pleasantly. "*Mezza* first, though."

"What?"

"Arabic hors d'oeuvres."

"Can you spell that for me?" the man asked and he took a pencil and small notebook from his breast pocket.

"H-o-r—"

"No, the other one, the one that begins with 'm.'"

There was a fuzzy announcement over the loudspeaker system, and the costumed dancers reentered the auditorium, most of them quickly surrounded by joyous families and friends. But not Jane.

She stood alone, taut and straight, until Kali found her and escorted her, without physical contact, to the food-laden tables. He picked up two plates and handed her one.

"Not before a performance," she said.

"But the others are eating."

"They have no hope of winning."

The man in the brown suit walked around the buffet tables, loading his plate. He didn't seem to know anyone there; he didn't speak to anyone, including Kali, whom he walked by without acknowledging.

And then it was time for the contest to begin. The lights dimmed, and Kali took his seat. As did the man in the brown suit. The man who had spoken to Kali on the sidewalk stood a few feet to Kali's left, leaning against the wall. When an usher asked him to take a seat, the man growled "Fire marshal" and flashed something in his wallet.

The music was deafening, filling every crevice of the room with its insistent pulsing. So when the curtains opened, and one by one the dancers appeared on stage—mysterious among clouds of dry ice and billowing panels of parachute silk set in motion by judiciously placed oscillating floor fans—the audience couldn't hear itself gasp.

Arms high, stepping in unison, their coin belts ringing like synchronized bells, the dancers danced. And the crowd roared. And incense burned in some out of the way place. And the strobe light spun.

It was exhilarating, a complete saturation of the senses. Not for the meek. Which is why few noticed that Kali appeared to pass out, and those who did notice were not alarmed.

As nearly one hundred women descended into a synchronized backbend, the man in the brown suit grabbed Kali's arm, and the fire marshal moved quickly to assist. Together they pulled Kali out of the row and out of the room to the elevator, which, surprisingly, descended the four floors quickly and smoothly. Through the lobby and outside.

"Drunk," explained the man in the brown suit to a passerby, as they dragged Kali's limp body upright, each holding a side.

"Passed out," said the fire marshal to the parking lot attendant as they threw Kali into the back of a dark sedan. The door slammed, the motor started; Kali's face pressed against the upholstered seat. Dead weight. Like a sack of loose-packed sand.

Kali didn't know where he was or how he got there. He couldn't move or speak. He was too drugged to fear. He didn't know that the two men from the auditorium were in the front seat. Dimly, he felt stops and starts. Dimly, he heard other cars.

They drove on a freeway and along a frontage road lined with wind-breaking trees. Down a side road poorly paved with asphalt. The car stopped. Kali's mind began to clear.

"What's going on?" he asked in a slow, tamped-down voice.

"Nothing."

"Who are you? Where are you taking me?"

No response.

"I have a right as an American citizen to know who you are."

"Don't talk to us about America, buddy," said someone in the front seat. "Your rights ended when you got into this car."

"Are you kidnapping me? Do you want ransom? I'm not a rich man. You have nothing to gain by keeping me."

In spite of the nausea that washed over him, he tried to sit up. But unseen hands pushed him down to the floor, where he lay wedged between the seats. A hood covered his head; handcuffs snapped around his wrists.

"I can't breathe."

"You could breathe fine under the covers at the motel," said a man's voice.

"What are you saying? Who are you?" asked Kali.

"Pretty damn fine as near as we could tell," said another man.

When the car started again, it rode on a different surface, which sounded and felt like gravel as the wheels dug into and over it. This part of the ride was short, and then the car stopped and the men in front got out and slammed their doors.

They dragged Kali out of the back seat and led him over a hard surface. Partly because he was still dizzy and partly because they moved fast and he couldn't see where he was going, he tripped repeatedly.

They took him into a building. A metal door clanged shut behind them. They walked awhile down a corridor and through another door. Walked a little more. Went through another door. Down two flights of stairs with a landing in between.

"Take off his hood."

Kali stood blinking, seeing, not seeing.

"Sit down, Huron."

When he didn't, they slammed him into a chair. Then pushed it forward to a small table. He was in a room with cinderblock walls. It had no windows. The fluorescent lights in the ceiling buzzed and hurt his eyes. Across the table from him sat the fire marshal. The man in the brown suit stood against the wall.

"So, here we are, Huron."

"You have the wrong man. My name is Hourani. Kahlil Gibran Hourani."

Each man took out a notebook and wrote down the name.

"Please, let me show you my driver's license," Kali said.

"Take off the cuffs," said the fire marshal, and the man in the brown suit obeyed him. "We want Huron to be comfortable."

As Kali reached into his back pocket for his wallet, he said, "This should clear up who I am." He handed his license to the fire marshal, who held it between his second and third fingers, tantalizingly, without looking at it.

"The information on it is correct?"

"Yes, everything's correct."

But the fire marshal didn't return the license. Instead, he handed it to the man in the brown suit, who looked at it carefully before putting it in a large manila envelope that he withdrew from a briefcase.

"My wife says it's a terrible picture," Kali said.

"I don't think it's so bad," said the man in the brown suit.

"We don't care whether the subject's picture is good or bad," barked the fire marshal. "It's irrelevant. It has nothing to do with why we're here."

"Subject?" asked Kali.

"Don't speak unless you're spoken to."

"But I—"

"What nationality are you, Huron?" asked the fire marshal.

"I'm Syrian, Lebanese."

"Well, which is it?"

"Lebanon was once a part of Syria."

"So, you admit to being an Arab?"

Kali leaned forward earnestly "You know, we're getting off on the wrong foot here. You obviously think I'm someone else."

"Oh, we do, do we?"

"Yes, I'm sure of it. There's been a mistake."

"The mistake was in letting you in this country in the first place."

"I'm an American citizen! I was born here!"

"You trying to get patriotic on us, Huron?"

"All right, all right. Let's start again. I'm going to assume you're not kidnappers. That you didn't take me for ransom."

"Assume what you like."

"Just please tell me who you are. Police? Secret agents? What's going on here?"

"You tell us, Huron."

11

"SO," SAID THE FIRE MARSHAL—WIRY, menacing, in charge—
"we have you on tape saying you were going to 'take your best
shot.' Do you recall saying that, Huron?"

"On tape? What are you talking about?"

"On tape," repeated the man in the brown suit. In the Palace
of Fine Arts, he'd seemed accommodating, approachable. Standing against the wall, he seemed capable of more than Kali wanted
to know.

"Twice, Mr. Huron. Do you deny saying that?"

"It was a figure of speech!"

"This figure," the fire marshal continued, "what does it look
like? What form does it take? What color—or colors—is it? How
long is it? Can it be seen with the naked eye from great distances?
So that it could be used as a signal? By an accomplice, for example? Your accomplice?"

"A figure of speech," Kali said, trying to keep his voice under
control, trying to suppress the fear and anger that rose inside, "is
a way of saying things. Saying something is like something else.
Instead of just saying it outright."

"Don't get fancy with us, Huron."

The man in the brown suit stepped forward to the table and
whispered something to the fire marshal.

"We also have signed statements from numerous witnesses," the fire marshal announced.

"Witnesses? Witnesses to what?"

"Your actions during the last thirty-six hours."

"I didn't do anything worth witnessing during the last thirty-six hours."

"That's not what these reports say."

"Can I see them?"

"Of course not. They're confidential."

"I have a right to see any statements against me."

"Maybe later; maybe not."

"Then, I don't believe you have them."

"You're not being cooperative, Huron."

"How could you possibly get signed statements in a day?"

"We don't mess around."

"I demand that you tell me who they're from." Kali's body, dampening with sweat, threatening to betray him, to communicate his agitation if it hadn't done so already.

"Let's see." The fire marshal looked at some pages on his clipboard and then, with a half-sneer, said: "Airline reservation clerk, security guard, airport car rental trainee—"

"Ruchelle?" Kali asked, flabbergasted.

"—desk clerk at Empire Motor Hotel, receptionist at Palace of Fine Arts, next-door neighbors at Empire Motor Hotel—"

"—They were drunk the whole time they were there—"

"—ticket seller at belly dancing event, who didn't have much nice to say about you, by the way."

"I don't have much nice to say about her either. She was unhelpful and rude."

"She said you tried to sneak in without paying."

"That's a lie. I bought a ticket and two CDs—"

"—from the CD vendor at the shopping bazaar who also gave us a statement—"

"—which I didn't really want—"

"—the parking lot attendant, the room service waiter who was in your room twice."

"I can't believe this."

"Believe it, Huron."

"Hourani: H-o-u-r-a-n-i," Kali shouted.

Each man wrote the name on his clipboard: the man in the brown suit, using capital letters; the fire marshal, underlining in red.

Kali said: "I'm surprised you didn't poll the RVers."

"None of them remembered seeing you. But we didn't have to rely on them."

The man in the brown suit shook his head.

"Because we put a nice little bug in your room," said the fire marshal.

"Top of the line."

"You bugged my room! But why?"

"That's the way it goes, Huron."

"Did you listen to . . . everything?" Kali asked.

"Everything."

The fire marshal paused a moment to let this information sink in. He exchanged looks with the man against the wall. Clearly, they thought they had him, that this development would persuade him to tell all.

"You may have some grudge against me," Kali said, filled with the powerless rage of a man who could not understand or alter his predicament, "but how could you do this to Jane? How could you violate her privacy like this?"

"Let's see here. Jane, Jane, Jane," said the fire marshal, thumbing through his notes. "She found you 'distracted by political rhetoric.'

She said you 'seduced' her. That you pursued her. That she could not escape your persistent attention. 'Stalking,' she called it."

"But she wanted me to find her," Kali said. "She left me a note."

The fire marshal moved to the edge of the table above Kali. The man standing in the brown suit shifted his weight from one foot to the other.

"You mean this note, Huron?" The fire marshal took the note from a manila envelope and set it in front of Kali.

"How did you get that?" Kali asked, visibly shaken.

"We'll ask the questions here, Huron."

"Is this it?" the fire marshal asked again.

Kali looked at the note: the paper torn from a drugstore tablet, the hole in it where it was nailed to her door, her handwriting, her words.

"How did you get it?" Kali repeated quietly.

"As I said before, we have our ways."

"Actually,' said the man in the brown suit, "you didn't say that before, but we do have our ways."

"Did Jane give this to you?" Kali asked, as he struggled to preserve his sense of what was true and what was false before this suggestion of betrayal.

"Hey, it's okay, buddy, it happens to the best of us," said the man in the brown suit.

The fire marshal read through his notes, lining out entire pages, writing in the margins of some with his pen. After an interval of several minutes, he looked at Kali with an expression that said all the news was bad, all the facts condemning.

"Now. The box. What was in it, Huron?"

"What box?"

"The box you carried into the Palace of Fine Arts, the box you held tightly under your arm up four flights of stairs. That box."

"Eyeglasses, of course. For Jane."

"You're wasting our time."

"It's not my intention to waste time. Quite the contrary. I'm telling you the truth," Kali answered with forced composure. "I'm doing my best to cooperate."

For it occurred to him that the faster he answered their questions, the faster he'd get out of the place. If this was a straightforward investigation, it was best not to argue, not to antagonize, and to give short, clear answers. After all, he had nothing to hide—except from Sophie. He'd help these men realize their mistake about who he was, so they'd let him go. He wondered if he should tell them he'd forgo a formal apology. That he wouldn't sue them, whoever they were, or report them to their superiors, whoever they were. That all he wanted was his rightful release. That he'd let bygones be bygones.

"You expect us to believe that the box was for the transportation of corrective lenses?" asked the fire marshal. "Surely you can come up with something better than that."

"Not merely lenses. Lenses fitted into my customized frames."

The man in the brown suit grimaced and Kali tried again.

"Please listen. I'm an established optician. With an excellent reputation. I've had a small business in the same location for many years. I filled Miss Plain's prescriptions and provided her with four pairs of glasses—"

"Nobody gets four pairs of glasses at once."

"On the contrary," Kali stated with renewed authority, "some people do."

Were they simply measuring his veracity before letting him go? Were they misstating facts to test him, to determine the amount of real information he had? Like in the movies when somebody confessed to a crime and the detectives asked questions about the condition of the body that only the perpetrator would know?

"You see, she was always losing her reading glasses. She would set them down and not be able to find them."

The fire marshal wrote down what Kali said.

"And I knew she needed them. So, when she didn't come in to pick them up, I called her to tell her they were in—"

"—Nineteen times, to be exact—"

Kali blushed. "Was it that much?"

"In an eight-hour period."

"Well, I was worried about her not being able to see well enough. So I packed the glasses carefully in a cardboard box and took them to her."

"This box?"

From another clear plastic bag the fire marshal withdrew the box. It was closed, flaps folded in an interwoven lock. He slid it across the table to Kali. Then waited, with great satisfaction, while Kali stared disbelievingly at it.

"Open it."

"You didn't take away Jane's glasses just to get me to identify them, did you?"

"Open the box, Huron."

"But you've interfered with her eye hygiene!"

"Just open it."

With sweating hands that left damp smudges on the cardboard, Kali opened the box and looked inside.

"What are those?" Kali asked, staring at the contents.

"You know damn well what they are."

"Ski goggles?"

"You mean night-vision goggles, don't you?"

"I've never seen these things before," Kali said.

"For use in illegal surveillance."

"I don't know what you're talking about."

"That's what they all say."

"Well, in my case it's true."

Kali felt like he was sinking in a pool of quicksand and the more he tried to help himself, the deeper he went. He had no sense of what was going on. He couldn't figure out how to proceed.

"At least," he said in a discouraged voice, "Jane has her glasses."

"She will—after we run some tests."

"Tests on the glasses? Why? What do you expect to find?"

"You tell us, Huron."

"But for now," said the man in the brown suit, moving toward the table, "just put the goggles back in the box. Slowly. Smoothly. No quick or unexpected moves."

"This is crazy."

"And close it up exactly as it was before."

The fire marshal said, "You know, Huron, your fingerprints were all over that box."

"Of course they were," Kali said vehemently.

"And now they're all over the ordnance."

"Ordnance?"

"You'd better come clean with us. This 'Jane Plain' was your accomplice, wasn't she?"

"Accomplice to what? I don't know what you mean."

"In the assassination attempt. You duped her."

"No! No!"

"Just tell us Jane Plain's real name."

'You mean that's not her real name?" Kali asked, struggling to keep the anguish out of his voice.

"She's used others."

The Kali who had never lied in his life (until Cincinnati) couldn't imagine that Jane—the Jane of the dulcet voice, the Jane of the pungent fragrance, the Jane of passionate abandonment—had lied to him about her name. Though from the first he'd thought her name unusual, to say the least, and wondered how her parents could burden her with it. But that she'd lie about it? To him? Before and after all they'd done together?

"I don't believe you."

"Believe what you want, Huron."

"You're mistaken about Jane." Kali rose from his chair, leaned over the table toward the fire marshal. "You're mistaken about everything, actually. Your questions are based on lies or gross misinterpretations."

"Sit down, Huron," he warned.

"But you don't know what you're talking about!" Kali, still standing, raised his voice, gestured intently with hands. "Why won't you listen?"

"Down," ordered the fire marshal as the man in the brown suit put his hand inside his jacket.

"Everything's crazy! You're making a mistake!"

Without warning, the fire marshal stood and picked up his chair and threw it across the room, effectively stopping Kali in midsentence and midfeeling. The man in the brown suit retrieved the chair and set it upright where it had been before.

"Now about this grandmother of yours—" the fire marshal began as though nothing had happened, as though everything could now go on as before.

"—'alleged' grandmother—" corrected the man in the brown suit.

"What name does she go by?"

"Please. This is unnecessary," Kali said, as he slumped in his chair.

"We'll decide what's necessary and what isn't."

"State the name, Huron."

"All right. Aziza Hourani."

"Now we're getting somewhere. Country of origin."

"Lebanon, formerly part of Syria."

The fire marshal and the man in the brown suit exchanged congratulatory glances.

"Present whereabouts?"

"Saints Peter & Paul Syrian Orthodox Cemetery when she's not appearing to me or, presumably, one of her other charges."

"Huron, do you think we're stupid?"

"I'm beginning to wonder," Kali said under his breath. It just slipped out. It wasn't what he intended to say.

The fire marshal stood and glared at Kali and, as Kali prepared himself for what might come, the man in the brown suit came forward as if on cue.

"Cuff the prisoner again. Confine him to lockup."

The room to which Kali was delivered was cold and dry. Piled floor to ceiling—except for a clearing in the center—with obsolete office machines and furniture: desks, chairs, typewriter stands, typewriters, adding machines with leftover scraggly tapes, dozens of black and gray telephones tangled together in their wires, and two metal cots.

Kali stood still for a few minutes. Getting his bearings. And though handcuffed, prepared to defend himself if necessary. Not against the remote, unlikely dangers about which he'd agonized for half a lifetime. But against whatever might come through the door. Against whatever might try to steal his view of the world and his place in it.

For in spite of his longstanding fears of random disaster, Kali clung to a belief in the order of things. As ye sow, so shall ye reap;

events will unfold according to laws of probability and predictability; mankind in general and individuals in particular are cradled by benevolent forces. Things, he reassured himself, work out in the end.

With a tentative, unfamiliar bravado, Kali knocked one of the piled up chairs to the floor, stood it upright, and sat down. Situe sat in the corner on her own stool.

"Thank God, Situe-bitue, what a relief to see you," he almost sobbed.

"I'm pleased to see you as well."

"How long have you been here, in this . . . dungeon?"

"Long enough."

"Have you seen what they're doing?"

She nodded yes.

"What's going on?" Kali asked her. "Why am I here?"

"They think you're a terrorist."

"How could they think that?"

"Nationality, demeanor, activity."

"Oh, no."

"You're an Arab—"

"—Even though I can't speak the language?"

"I blame your father, my son, for that."

"He wanted to be an American."

"He could be both Arab and American."

"He wanted us to speak English. To eat American food."

"Such food! May your grandfather rest in peace!"

"A terrible thing, I concede that, Situe-bitue. But let's get back to the topic at hand. What shall I do now?"

She lit a cigarette as though she needed it.

"You haven't helped yourself so far. The way you looked at the airport, sweating, nervous, clutching that briefcase of yours—"

"—it had Jane's glasses in it." He stopped, winced when he remembered how Sophie had tried to carry it for him. His expression changed and he leaned toward Situe, forgetting himself for a moment.

"By the way, how's Sophie doing with all this?"

"She and her sisters went to church together."

"To pray for me?"

"It's Sunday. They always go."

"But, is she worried?"

"Why should she be? She thinks you're in Cincinnati, remember? You're not supposed to be home until tomorrow night."

Kali bowed his head forward. "So she doesn't know?"

"Not yet."

She blew giant smoke rings through her mouth and small doubles through her nose. Kali watched them dissolve as they floated toward the ceiling.

"I took my best shot, like you said, Situe-bitue."

"An unfortunate choice of words, as it turns out."

"I've ruined everything."

"You're not that powerful, dear grandson."

"I want to ask you," he hesitated before completing the question, "about Jane. Did she win the contest?"

"No."

"I'll never forgive myself for getting her into this. Is she under arrest, too?"

"Don't worry about that girl. She floats to the top. It's a gift."

"Now she won't get a job as a belly dancer on a cruise ship."

"She's had another offer. Two, actually. One from a photographer with a stutter. And . . . " Situe stopped as if thinking of how to phrase the rest of her statement.

"Yes?"

"One of the men who is questioning you—the one who wears the brown suit—is letting her stay at his place."

"No!"

"Yes."

"Isn't that against the rules?"

"Many things are against the rules, but that doesn't stop them from being done."

"My God, my God, my God."

"This is not the time for incantatory statements. Focus, Kali."

He stretched his arms above his head as far as they would go, notwithstanding the handcuffs, and tried to breathe deeply.

"You're right. So, exactly where am I?"

"In the basement of an abandoned building."

"In Santa Vista?"

"About fifteen miles north."

"Are there any other buildings around?"

"No."

"Why here?"

"It was close and available."

Kali sighed.

"And private. Convenient for questioning, for faking a death when you want it to look like the accidental fall of a drunken member of a belly dancing audience . . . "

Kali gasped. "Death?"

"That's what I said."

"How long have I been here?" he managed to ask.

"Since the beginning of time. The past and the present merge on a great continuum."

"Please, Situe, spare me the philosophical lecture."

"I speak the truth."

"Yes, yes, I know, but on a more mundane level, how long?"

"About eight hours."

"It's the middle of the night?"

"Yes."

He looked intently into his grandmother's face. "I need to get out of here alive and without causing repercussions to those I love."

"If you get out, where will you go?"

"I'm not sure."

"Finally," she said, "intelligent flexibility, a reasonable acknowledgment of the unknown. I congratulate you for that. It's a movement in the right direction." She gazed intently at him. "Even though you don't yet have answers."

"Then everything will work out?" Kali asked.

"There are no guarantees."

"Can't you just get me out of here? With heavenly magic or something?"

"You know the rules," Situe said quietly.

"Then I reject your rules. I reject all rules. The hell with them all."

"Calm yourself," Situe said. "Listen. He's coming back."

Kali heard approaching footsteps.

"Who are these people?" Kali asked her.

"The cast varies, but the script remains the same."

"What kind of answer is that?"

"How about this: it's the same everywhere; only the uniforms change."

"They're not wearing uniforms."

"Exactly."

"What now?"

"Now is the time for bravery, dear Kali. And vision. You have the means. You have the ability."

The door opened and the man in the brown suit appeared.

"Time to go."

"Go where?" Kali asked.

"Just get up."

As the man led Kali down a hallway, Kali felt the proportion of fear to courage shifting slightly. More courage, less fear. He thought of Situe's words; her comforting image rested in a corner of his mind.

The fire marshal sat at the same table as before. He motioned to Kali to sit in the same chair. Indicated that the handcuffs should be removed. Kali resisted rubbing his wrists so he wouldn't give them the satisfaction of his discomfort.

"Kahlil Gibran Hourani, please state your full name."

"You just stated it."

"We want you to say it."

"I don't see the need."

The questioner tossed a pair of leather gloves in the center of the table. Although Kali did not understand the exact nature of the threat, he answered.

"Kahlil Gibran Hourani."

"So, Mr. Huron, where do you live?"

He told them.

"Are you married?"

"Please leave Sophie out of this." He was prepared to suffer his own fate, but to drag Sophie into this—whatever it was—after already dragging Jane into it (although Jane sounded as though she was making out pretty well) was a cruel blow.

"Is Sophie, your wife, the woman who dropped you off at the airport?"

Kali said nothing.

"The woman who thinks you're in—" he checked his notes— "Cincinnati at an obstetricians' convention?"

"Opticians."

"Excuse me. Op-tic-ian," the questioner repeated with a mocking, staccato bounce to each syllable. "We don't like being corrected, Mr. Huron."

"Even if you're wrong?"

"Especially if we're wrong."

The fire marshal and the man in the brown suit looked at each other with satisfaction.

"So, Mr. Huron, do you know what an admission against interest is?" the fire marshal asked, as he turned a page on his clipboard, crossed off a line with his pen.

"Vaguely."

Kali felt the room tighten. He looked at the faces of the two men and saw the failure of empathy, the corruption of unchecked power.

"What are you looking at, Huron? Are you playing some sort of game?"

"I'm looking at you. I'm looking at you as fellow humans, as members of my species. Trying to find a common ground. Trying to figure out why you're doing this."

"Are you threatening us, Huron?"

"No, no, of course not."

"Who do you think you are?" asked the man in the brown suit.

"It's just that I don't always understand what you mean," Kali offered.

"Those are fighting words, Huron," said the fire marshal.

"How can you interpret my words that way? I have the right to express my opinions. The right to ask questions. I'm a citizen. For God's sake, we're all citizens."

"Right. What of it?"

"I want to know who you are," Kali said firmly.

"Keepers of the peace."

"That answer is insufficient. You need to give me more information."

"Make us." They thought this was very funny.

"I have a second question. Why am I here?"

"You tell us."

"That's your answer?"

"Any more questions, Huron?"

"Please don't call me 'Huron.' That's not my name."

"All right, *Mister* Huron. Anything else?"

"Anything else?" echoed the man in the brown suit.

Kali hesitated. He was reluctant to have them know that he needed anything, especially information. He didn't want to appear more vulnerable than he was. But his need to know overrode his reluctance.

"I want to know how long you intend to keep me here against my will."

"That all depends on you."

"Does anyone know I'm here?"

"*I* didn't tell anyone," said the man in the brown suit, with a malicious grin.

Kali started again. "I want to know whether anyone knows about my—"

"—espionage?"

"That's insane. I've done nothing like that. I was—disloyal—to my wife, to Sophie, I admit it. I was trying to find answers. Answers I should have searched for in another way and in another time. But I didn't commit espionage; I wasn't even unpatriotic. And I—"

"—About those answers, Huron. Where'd you go? Who'd you see?" The fire marshal slapped a yellow legal pad on the table in front of Kali and tossed a ballpoint pen on top of it.

"Write it all down and save yourself a lot of trouble," said the man in the brown suit.

Kali said nothing. He left the pen and paper where they were. The fire marshal leaned over the table and stuck his face close to Kali's. So close that Kali could smell the alcohol from the night before.

"It's now or never, Huron."

The fire marshal stayed bent, threatening. He stared intensely into Kali's face.

"Well," Kali started slowly, and the man in the brown suit, sensing something important, picked up his pen, ready to write.

"There is something you should be aware of." He stopped for an instant, recognizing their intense desire to hear what he had to say. Dangling them for a few more seconds, unable to let go of the first shred of control he'd had with them, unable to resist magnifying the dramatic effect. He could feel the tension in the fire marshal's face and neck; he could feel the heat of the laser beam stare.

"Something you may want to know," Kali began again, strengthening and expanding his voice, as the fire marshal lessened the distance between them; they came face to face, nose to nose, eye to eye.

"As I told you, I am an optician, a man who has looked closely into hundreds of faces and thousands of eyes."

Kali paused. "In my profession I have seen many things. For example, right now, I see something you may want to know about." He paused again.

"Right now, as we sit here, I can—and will— tell you that . . . probably for your whole life, and probably without being aware of it, you have had . . . a wandering eye. The left one, as a matter of fact."

He picked up the pace and increased the volume of his voice: "But do not let it defeat you, for help is on the way. A few exercises, conscientiously performed for a relatively short period of time, may rid you of your problem. Or at least significantly improve your condition."

The fire marshal squinted and, with one forward thrust of his head, smashed Kali's nose across his face.

12

"WELL, THAT WAS AN AUSPICIOUS ENDING," Situe said, bending over him.

Kali moaned in pain. His nose was caked with dried blood. His face was swollen. His eyes were black.

"Although we're proud of you. We didn't know you had it in you."

"We?" he managed to ask.

"The colleagues I persuaded that you were worth the trouble."

He lay on his back on the floor, drifting in and out of consciousness, while the towers of furniture around the perimeter of the room rocked back and forth like skyscrapers in an earthquake.

Situe's hand reached out to touch him, stayed suspended between them, as if she were struggling with a rule she knew she shouldn't break.

"Why are they doing this?" Kali asked.

"Death by inches. The theory being that before too many inches are accumulated on their measuring stick, you'll tell them what they want to know."

"But I don't know anything."

"You're beginning to know, dear grandson."

"Thank you for the compliment, Situe-bitue. It almost makes this ordeal worth the pain, but not quite." He tried again to sit up.

"How long have I been here?"

"Half a day."

"So I have two days to get out of here before Sophie finds out."

"I don't think you appreciate the gravity of this situation. Sophie is the least of your worries."

"But I'm innocent."

"Innocent of what?"

"Surely, they'll find out that I'm just a middle-aged—"

"—fool?"

He couldn't finish his own sentence.

"They don't think you're a fool, Kali. They take you seriously. Isn't that what you've always wanted?"

"So I said."

"Ironic, isn't it?"

What little food remained in his stomach squeezed up his esophagus. He couldn't swallow his saliva fast enough and began to drool. He alternated between leaden pain and numbness induced by shock. Never before had another man intentionally injured him. That one man could so desire to hurt another filled him with surprise and grief.

"Ah, dear grandson. See if you can sleep. Conserve yourself. They'll be back."

He tried what she suggested.

"It's impossible."

"Keep trying. You must learn to ease your own pain."

"I can't. My mind is galloping everywhere."

"Then together we shall tether it."

From nowhere Situe's stool appeared and she nodded gratefully and sat down. Kali lay as comfortably as he could. Situe lit a cigarette and inhaled deeply, then closed her eyes and began:

It had long been a concern among half the people of the village that securing water from the fountain was too great a burden. The half that complained? The half that had to carry it in jugs on their shoulders or heads or however else they managed: the women. And the women that lived farthest from the fountain complained the most. Naturally.

There was so much complaining that their husbands and fathers and sons could no longer tolerate it. Rather than pitch in and help carry, which would have violated all the rules they lived by, they decided to dig another well in the other half of the village and build another fountain over it. Concerns over whether there would be enough water to support two fountains were overridden by fears of continued discontent in the households.

The new fountain was built exactly as the old and everything went smoothly for a while. But people inclined to complain will always find something to complain about.

"I don't know anymore what goes on with the Maloofs in the other half of the village."

"The eligible daughters are cut off from half of the eligible sons."

And so forth.

Soon, people could say only bad things about the new fountain and wondered why they wanted to build it in the first place. In fact, they couldn't find anything good to say about any fountain, old or new. They sat around in the evening and recalled every gloomy fountain tale they could recall.

Remember those scraggly Bedouins who stopped here when they were dying of thirst? asked a great grandmother with the longest memory in her family. And we gave them water from the old fountain and fed them and gave them a place to rest? And when they left, they helped themselves to a few goats, a camel, and a foolish widow who wandered outside her door alone at night?

Everyone nodded. Yes, they remembered.

And who could forget the Boulos sisters, Tameen the Older and Tameen the Younger?

"Two sisters with the same name?" Kali said, and Situe was relieved that he could pay enough attention in his state of mind to formulate a question.

"The older one was named in joy after her mother; some said the younger was named Tameen so that their father would have someone to blame for the mother's death, for she died giving birth to their second daughter."

The two Tameens gathered water from the old fountain twice each day.

Now, a young man named Youseff Ibrahim managed to be at the old fountain each evening because he loved Tameen the Elder. And she loved him. But there was bad blood between their fathers. And when the Tameens' father realized that his older daughter loved his enemy's son, he forbade her from going to the fountain. Which meant that Tameen the Younger, the runt of the village, had to carry the water by herself. She lasted a week before she tripped and fell and broke her neck.

Somehow the jug survived the fall. But who would take it to the fountain now? For Tameen the Elder, crushed with sorrow by the death of her younger sister and the loss of her lover, wasted away. Dying of a double broken heart.

And Youseff who loved her? Stabbed himself at that fountain and watched passively as his blood, sparkling in the moonlight, seeped into the sand.

Situe stopped and sighed—for herself, the two Tameens, the lover, Kali. She looked at him on the floor below her. Unable to tell if he was asleep or listening. But this story, with its endless plot possibilities and choice of characters deserved telling whether anyone heard or not. So she went on.

Those same eyes that saw nothing good about the old fountain turned their gaze on the new fountain.

"The water tastes brackish."

"This miserable ledge is too narrow to sit on. How poor and scrawny do they think we are?"

The men, of course, still worked all day in the fields, as they had in the past. Leaving the village and returning in the evening to the close arrangement of houses where they all lived. Houses that grew topsy-turvy, for when a son married and brought his wife home, another room or two had to be added wherever it would fit. Amidst this labyrinth of sleeping rooms and living rooms, the talk was fountains, fountains, fountains.

Just when it seemed that the impasse would never be overcome, the orthodox priest made his semiannual visit. Dirty, tired, bearded, and far too young to be on the road for weeks at a time without a wife, he dismounted his horse on the side of the town near the old fountain. And took a long, deep drink.

"Ah, just what was needed, a drink of this sweet, clear water." He was then ushered to the new fountain without being given a chance to rest or change or gather his thoughts, where he was invited to take another drink. "Ah, just what was needed, a drink of this sweet, clear water." A crisis avoided, upon his arrival at least.

The villagers feted the priest with everything they had to offer. A sponge bath, sleep on the richest family's finest rug. And to eat? Kibbe, bread, hummus, luban, dolmas, tabbouleh, roast lamb, figs, olives, lentils, cheese, tomatoes. It was a great feast, and everyone came.

Afterward he conducted services in the open air because the church was too small to accommodate the entire village. He blessed the few marriages that had taken place in his absence, christened babies, dissolved curses with holy water, erased bad luck by his presence. He read a half page letter sent the year before to a villager from a cousin in Damascus. He counseled against interpreting dreams without priestly assistance and reminded families that outside the commandments and the teachings of the church, there was no salvation.

And with great vigor, he admonished the elders to protect the purity of their daughters, although he blushed and felt a physical response when he said these words, for he couldn't help but imagine himself in bed with one of them, any one of them, despite himself. While the mothers paraded their older and less attractive unmarried daughters in front of him. Assuming that as a priest, he wouldn't be so vain as to demand the most beautiful or the youngest; that he would remain humbly grateful for whatever God provided him. But the priest's head was turned by all the attention and he started using the editorial "we" when referring to himself in conversation, and borrowed the grand gestures of the patriarch to illustrate his points. And he decided that none of the girls brought before him deserved to be his wife. Which was probably true.

Nevertheless, for a few days the villagers set aside their disputes over the fountains.

On the last afternoon of the priest's visit, during his sermon urging them to love God unto ages and ages, the sound of approaching horses settled on the congregation. At least a dozen. Fast moving. Snorting and neighing upon their arrival. The Turks: coming to conscript their young men, to take them to die or starve or fade away from homesickness.

No one moved as if stillness and silence alone would drive the soldiers away. Except the young priest who, though terrified, believed he had the power of God behind him. He went forward to confront them, to tell them, in God's name, to leave them alone. He approached the apparent leader, a massive man on a massive horse, who'd halted his followers near the old fountain.

Holding a Byzantine cross in front of him as though he were casting out the devil, the priest walked boldly toward the men and their horses. Just as he reached the leader, a snake slithered out of its hole. One horse bucked and screeched, spooking the others, who also bucked and screeched, thereby igniting the riders, who cursed and drew their weapons, thinking they were being ambushed.

The people in the village panicked and began crying out. In the confusion, the young priest—never an agile man—was struck in the chest by plunging hooves. He dropped to the ground and within seconds a fatal blow was delivered.

"They killed him," screamed an old woman.

The men of the village ran toward the Turks, without weapons, without thinking, without a plan except to remove the body of their priest from certain destruction, this priest, whose young and unconsummated life was ended by a hoof to the head.

There was no love lost between these groups. The soldiers, in self-righteous anger, sliced and shot their unarmed attackers. Many villagers were killed. Of the women who rushed to the aid of their husbands and sons, there were no fatal injuries, although one was taken by the soldiers and never returned.

How could this have happened? the villagers wailed and sobbed and beat their breasts.

Pride and envy, they were forced to agree. They'd ignored God's plan and substituted their own. They argued and complained. They built a second fountain when they had a perfectly good one already. And so on.

But here Situe stopped. Though it was a saga she could have sustained, bringing the descendants of the villagers up to the present. Modernizing the societies, reframing the beliefs, the politics, expanding the conflict to include cities, states, nations. Tying it all together with the braided string of human strengths and frailties.

She looked at Kali, snoring heavily below her: Kali, the continuation of the strongest and feeblest of human nature. Was he ready to move to a higher level of instruction? Could he comprehend in direct discussion the principles she was trying to teach him? That the only thing certain is change itself; that tradition counts for everything; tradition counts for nothing; that individual courage and prowess matter; that community matters. That the world is good, the world is bad, and so forth.

They were about halfway through the required course of study. Following a curriculum developed over centuries. One that Situe learned through intense discourse with her new contemporaries, her new peers.

Though sometimes she was impatient with them, with their endless theorizing: is the man drowning, they'd ask, because he cannot fathom the true nature of water, or because the gap between what water is and what he thinks it is, is unbridgeable? Or: did the man's reliance on mere words about water deprive him of the knowledge that if he breathed it in, it would fill his lungs and he would die? Or: does a great difference in quantity change its quality? That is to say, if the man were doused with a pail of water as opposed to being flung into the middle of an ocean, is the water's essence changed from life-preserving to death-inducing?

Enough! Situe would shout. Pluck the man out of it, dry him off, and give him something to eat. Do you know nothing of Arab hospitality?

But now, in this moment, her dear grandson, wounded, braver than before, slept soundly at her feet. Would he prevail? Or merely survive? Or neither? She had a limited time to teach him. And the lessons she wanted him to learn required great strength. She must teach him to see clearly, knowing he saw little; to seek what he desired, with no guarantees.

As Situe faded away, Kali stirred slightly and sighed. When he woke up, he would see that she was gone. And despite his fear, he would proceed on his own—a little longer, a little stronger, each time. For he was learning, whether he knew it or not. And she would return when he needed her, whether she could help or not.

13

"LET'S CUT TO THE CHASE, HARARY," said the fire marshal. But he changed his tone after the man in the brown suit whispered something in his ear.

"But first, how's that nose? No hard feelings, right?"

Kali didn't answer.

"It's nothing personal. Just following procedure."

Kali stared at them; he couldn't believe what he was hearing.

The fire marshal found his place on his clipboard and showed it to the man in the brown suit. Neither seemed concerned that Kali had not responded.

"Now, back to business." The fire marshal undid the top button of his shirt, having already removed his tie.

"Harary, on that tape we got from your room at the Empire, we heard you say, 'you've gotta take your best shot.'"

"We went over this before," Kali said, his words slightly slurred, since the swelling in his face made it hurt to talk and pushed his eyes nearly shut. To be able to see the fire marshal, he had to tilt his head back. And if he moved too much, he lost the chin or the forehead, and the fire marshal looked like nothing more than a pair of sullen moving lips.

Kali's head ached; his face ached. He longed to sleep; he longed to fight back; he wanted to escape into unconsciousness; he wanted to spring upon them like an animal and tear them apart. He desperately wished that none of this was happening.

"Yes, indeed. We heard everything on that tape." The fire marshal's voice—swaggering, boastful, insolent.

"Everything," said the man in the brown suit.

"What do you want me to say?" Kali asked. "I'm not denying what I did."

"We want you to tell the truth."

"I've told you the truth."

"I don't see why you're so modest. You were quite a guy back there at the Empire."

"You had no right to invade my privacy that way. I'm a citizen of this country. I was born here. We have laws against this kind of thing."

"I know how you feel, Harary. We—us men—well, we have it a lot harder—forgive the pun—than the women," said the fire marshal.

"What you've done is illegal."

"Was it the frustration of not being able to get it up that made you say that?"

"Say what?"

"You'd take your best shot?"

"I didn't say that!"

"Because you were having trouble shooting something else off?"

"Are you mad?"

"We're not the ones who went to a shrink, Harary. You are."

"Why are you doing this?" Kali shouted.

"Frankly, I'm getting sick of your lack of cooperation," said the fire marshal, dropping any pretense of understanding or sympathy. "We have a profile on you, you know."

The New Belly Dancer of the Galaxy | 107

"On me?" Kali felt dizzy. In danger of losing his new resolve to resist and try to escape.

"You think we just heard about you yesterday?" asked the man in the brown suit.

"You think you blipped on to our radar screen only because of the assassination attempt? We've been watching you for a long time."

"There's been no assassination attempt."

"You couldn't get a clear shot?" asked the man in the brown suit.

"Tell us you didn't know the lieutenant governor was making an appearance at the RV convention at your hotel. Tell us you didn't request a room with a birds-eye view of the podium by the half-barrel barbecues."

"What?"

"You intended to assassinate the lieutenant governor, didn't you, Harary?"

"I voted for the lieutenant governor."

"Which is neither here nor there."

"This is how it happened, isn't it: you lay in wait at the window in your room."

"You can't deny that," said the man in the brown suit. "Your fingerprints are all over the windowsill."

"Of course they are. I was staying there. I don't deny opening the window. I needed some air—"

"—I bet you did," said the man in the brown suit, snickering.

The fire marshal said, "Make a note—suspect makes second admission against interest."

Poor Kali. Poor Situe, who grimaced from her place of observation behind him. She hadn't intended to be there, afraid her presence would distract him and make him seem more evasive than he already did. This conclusion she came to after a simple cost/benefit analysis—a technique she'd recently learned. On the one hand; on the other. A time-tested, respectable approach, they'd advised her. Usually reliable. Hah! It didn't reckon with a *situe's* intensity of feeling for one specific, beloved grandson. Her immediate and unswerving concern was for Kali, theoretical restrictions notwithstanding, and she could not stay away. She hovered behind him, watching, hoping.

"All right, Harary, let's talk about something else. Your false foray into the airport. Your fraudulent behavior with your wife—that is assuming she wasn't in on it with you."

"Oh, no, not Sophie. Please, not Sophie. She's completely innocent."

"Then you admit that you're the guilty party."

"I admit no such thing. I'm telling you that, whatever you think I did—which is nothing, nothing at all—leave Sophie out of it. She doesn't know anything. She didn't do anything."

"So you did act alone. No fellow conspirators?"

"No conspiracy at all."

The questioner wrote down "suspect acted alone" on his clipboard.

"That phony trip to the airport. Trying to throw us off track?"

"No. Trying to throw Sophie off track, may she forgive me. All I wanted to do was deliver Jane's glasses."

"And you expect us to believe that?" said the man in the brown suit.

"You expect us to believe that you weren't going down there to get a whiff of Jane again? To inhale those perfumed oils she wears?"

"Citrus and ginger," said the man in the brown suit, "she mixes it up herself."

Kali winced.

"Hey, we've all been there, trying to get away from the wife."

"It's not like it sounds."

"Now we're getting some place."

"Let me explain," Kali began again, knowing his efforts were futile, yet unable to stop. "She didn't pick up her glasses when they were ready."

"What glasses?"

"Her eyeglasses, of course," answered Kali, with exasperation.

"You mean Jane's?" asked the man in the brown suit. Kali hated him, wanted to knock him on the floor, but remembering his nose, decided to let the moment go by without telling him or trying it.

"I took them to her apartment and she wasn't there. She left me a note—I honestly don't now how she knew I was coming, do you?"

"Of course not. How would we know?"

"But everything got away from me."

"Tell us about it."

Kali breathed deeply. "Everybody thinks I'm unbalanced, you know."

"Because of your extreme political beliefs and your assassination attempt? Or is there another reason?"

"No, because, after the dream, I tried to contact my grand-mother and then I did and, since then, she's been visiting me and telling me stories—

"What kinds of stories?" The fire marshal was poised again to write down what Kali said.

"We have ethical discussions."

"Well, it looks like they didn't do any good with you here on the brink of committing murder."

"Don't you listen to anything I say? Didn't you find out anything true about me?"

The fire marshal and the man in the brown suit conferred in private in the corner and when they finished, the man in the brown suit had a smile on his face.

"Hey, I think we should get our friend here a nice warm washcloth for his face. He can't be too comfortable with all that dried blood caked around his nose."

He brought Kali a cloth and Kali wiped his face, shocked by what came off it. His nose felt numb, which made it harder to wipe. His swollen eyes were tired and hurt when he touched them or tried to move the lids.

Everyone sat still for a few minutes. The man in the brown suit brought in a glass of chilled orange juice.

Kali drank it.

"How about a bathroom break, Harary?"

When Kali returned from the bathroom, there was a sandwich on the table and an apple. He ate both.

"What shall I do with the core?"

The man in the brown suit reached over and put it in his pocket. After a few minutes of quiet, the fire marshal stood and sat on the edge of the table. Then without warning, he bellowed, "All right, you Bedouin sonofabitch, speak English around us. No foreign language clues; no coded messages." He banged the table with his clipboard.

Kali's whole body flinched at the unexpected noise. "Have you heard me speak one word of Arabic?" he shouted angrily, "except for the word *situe*?"

"Which means?" asked the man in the brown suit.

"This is ridiculous."

"Which means?" repeated the man in the brown.

"'Grandmother,' like I said before," Kali answered, a man resigned to his fate.

"What other words, if any, do you know?"

"*Jiddue.*"

"Which means?"

"Grandfather."

"Any others?"

"*Keefak.*"

"Which means?"

"Hello, how are you?"

"Just fine," the man in the brown suit answered genially. The fire marshal hastily scribbled the three Arabic words and their translations on a page on his clipboard.

"Listen here, Harary, let's get one thing straight. We may not be fluent in Arabic like you are. But you can't fool us. You can't smuggle any Arabic messages to your compatriots and you'd better not try."

"How could I possibly get a message to anybody? Much less in Arabic which I don't speak?" asked Kali. "I'm being held in here forcibly, with the two of you. Nobody knows I'm here. Nobody else can hear what I have to say. Unless the room is wired for sound or something. In which case, you did it, not me. I've never been here before. Remember?"

The implication of Kali's words appeared to stagger the fire marshal, who immediately surveyed every inch of the room. Where the walls and floors came together. Electrical outlets. Worn spots in the floor. Cracks in the ceiling.

"Well, Harary, we can't find the bug or the wire, but that doesn't mean we won't."

The fire marshal and the man in the brown suit left the room. Only the man in the brown suit returned. He looked grim.

"I forgot to search you."

"There's no reason to search me."

"Take off your clothes."

"What?

"Just do it."

"Why?"

"Just do it. Please."

"I refuse."

"Don't refuse."

"Shirt first. We already have your jacket."

"If I won't?"

"Don't ask."

"Well, I'm going to ask."

The man pulled his coat back, displaying a gun sticking out of a pocket.

"It's real."

Kali unbuttoned his cuffs, noticing for the first time how dirty they were. As were his fingernails. There were cuts and scratches on the backs of his hands which he didn't remember getting.

Next, the buttons on his shirt—a favorite shirt—of light cotton, a tasteful plaid of gray and burgundy that flattered him, Sophie always said.

The shirt was beyond repair. Bloodstained down the front, from his nose, no doubt. Plus general filth from the outside of the cloth to the inside. He laid the shirt across the back of the chair on which he'd been sitting.

"Arms out straight."

A kind of metal detector, Kali assumed, ran over his arms; the device was cold, but not sharp. The same shape as those automatic barbecue lighters that never failed. The process seemed like nothing to worry about until the man forced it into Kali's right armpit.

"Hey!"

The man plunged it in again. Harder, like he was poking at some vermin down a hole. Kali reached out to grab him, but the man was quicker and jabbed him in the solar plexus. Kali lost air, wove, caught himself. Doubled over.

The probing continued. Four or five times under each arm. Pitiless and deep. The sour, rancid smell of Kali's body filled the room.

"Now, stand up straight."

The man swept the device slowly over Kali's chest, top to bottom and side to side. Twice.

"Anyone can see that I have no place to conceal anything. Look, there's nothing, nothing hidden anywhere."

"Quiet."

The man set the device on the table and placed his hand in the hollow of Kali's throat. Kali tensed, waiting for the infliction of some kind of pain. Instead, the man stroked Kali's sweating skin. Then, with the fingers of that same hand, firmly but gently, he combed the coarse black hair that covered Kali's chest. Kali stiffened but did nothing. The man circled one of Kali's nipples; he circled the other one. They became taut, erect, in spite of Kali's mental efforts to prevent it. The man breathed deeply and regularly. He touched a spot marked by a freshly made bruise.

"I'm sorry."

When the man stepped back, Kali braced himself. He had no idea what would happen next. Sweat nearly blinded him and burned the abrasions on his face. He moved to wipe it out of his eyes, and the man ordered him to hold still—the almost tender expression on the man's face contrasting with the stridency of his voice.

"Open your mouth."

"I can tell you're a decent man," Kali said. "You don't have to do this."

"You don't get it, do you?"

"Get what?"

"Just open your mouth and shut up."

"Which is it?" Kali asked, "open or shut?"

The man responded with a hard clip to the back of Kali's neck. Kali's head rang and his vision doubled. Then the man shoved the device in Kali's mouth, chipping one of his front teeth. The man ran the device over the surfaces of Kali's mouth, under his tongue, the inside and outside of the gums. Nothing, apparently.

"Wider."

He thrust it down Kali's throat far enough to make him gag. A quick, rough insertion. In once; out once. Kali resisted the impulse to throw up. The man made a guttural sound, then continued the examination, probing Kali's ears and neck, leaving the nose alone.

"Take off your pants."

Kali hesitated.

"Drop them, Harary."

Kali dropped them to the floor. They'd already taken his belt; he'd been shoeless since the first minutes of questioning.

"Your shorts."

"No."

What did he have to lose? His life, his integrity, his pride? Maybe all of the above. He lunged for the gun in his new all-cotton underwear and the socks they matched so perfectly.

14

THIRD SESSION: each in his usual position. All fully dressed, though one precariously. One, filthy; two, rumpled. One, hurt yet emboldened, though unsure of the outcome.

"We don't know how you hid it—or them—but you won't get away with it, Harmouni. Have no doubt. We'll find everything we need to send you away for a long time."

"Every goddam thing," growled the man in the brown suit. His lips were split top to bottom in several places; there were handprints around his neck; he bore invisible internal wounds.

"And then you'll be of no further use to us," continued the fire marshal.

"None whatsoever."

"You'll be expendable."

"Completely."

"Go to hell," Kali thought. He wore a new gash on the side of his head—clotted and sticky—and took in the smell of his own blood with every breath.

As the fire marshal consulted his notes, Kali wondered what could be asked that had not already been asked; what pain inflicted that had not yet been inflicted. Maybe they were going to kill him outright and hadn't gotten around to mentioning it.

In spite of this grim possibility, however, Kali stood his ground. He no longer dreaded what might happen, because it seemed to have happened. He had confronted a real calamity, an unavoidably immediate and personal event, and made it through.

He had lunged for a gun.

Not that he had covered himself with unqualified glory, so far. But two steps forward and one step back was progress of a sort. Had the earth shifted on its axis? Was there a change of seasons? He didn't know, but whatever the explanation, he clung to its inner results.

"Tell us, Kali—"

It was the second time they'd called him by his first name and Kali wondered what they thought they were accomplishing by it.

"Why did you climb the stairs at the Palace of Fine Arts?"

He wanted to shout, "Because they were there," but said instead, "Because the elevator was broken."

"Nothing to do with surveying the premises?"

"Nothing."

"The short man behind the counter in the lobby told us you had a box under your arm—"

"I did. Jane's glasses." The whole time he talked now, he tried to think of ways to escape. Looking for vulnerabilities in his questioners, weaknesses in the physical prison around him.

"The woman at the card table said you carried that box into the Middle Salon."

"I already told you the box had Jane's glasses in it and I was going to take them to her." He steadied his voice. "She left me a note saying that's where she'd be and that's where I took the glasses."

"Like a trained poodle," sneered the fire marshal.

Kali looked at the man in the brown suit. "You'll find out how what it's like soon enough."

"You shut your mouth."

"What's going on here?" asked the fire marshal.

"Did he tell you where Jane's staying?" Kali asked.

The fire marshal glared at the man in the brown suit, who withdrew a handkerchief from his pocket and blew his nose and wiped his injured face.

"How," the fire marshal asked Kali, "do *you* have any information about *us*?"

"I have my ways, too," Kali said mysteriously.

The man in the brown suit came forward and knocked Kali off his chair. As he lay on the floor, the fire marshal continued the questions.

"Now, let's see. The woman at the card table said you lied to get into the Salon."

"I told you before that's not true," Kali answered, with as much dignity as he could muster from his inferior position. Slowly, slowly he lifted himself from the floor, trying not to provoke another attack; watching so that if it came, he'd be able to anticipate it. Perhaps, deflect it.

"Do you deny that the woman said you couldn't go in unless you shopped?"

"No."

"But you didn't shop, did you?"

"I bought two CDs."

The man in the brown suit set two CDs on the table in front of Kali.

"Are these the ones?"

"You know damn well they are."

"What's hidden in these CDs? What's their real message?"

"I haven't even listened to them."

"Well, the seals are broken."

"Don't try to tell me you didn't do that."

A few minutes elapsed while the fire marshal stared silently at the surface of the table. "Let's focus on this alleged language deficit of yours. Is this part of the grand plan to keep the conspirators delinked?"

"As I told you before," Kali answered calmly, "I don't speak Arabic. We didn't speak Arabic in the house because my father wanted us to be 'American.'"

"We get it, Harmouni. Only the Arabic-speaking few are in on most of the info? Need to know basis, correct?"

"I simply never learned to speak the language."

"Like separate cells," the fire marshal continued, disregarding Kali's answer, "no one knows what anyone else is doing; each performs his part of the job only."

"I don't know what you're talking about."

"The hell you don't, Harmouni." The fire marshal became very still. And his breathing deepened and slowed. He lowered his voice as though he was about to reveal a message so potent its mere statement could affect the course of history.

"I'm talking about *hummus*."

"*Hummus*," the man in the brown suit intoned.

"I'm talking about *dolmas*."

"*Dolmas*."

"I'm talking about *cousa*."

"*Cousa*."

"Do you understand what I'm saying, Harmouni?" the fire marshal asked calmly, soothingly.

"Everyone knows what *hummus* is," Kali answered.

"So you *do* know Arabic!" the fire marshal said triumphantly, as though Kali had fallen into a well-laid trap.

"I know the names of Arabic foods."

"Tell us the ones you know," the fire marshal said, pen poised.

"The ones you just said and others."

"Which others?"

"Well, you forgot *tabbouleh*."

"Which is?"

"Parsley salad."

"And *kibbe*."

"Which is?"

"Raw or cooked lamb—"

"Raw lamb! Raw meat! That's disgusting!" The fire marshal jumped up and stomped around the room. "It's sick, I tell you! Sick! Your people make me sick! *You* make me sick! Sick! Sick! Sick!"

The fire marshal's saliva landed in the middle of the table and beyond and dribbled down his chin. Which he didn't seem to notice even when the man in the brown suit handed him the half-dirty handkerchief from his pocket. The fire marshal stood there purple-faced, clutching the handkerchief, while the veins in his neck pumped full.

"Let me remind you, Harmouni, that you are outnumbered, unarmed, and incommunicado."

"I was just thinking the same thing," Kali said quietly.

The fire marshal shoved the handkerchief in his pocket.

"I'm not going to beat around the bush any more, Harmouni."

"Is that what you've been doing?" asked Kali.

"Mano a mano, that's how we're going to proceed from now on."

"Fine. Whatever you say."

"You won't think it's fine for long," warned the man in the brown suit. Whatever benign or neutral feelings he had felt for Kali dissolved when Kali lunged for the gun and won. At least for a few minutes.

"Getting back to the *hummus*, Harmouni," the fire marshal said roughly, insistently. "This is your last chance to tell us about it."

Kali didn't know what to say and said nothing.

"Don't be coy, Harmouni. We already know it's a dip."

"That it is."

"And that it's made of chickpeas, sesame paste, lemon juice, garlic."

"Indeed," Kali answered.

"Now we're getting somewhere," said the fire marshal. "And that there was some of this '*hummus*' at the party before the belly dancing contest, was there not?"

"There was," Kali responded.

"Did you eat any?"

"Yes, it was very good."

"Well, I didn't like it," growled the man in the brown suit.

"Nobody cares whether you liked it or not," hissed the fire marshal, returning to his chair.

"Ah, *hummus, hummus, hummus*," mused the fire marshal. "The stuff of antigovernment plots. The perfect medium for the transport of contraband or explosives."

"Or both," added the man in the brown suit.

"And we're giving you this one opportunity—and make no mistake, this is the only one—to come clean, to tell us how the stuff is hidden."

They waited.

"Last chance."

Kali replied slowly. "Theoretically—"

"Of course," the fire marshal winked at the man in the brown suit, "only theoretically."

"—it could be done."

"Go on."

"But you'd need some very, very large containers."

"Continue."

"And, frankly, I've never seen a full one larger than this—" he made a circle with his hands about the size of a cantaloupe— "except at my mother-in-law's—"

"We're listening."

"—when she put the *hummus* in a half-gallon container which had been used for something else—"

"Do you remember what?"

"Popcorn I think. And the top came off in the car when she was taking it to the church—"

"A meeting of the cell at church, eh—?"

"—and the *hummus* spilled all over the back seat. The stain never came out. And she had to sell the car."

Something shifted in the room. Kali felt it. Molecules realigning, elements recombining. He had sealed his fate. He could tell by looking at their faces.

"So that's how it is," said the fire marshal. "You give us no choice." And he started toward the door, while the man in the brown suit held his position against the wall.

When the fire marshal returned, he carried one five by seven index card, which he fluttered in the air like a fan in front of Kali's face.

"Layla and Philip," he announced.

Kali froze.

"The girl is five foot seven, dark hair, dark eyes, would like to lose about six pounds. When she watches television, she crosses her legs and jiggles her foot."

"They have nothing to do with any of this. They're just children."

"Well, not exactly 'children,'" said the fire marshal. "It says here that Philip is twenty-four and Layla's birthday is next week." He looked at Kali and smiled. "I wonder what she wants for her birthday?"

"No," Kali said, choking.

"Now Philip, on the other hand, shouldn't get any presents," said the fire marshal throwing Kali a disgusted glance. "We know what Philip is, don't we?"

"I don't care. I've never cared," Kali cried out.

"Because of his, uh, predispositions, he sometimes goes to out-of-the-way places. Places where he could easily be hurt."

"You must listen to me. I'd tell you anything I knew to prevent injury to my children. But I don't know anything. I have no information. I am nobody. I'd tell you anything, but I have nothing to tell!"

"And, let's see here," the fire marshal continued, "it says that Layla writes poetry, most of it terrible."

"I beg of you."

"And Philip's motorcycle is vulnerable to blowouts."

"I know nothing."

"Last chance."

"Well, it doesn't really matter," the fire marshal said matter-of-factly as he clipped the index card to the board. "Events are already in motion."

A chill passed through Kali, a fury that soaked him, drenched him, nearly drowned him, then held him up and hurled him forward on its strength, and he was a tidal wave and he heaved himself into the fire marshal and then into the man in the brown suit. Smashing them against the rocks, bashing them to bits, swelling, uncontrollable, a force of nature, answerable only to the gods.

But the tide went out, inevitably, and its strength ebbed, and in retreat, though it left behind evidence of its presence, it succumbed to opposing forces that punched and kicked until the protecting father passed out.

∽ 15 ∽

KALI KEPT HIS EYES CLOSED until he was sure he was alive. Which he confirmed by acknowledging each painful part of his body. In particular, his throbbing sides. He thought some ribs were broken.

"What the fuck happened to you?"

Two unfamiliar faces stared down at him. A hand reached out to help him. He took it and it led him to a cot and helped him slowly lower himself on to it.

"Painful, I'm sure, but you're going to live."

The room swirled. The presence of vomit overpowered him. In his mouth, on his clothes. The two men still there, faces becoming more distinct.

"I don't suppose there's any harm in telling you my name," said one. "It's Orville Mason Johnson IV. My friends and associates call me Orville."

When Kali didn't respond, the man said conversationally, "Well, there's certainly no shortage of places to sit in here."

Kali managed to get himself up on one elbow and to find a spot of cold wall to lean against. Another push and he was nearly upright. He was in the same room he'd been held in before.

"Head throbbing?" Orville asked pleasantly, as though they were friends who'd spent an innocent night drinking and had to sleep it off. "Allow me to introduce myself further." He bowed slightly. "I am a spinner of retirement dreams. Or, in more prosaic language, an investment counselor. Under different circumstances, we might have had a professional relationship. You look like you might want to retire in a few years."

Kali was having trouble keeping things straight. Slipping in and out of memory. He looked around the room again to figure out where he was. After a few minutes, the second man came into better focus. He was thick and squat and stood very still. He seemed planted in the floor.

"*Keefak*," Kali said to him, startled when that word slipped out, a word he rarely used, and certainly not with strangers.

"What's this keefit shit?"

"*Keefak*," Kali corrected, though it hurt to speak.

"I don't keefit nothing."

"What?" Kali responded, trying to fit this conversation into a form he could recognize.

"Don't let him bother you," Orville said. "You should try to rest. It takes awhile to recover from the kind of physical and emotional trauma you've undergone."

"Who are you again?" Kali asked.

"As I said before, I am Orville Mason Johnson IV. As I also said before, you can call me Orville."

"And you can call me—" the other one growled.

"That's enough for now," Orville interrupted pleasantly. "We'll get to that soon enough."

Kali lay back and closed his eyes. It hurt to breathe; it hurt to remember. After a few minutes, he asked, eyes still closed, "What are you doing here?"

"Extending our commiseration and concern to you," said Orville.

"No, I mean, *why* are you here?"

"Ah, that," said Orville.

"Wrong place at the wrong time," snorted the other one.

"That's one way of putting it," said Orville. "Tell him where and when."

"Shut the fuck up, man."

Orville turned to Kali, "I will explain. Wrong place—on top of a woman in her motel room; wrong time—while she was screaming."

"I wasn't going to hurt the fucking broad."

"Of course not," Orville said contemptuously," just rob her of her virtue and everything she had left. You're a foolishly greedy man."

"What makes you so fucking superior?" he asked, leaping from his chair. He stood threateningly over Orville, who appeared unconcerned.

"What he's trying to say in his vulgar, inarticulate fashion," Orville said, "is that I'm no better than he is. He's wrong, of course."

Kali stared at the two of them. Through what cosmic error had he been put here in this room with these two? Had he violated some fundamental law of nature? Was he trapped in a time warp? Or simply hallucinating? A slight shift in position and his aching body reminded him that this was real: he was here, in this room, on this cot, with two sadistic maniacs nearby—maybe four.

"And your name is—?" asked Orville.

"Kahlil Gibran Hourani."

"A fucking terrorist," muttered the other one.

"I take it that you are of the Middle Eastern persuasion, Kahlil," responded Orville lightly. "That explains the eyes, the nose, the rest of you. You're quite a mess, you know. Terrorists are getting even poorer treatment these days than we are."

The other man nodded.

"I'm not a terrorist."

"Whatever you say," Orville agreed. "Now, as I was about to explain, there's a vast difference between what I do and what Shadrack here does."

"I told you a thousand fucking times not to call me that."

"And why not? What other name should you be called?"

"My mother gave me that name. Just before she died. Said it was the most beautiful name she could think of."

"I'm sorry about your mother," Kali said, in spite of the pain and the nature of his companions.

"Don't be, Kahlil," said Orville. "Shadrack here lies like a rug."

Kali felt less dizzy than before. "I'm not a terrorist. I'm an optician."

"That's a relief, Kahlil," said Orville.

"And I need water."

"Of course," Orville said. He gestured to Shadrack who produced three bottles of water from on top of one of the piled desks.

"Pure as a mountain spring," said Orville.

Orville and Shadrack took a drink. Kali held his bottle in his shaking hand until Orville reached over and twisted off the top for him.

The water spilled down Kali's throat, cooling off his overheated insides; reassuring him that his body though damaged, was not completely broken, that he was capable of doing something physical, if only take a drink. He was too grateful to ask where the water had come from.

"The great restorative," proclaimed Orville. "Now, where were we?" He sat in an old oak swivel chair on wheels, which he turned with a flourish toward the person he spoke to. Like it was a meeting of some kind and he was in charge.

"Tell me again who you are," Kali said as his mind progressively cleared.

"Just a fucking maintenance man at the fucking Empire Motor Hotel," said Shadrack.

"Oh, God. Not the Empire again," said Kali.

"And I," said Orville, "was one of its more distinguished guests. Conducting small private investment counseling sessions."

"Yeah," said Shadrack, "what he doesn't mention is that he'd already robbed the fucking broad before I went into her room."

"Ah, finally you admit it," said Orville.

"I don't admit nothin'."

"Kahlil," said Orville, "impossible though it may seem, Shadrack and I have been partners in a variety of ventures."

"Right," added Shadrack, "he fucks 'em over and I just fuck 'em."

"Con men?" asked Kali.

"You should choose your words more carefully, Kahlil. You're not here because you've won a medal, you know," said Orville. "We all appear to be in the same boat."

Kali took in as much of them as he could. They didn't seem to mind as, silently, they submitted to his examination, to the up and down sweeps of his head. Suddenly Kali said, "I need to get out of here."

"Indeed you do, Kahlil. As do we."

"There has to be a way—" Kali went on.

"Pray continue."

"—but as you can see, I haven't done very well on my own behalf—"

"—No one's perfect, Kahlil," Orville said, wheeling his chair forward, encouraging Kali to go on.

"—or anyone else's."

"Why not join forces then? Three heads are better than one," said Orville, as Shadrack, motionless and silent, stretched out on his back on the other metal cot. "After all, Kahlil, you're responsible for our being here, however accidental it may be. But for you, the police wouldn't have scooped us up. There we were, conducting our business at the Empire Motor Hotel—"

"May it burn to the ground," said Kali.

"—and we got scooped up in your net."

"It's your fucking fault, all right," Shadrack said, rising from the cot.

"That attitude, Shadrack, is not helpful," said Orville. "Kahlil here is doing his best to communicate honestly with us. Aren't you, Kahlil?"

Kali stared at them as blankly as his distorted, bloodied face allowed.

"And we will give him every opportunity to express his thoughts to us. To tell his side of the story. It may yield a solution to our entire dilemma." Turning his chair once again in Kali's direction, Orville asked, "So, exactly what were you doing at the Empire to cause them to, as they say, cast such a wide net?"

"Nothing illegal," Kali answered vehemently.

"Join the club," sneered Shadrack.

"All I intended to do was escape for a few days, to meet up with a woman—"

"There's always a woman involved in these things," Orville nodded sympathetically.

"—and my departure got complicated at the airport through no fault of my own."

"It's never our fault, Kahlil."

"And my wife, Sophie, wouldn't leave and I was getting nervous."

"A fucking broad," said Shadrack.

"Don't refer to Sophie that way," Kali said sharply.

"Don't be offended, Kahlil," said Orville. "It's practically the only word he knows, as you may have noticed."

Kali tried to get up: he wanted to get to the door, fling it open, get out. He broke out in a cold sweat. He thought he was going to throw up. He lay down again on the cot.

"Need to recuperate a little longer, Kahlil?" asked Orville.

"They're going to kill me, you know," Kali said.

"Who's going to kill you?"

"The other two. Haven't you seen them?"

Neither Orville nor Shadrack responded.

"They can't let me go after what they've done. They have no choice but to kill me."

"I think you're getting delirious, Kahlil."

"I'm seeing things clearly for the first time."

"You're too morbid. Try to cheer up."

"How did I get myself into this?" Kali moaned.

"That," said Orville," is a question I ask myself every hour on the hour."

"Every fucking hour," said Shadrack.

No one spoke for a few minutes, and the room descended into a deadened quiet. There were no windows. There was no clock. There was no sound from the outside world. There was little smell except for what the men provided.

"I don't think they want *you*," Kali said. "It's me they're after. They probably arrested you because they were forced into it by that screaming woman."

"Extraordinary lungs," said Orville.

"Loud fucking broad," said Shadrack.

Each silently reviewed his present predicament, dwelling on the past acts which had gotten him where he was. Kali felt remorse for the pain he was sure to inflict on his family; Orville regretted that he hadn't detached himself from Shadrack when he had the chance; Shadrack wished he'd stuffed a pillow down the woman's throat.

"If only," sighed Kali.

"If only," said Orville.

"Fuck," muttered Shadrack.

Orville bowed his head and closed his eyes. "Lord, help us," he said.

"Amen to that," Shadrack responded softly.

Out of courtesy, Kali also said amen.

Louder, Orville said, "Lord, give us hope."

"Amen," Shadrack said, also louder.

Orville stood and turned toward Shadrack. "I believe in the Lord. I know His goodness and I know His power." He raised his arms and called out, "Lord, help us!" Then he moaned like he was going into a trance. In a deep, vibrating voice, he said, "I've heard the voice of the Lord and He said that He's with us. That He will help us escape! Even the apostate Kahlil! And anyone we don't want to find us will never find us again!"

At this, Shadrack leaped off the cot and started to twist and sway and hop around the floor, while Kali watched in wonder.

"The spirit is in you, Shadrack!" Orville shouted.

"Thank the Lord!" Shadrack shouted back.

"The spirit is in me," Orville shouted.

"Bless the Lord!" Shadrack shouted.

"Is the spirit in you, Kahlil?" Orville asked.

When Kali didn't answer, Orville chanted over him he was casting out the devil. "Lord, heal your sinful servant, Kahlil. Lend him your strength. Anoint Kahlil with Your holy oil so he will be slick enough to slip the hell out of here unnoticed. Amen."

"Amen," Shadrack responded.

"And let us sneak out right behind him."

"Fuck, yes!" shouted Shadrack and he and Orville burst into laughter.

"We still fuckin' got it, don't we?" said Shadrack.

"Indeed we do."

"And no one can take it away."

"Not on your life!"

"So, what's the plan?" Shadrack asked as he continued to bounce around the room like he couldn't turn himself off. "How are we going to get the fuck out?"

Face flushed, short of breath, Orville sunk into the swivel chair and spun it around toward Kali.

"Kahlil has the answer."

"The answer to what?" Kali asked.

"To why you're here. And, secondarily, to why we're here. Who else would know but you?"

"I don't understand."

"We shall help you understand. We'll sift through the vastness of your knowledge, and help you find the key. There must be something in your life that propelled you to this place. You just need to identify it."

"You mean something I did?"

"Perhaps. Or some plan you had. Or someone you were working with."

"That doesn't sound right."

"Kahlil, you must relate everything in detail. From the beginning. Leaving out nothing. Starting with when Jane Plain brought in her three prescriptions and ordered four pairs of glasses, to when you were brought here. That's taking the long way, I know, but it's necessary. And speak loudly and clearly so there's no mistaking what you mean, Kahlil. And then, if there's time, well, Shadrack and I will tell our stories."

"How did you know she had three prescriptions?" Kali asked, jolted to hear this information spoken by another.

"You told us, Kahlil."

"How did you know she ordered four pairs of glasses?"

"You told us that as well, Kahlil," Orville said, "when you were semiunconscious. You were raving. It was a tragic thing to see."

Somewhere in Kali's fog of uncertainty and pain, a warning sounded. Low and indistinct, but clear enough. Kali had the impression that Orville and Shadrack already knew the answers to most of their questions about him. That they were waiting for the next act of a play they had already seen. He looked around the room for Situe, but she wasn't there. He was on his own and he needed time to figure out what to do.

"I don't feel well enough to talk," Kali said.

"I was really looking forward to hearing of your experiences, Kahlil."

"I can't think yet. You go first."

"I appreciate your condition, Kahlil, but from an organizational point of view, you should be the one to go first. Since it all started with you and it was your involvement, if I may be so bold as to point out again, that pulled us under the umbrella of the police."

"I can't."

A moment of invisible tugging. A rope—vibrating, taut.

"Right now, I have only enough strength and clarity of mind to listen," Kali said, and he lay back down on the cot and closed his eyes.

"Ah, I see, Kahlil. Very well, then." Orville paused. "I'll contribute what I can. As you request, I'll relate my personal saga.

Briefly, and without interruption," Orville said, throwing a warning look to Shadrack.

"Start at the very beginning," Kali said.

"Fair's fair," said Orville.

"Leaving nothing out."

"As you wish."

As Orville prepared to speak, he leaned back in his chair, closed his eyes, pressed his fingertips together, and waited until the perfect opening sentence came to him.

"Growing up poor in a small town in the southeastern portion of this great country of ours formed my profoundly flexible character." A deep breath as he luxuriated in the sound of his own voice.

"Dirt poor," he added.

Kali, eyes closed and still, made a small sound to suggest that he was listening, as his mind explored possibilities for escape.

"I was a precocious adolescent, and my high school teachers had no idea what to do with me. Accordingly, I enrolled in our local city college before I had reached my seventeenth birthday. It was there that I had my first adventure with an older woman."

A look of fond recollection crossed his face.

"She was a professor of English composition, a distinguished and competent woman. Middle-aged. Unmarried in a day when that meant the preservation of chastity. Now. Despite my perceptible skill in elocution, I had neither the patience nor the interest to master the written language and I was failing her class. She was sympathetic and I was in need. She was lonely and I was there. Admittedly, there were yearnings on both sides."

Orville stretched out his legs at the sheer pleasure of telling his own story.

"You might say we tutored each other. A May/December coupling of considerable mutual benefit and discretion. I never learned the value of a well-placed comma, but I learned the value of a well-placed hand."

Shadrack rolled his eyes at a line he'd obviously heard before.

"Naturally, I passed the class. And thus began my life of bringing joy to women of a certain age and type. Which I developed into a profession. In nearly every state of the republic."

A lifetime of deception, thought Kali. Nothing but lies. With no sense of shame and no intent to change. How could he sleep at night? How could he live with himself? Perhaps there was a perverse justice after all: Orville and Shadrack might never have been caught if he hadn't been wrongly accused. The proverbial silver lining. He imagined Situe, nodding with approval at his appreciation of the moral complexity of the situation.

"Yes indeed," Orville concluded proudly, "I've never once had to get my hands dirty to support myself."

"Fuck you," Shadrack said sullenly.

"Did you ever go to jail, Orville?" Kali asked, having learned to ignore Shadrack's comments as Orville did.

"I shall provide a delicate answer to an indelicate question," Orville responded. He leaned back in his swivel chair. "There were probably times in my life when I should have and didn't, and times when I shouldn't have and did." And here his eyes turned thoughtful, though the rest of his face didn't follow. "You see, Kahlil, given the kind of life I've led, there was little reason to expect that when I told the truth, anybody would believe me."

"I know what you mean," Kali said.

For the truth had done Kali no good whatsoever since his abduction from the Palace of Fine Arts. When he told the truth, it was twisted and used against him; the substance of what he said was irrelevant—truth or fiction, it didn't matter. Yet the truth was all he could tell. Or had been, before Cincinnati. He shifted position to take the pressure off a bruise on his thigh.

"All right, Kahlil," said Orville, "your turn."

"I'm not sure where to begin."

"As they say in the songs, begin at the beginning," said Orville. "A deal's a deal."

Kali looked around the room for Situe. This would have been a useful time for her to appear. So where was she? Advising one of his ineffectual cousins? Or some other relative who thought he was crazy?

But, Situe or not, this might be his last—and only—opportunity to make a complete record of all the things he wanted to say. Even if the only witnesses were Orville and Shadrack. Because he was probably going to be killed before this was all over. He'd seen one gun and, for all he knew, there were more. Death by revolver, who'd have thought he'd end this way?

Two shots to the head, close up. Maybe four, depending on the gun supply. A quick and easy extinction. Unless they missed and left him merely gravely wounded; to die lingeringly, agonizingly. Or worse, not to die.

Why should he think they could get his execution right? They'd bungled everything else—taken the wrong man, misread the obvious. They'd probably left a trail of failed killings behind them. Attempts which merely maimed the victims and bloodied the floors. Leaving the undeceased in the hands of resentful or pitying relatives and, depending on the severity of the injury to the brain, entombed forever in an unresponsive body, unable to turn over, dissolving into bedsores and atrophied muscles.

Kali decided to talk. If it turned out he was going to die here, he'd die having said it all. And if he didn't die, it would be good practice, a dress rehearsal for when he got outside again.

"Even if you don't believe me," Kali said out of the blue.

"We'll believe you, Kahlil."

"Even if I never get out of this room."

Orville leaned forward in the swivel chair, expectant, attentive, his eyebrows lifting slightly and whispered, "That's the spirit," while Shadrack seemed to doze, flat on his back on the cot, as a small well of drool collected in the corner of his mouth.

"I shall relate my errors and omissions as well as my achievements. Not that I assume that I alone caused things to happen—as Situe continually reminds me, I have little control over external events."

"Situe?" asked Orville.

"My grandmother."

"Ah."

Kali inhaled deeply, intending to go on. But nothing came out of him except a furious sweat that exploded through the pores of his skin, scalding his assorted cuts and scratches. The muscles in his lower back tightened like fists, and his innards tensed as if fighting off blows. His struggle to see and understand the collision of personal decision with the forces of history had shut him down. He'd lost the power of speech.

"Kahlil, we're waiting with bated breath," Orville said, somewhat impatiently.

He struggled to put the words in the right order. To make them say what he wanted. For once he said them, they were beyond his control. They'd travel past Orville and Shadrack and outward to the end of the universe, never to be reclaimed. They'd be turned over and inside out and branded and fingerprinted and rearranged.

"Kahlil?"

Kali tried again. And this time the words came, haltingly at first, then picking up speed and settling into a strong, steady pace. With renewed confidence, he plunged into the disasters: flood, famine, political collapse, parts of the state falling into the sea, and so on. He described each in arduous detail, emphasizing his fear of their unending consequences.

"We got the fucking idea, man."

He moved on to the dream and told how he lost Situe and, for a time, couldn't get her back. He told why Sophie made him go to the first doctor.

"It happens to the best of us," Orville said, "so I hear."

"It never fucking happened to me," said Shadrack.

He said why he went to the psychiatrist. And blurted out that he didn't know that Sophie's sisters were part of the package.

"Every man's curse," said Orville.

With a change of tone, Kali spoke of Layla, who rarely came to visit and of Philip, who sought but rarely found—both of whom he loved more than they loved him. He could have done more for them; he probably did enough.

"That's the nature of things," responded Orville.

Kali spoke of gazing deeply into women's eyes. And earning their trust through lenses and frames. All made possible by the glories of opticianry. And he talked of Jane's smell, and the note on her front door, and the airport, and being at the Empire Motor Hotel.

"With Jane, I presume?" Orville asked.

"Yes."

"And?"

"And what?" Kali collected himself. He didn't want to say more about Jane. Not yet. He knew Situe would be disappointed that he couldn't resist reporting this and, for the first time, was glad she wasn't there.

"There was another girl at school—" Kali began.

"Oh?" Orville laughed, with a sly wink at Shadrack.

"She was the one that I ached to follow, but didn't."

The New Belly Dancer of the Galaxy | 139

He spoke again of Sophie, whom he probably hadn't given enough credit.

"You're not alone, Kahlil. Where's the man who gives his wife enough credit?" said Orville.

"Are you speaking from experience?" Kali asked.

"I'm afraid so, Kahlil."

Kali continued. "Until Jane I was completely faithful."

"And now?" asked Orville.

"I'll try to go on as before."

"So it was just a fling?" Orville asked.

"Not a fling. What I did was part of a larger philosophical scheme."

"Is that what you tell yourself, Kahlil?"

"Let me explain. Before all this, I had dreams but I never acted on them. I simply followed my habitual pattern: I went to my store, I went home, I went to church—although I'm not a believer."

"Frankly, Kahlil, you surprise me. I thought you were an innocent, a moral transparency."

"You don't understand. I give the church money, I sent my children to Sunday school there, I got married there. I just don't believe in it."

"And I thought you didn't have a deceptive bone in your body, except when it came to your wife."

"That is a cruel and unnecessary thing to say," Kali cried out.

"But true, Kahlil," Orville responded.

"I didn't have a choice. My people are Syrian Orthodox."

"There are many paths to God, Kahlil."

"Not for me."

"Surely some of your Arab brethren belong to other religious groups?"

"My 'Arab brethren'?"

"The Mohammedans, for example. Those that subscribe to the jihad."

"How would I know?"

"What about you, Kahlil? Do you embrace the jihad?"

In spite of the needles which jabbed at his insides, Kali bent toward Orville and spoke slowly and evenly. "My grandparents came here at the end of the nineteenth century." Kali's voice got louder. "My parents were born here. I was born here. For God's sake, I'm a member of the Chamber of Commerce."

"A typical history, Kahlil. But one that fails to take into account the specifics of your heritage."

"I don't divide the world into Arab and non-Arab or Muslim and non-Muslim. I don't think in those terms."

"Then you're one of the few these days who doesn't."

"I've just tried to live a good life."

"You can't live in a vacuum. You can't deny who you are."

"I was the kid down the street in the family down the street. Or the optician who fixed his next door neighbor's glasses. Nothing unique. Nothing special."

"Kind of bland weren't you, Kahlil?"

"Do you want me to invent a history that doesn't exist?"

"Tell me about your dreams."

"That's what I've been trying to do," Kali said. He ached in a hundred places.

"Tell me about your dreams," Orville said again, kindly and persuasively.

"They're the same as everyone else's," Kali responded.

"You're being too modest, Kahlil."

"You're trying to flatter me into continuing."

"Not flatter. Persuade."

"I see no reason to continue."

"Try to appreciate my position," Orville said. "Our position," he continued, by a tilt of his head, including Shadrack. "It is not an exaggeration to say that we shall sink or swim in the sea of your words."

When Kali didn't answer, Orville suggested he lay back and be comfortable, that he breathe regularly and deeply, that he and he alone determine the direction and scope of the remainder of his narrative.

"That's the only condition under which I'll speak," Kali responded.

"One must adhere to an internal standard," Orville acknowledged.

"And the only reason I continue is to complete my record."

"I understand," Orville said, offering Kali his own bottle of water. "Can you tell us about the Hashanian Mutual Aid Society?"

"How do you know about that?"

"Your delirium, Kahlil. It was of long duration and you covered numerous topics." Orville leaned closer. "You said you were an officer."

"I am. The recording/corresponding secretary."

"Most impressive. Is it your responsibility to keep your chapter of the society in touch with its network?"

"There is no network. There's only one branch."

"Is that the official line? Some are underground?"

"Most of them are underground."

"Martyrs?"

"I can think of one man who might call himself that."

"Who would that be?"

"Fred Kibby. He's kept the books for thirteen years and says nobody appreciates him." For an instant, Kali thought he might lose control, might start laughing and never stop.

"I shall overlook that joke at my expense, Kahlil," Orville said cheerfully, "if you tell me where the society meets?"

"At the church, when we're not at the cemetery."

"Does the society donate money to various causes?"

"One cause. We bury people."

"When?" Orville asked.

"—they're dead."

"I assume the books of the society reflect accurate expenditures and income?"

"You haven't met Fred Kibby."

"Remember, Kahlil, that this inquiry is for your benefit. To help us discover if you have any information which can get you—and us, secondarily—out of here."

"So you keep reminding me."

"And so we need to know about the society's finances and whether, for example, any funds are diverted elsewhere."

"Sometimes at the recommendation of the president, we donate money to the Altar Society."

"Anything else, Kahlil?"

Kali's head began to throb.

"All this is beside the point. It's not important."

"Then tell me what is important."

"What's important is that my father was a good man," Kali said vehemently.

"I have no reason to disagree with you, Kahlil," answered Orville calmly, steadily.

"But in the old days, nobody cared who he was. Or what he was. And when I explained they didn't understand. So I said we were Italian. Does that make sense to you?"

"It does."

"Nobody knew the difference."

"That's it?"

"Mostly."

"Speak, Kahlil. Unburden yourself."

"There was something else."

"Go on."

"It was nothing that happened. Just something I thought."

"And kept to yourself?"

"Nobody else knew."

"But you knew, didn't you, Kahlil?"

Kali's headache had expanded to a neck ache, a shoulder ache, a heartache.

"My father was a good man."

"You already said that."

"And dark, much darker, than I am."

"It's never been easy to have dark skin in this country, Kahlil."

"And we were close to being poor, I guess."

"Poverty is frowned upon as well."

"One afternoon he came to pick me up at school."

Kali stopped and Orville waited.

"And the next day the kids asked me if the colored man was my father."

"Suffer the little children . . . " Orville said softly.

"And I said no." Kali lay back on the cot and closed his eyes. "Do you think he knew?"

"Probably," Orville said, for the first time swiveling his chair away from Kali and turning to face the wall.

The air was stale. The door was locked. Kali closed his eyes. The room was quiet. Orville's head drooped forward. Shadrack, who'd been sleeping since Kali's narrative began, occasionally whistled as he exhaled, the only real sound in the room.

16

"NOW, ABOUT THIS GRANDMOTHER OF YOURS . . . " Orville began.

"Not 'this grandmother.' My grandmother. We call her Situe."

And the memory of every dish Situe made filled Kali's mind and rolled off his tongue: starting with *kibbe, tabbouleh, cousa*, and her version of spaghetti, and ending with the bread she rolled on her knees on the bare kitchen floor, which she'd swept, scrubbed, and floured. Kali could smell the lamb; he could feel the crunch of the pine nuts in his mouth.

"The table nearly collapsed under their weight."

"A common ethnic myth, Kahlil, held by members of every culture," Orville responded.

Kali described the *maharajans*, the summer festivals, when everyone got together and pushed eligible sons and daughters into each other and the men twirled handkerchiefs as they led the *dubke* across the patios.

"Not my father, though."

"Why not?"

"He liked to waltz. Because it was American."

"Austrian, actually," responded Orville.

And then Kali talked about his Neighborhood Watch group, which had little to watch, thank goodness, and of a child he often heard cry somewhere near his house. Sophie said he over-reacted, that he shouldn't try to find it or find out why. But he tried, nevertheless.

"And I love books," Kali continued, talking fast, because now his words flowed unabated.

Though he seldom read. Not from lack of time, but because there were so many, he couldn't decide. At the library, at the bookstore, towers of shelves, miles of aisles, alphabetized lists, arrangements according to topic or print or age—they made his chest constrict and he'd have to look at the floor or get out or be overwhelmed.

"What of Jane?" Orville asked.

Oh, the pain. The great pain, Kali raved. He told how she smelled. And made clear that he had smelled other smells before that had captivated him—of food, mostly—but he'd never been so foolish about a scent as he was about hers. Nor did he under-stand why he crossed over that invisible line this time. And lied to Sophie.

"Age, maybe, among other things," said Orville.

"And Sophie was the only person I lied to," he said emphatically to both Orville and Shadrack, now awake and coming to life.

"I should have been most loyal to her."

"We only hurt the ones we love," Orville said.

"If it hadn't been for her sisters, I wouldn't have lied," Kali said.

Shadrack snorted a short, contemptuous laugh.

"So you went to the airport . . . " Orville led him.

"Right. To the airport, by the security guard, to Ruchelle, to the Empire Motor Hotel—but you two know about that, don't you—and to the New Belly Dancer of the Galaxy Contest."

"And there you were at the Palace of Fine Arts," Orville prodded.

Which reminded Kali of the lady at the card table, and how he found Jane ("Jane, oh, Jane") but didn't recognize her at first, and how the belly dancing teacher was the only authentic dancer in the room.

"The only Arab."

With great discretion, he reported on the times with Jane in the room at the Empire. And indicated that the eyeglasses were a professional success.

"Success in any other area, Kahlil?" asked Orville.

"Success in that area, confirmed," Kali responded somewhat embarrassed.

Then on to being kidnapped by the two men who were responsible for the physical injuries they saw before them, on to meeting Orville and Shadrack. He did not describe how his nose was broken; he did not describe the search with the metal detector; he did not describe being beaten into unconsciousness. He did say that he lunged for the gun; that he fought back; that he defended Sophie against insults; that he would give his life for her and for Layla and Philip. And that they almost took it when offered. He added that he heard that Jane had not won the contest, but did not say from whom he got the information. He admitted to them that he never thought she was a very good dancer.

"So, here I am. Physically debilitated. A prisoner. And unable to change the past which made me that way."

"We appreciate your dilemma, Kahlil," Orville said.

"I'll never be able to correct all the false perceptions about me."

"Truth is forever elusive."

"How could I persuade the security guard that I wasn't sweating for the reasons that he thought, that I wasn't nervous because

I was about to commit a criminal act, but because I was lying to my wife?"

"A question without an answer," Orville responded.

"And how could I tell Ruchelle that of course cost is a relevant consideration to me when renting a car?"

"How indeed?" Orville responded. "Is there much more, Kahlil?"

But Kali didn't acknowledge the invitation to wind it up. He wanted to finish. He wanted to tell what happened from beginning to end.

Delicately, he broached Jane's betrayal, her throwing in with one of the questioners. That was the bitterest pill. Why didn't Jane tell them the truth? Show them her new glasses. And, incidentally, how well they fit, so all wouldn't be in vain, so they wouldn't think him such a fool. So they'd appreciate that he was a professional, a fine optician, a man who truly cared about the vision of those who came to him without reference to race, creed, national origin, eye type or condition. Although, he'd already decided that if the fire marshal or the man in the brown suit came to the Oasis, completely blind in both eyes, they'd have to find their own ways out and have their prescriptions filled elsewhere. There were, after all, limits.

"Fuck yes," said Shadrack.

And as for Sophie: maybe she didn't know yet that he wasn't in Cincinnati, that he'd ruined the new underwear and socks she'd bought for him. That he'd betrayed her in every way. But she'd find out. He didn't expect her to forgive him. For all practical purposes, his life with Sophie was probably over. When it came to Layla and Philip, he'd try to explain that he did his best to protect them, suffering great physical injury. And hope for the best.

His business? The Oasis? Hard to say what would happen there. Sometimes scandal helped. Any kind of name recognition was good, they said. Still, the effect on other members of the family, people at church, neighbors, would be bad, he was sure. Perhaps the only good thing to come out of this would be that Sophie's sisters would never speak to him again.

He smiled. His first smile since he was forcibly removed from the Middle Salon at the Palace of Fine Arts before getting to see Jane dance on a stage. Jane, who wasn't very good. An awkward, inarticulate belly dancer. He hadn't dared to think it when he was with her. He'd excused her performance in the motel room on the grounds that she had no music, the setting was wrong, she was self-conscious. But the truth was, it wasn't in her blood.

And now she was with the man in the brown suit, whoever he was. Policeman? Federal agent? Vigilante? Or maybe she wasn't, since the man was undoubtedly still here, in the wings, probably spying on him through some concealed opening, waiting for the next interrogation session. Kali reminded himself with grim cheer that the man's face was no longer bland.

Kali spoke of his immortal soul. For, it seemed to him as he spoke, in that particular room, that he had one. At least then. Or maybe "immortal soul" was just a phrase he used because he learned it growing up. As a way to refer to the essential human-ity of a person. A linguistic reference, more than a religious one. After all, when Khrushchev (or one of those Communist leaders) said "My God" (or words to that effect) and the rest of the world lurched smugly and said I told you so, it was probably not that Khrushchev actually believed in God, but that he was employing a common phrase to express a common feeling.

"Let's wrap it up, Kahlil."

And speaking of common: didn't statistics show that adultery was a common occurrence in modern society? Not the end of the world by any means. There, he admitted it: he'd committed a simple act of adultery. Or two. And he was appropriately ashamed. What would they think of him at Saints Peter and Paul? He could be ostracized, in spite of cleansing his heart. He smiled again. He might be asked to resign as correspondence and recording secretary for the Hashanian Society. Small compensation, but a compensation, nevertheless.

"You've moved in a very narrow world, Kahlil."

What had he done that other frail humans hadn't done before? He wasn't especially horrible, was he? Were his transgressions much worse than those of others? And what exactly were his transgressions anyway? He wasn't a public figure. His violations, if any, were private, personal. They had no effect on anyone but himself.

"That doesn't sound like you, Kahlil," Orville said, causing Kali to flinch, stop, swell with regret. Even Shadrack seemed touched, however slightly.

And again, Kali spoke of Situe. Whatever he had done or not done, he knew he could depend on her. She'd come back from the afterlife (if, indeed, there was such a thing) to help him. And they should see her! What a woman of the world she'd become! A sophisticate! An intellectual! She wouldn't be shocked by him, or disgusted, or unforgiving.

He stopped. He had nothing more to say. A glorious emptiness suffused him. He felt the lightness of a man who had held nothing back. Who had purged himself. Except for one last thing.

"Orville, there's one last thing," Kali said.

Orville inclined his head, dutifully listening; Shadrack muttered his favorite word under his breath.

"Why are you and Shadrack so intent on getting me to talk? Are we on the same side? And if so, do you know who's on the other one?"

∞ 17 ∞

THE CASH FROM KALI'S WALLET protruded from the heel of his left shoe. The change from his pants pocket occupied the toe. A panel of light illuminated the floor by the half-open door where the shoes had been set neatly together. He was alone.

Freedom?

He shoved the shoes on his feet.

Unerringly, he found the stairs. How? He didn't know. Unerringly he found the front door and went out. There was no one behind him and he ran.

It was a painful, frantic run. Oh God. Oh God. Oh God. Oh God. Each time his foot hit the pavement a cry—half grunt, half growl—came out his mouth. At the edge of the lot he stopped and looked back. The building seemed so tame from the outside. So nondescript, but he knew he'd remember it.

For a few yards, Kali followed the road before slipping into the wooded area which abutted it. The middle of nowhere. Dark as hell, except for the telltale glow in the distant sky of headlights on the freeway. Quiet as hell, too, except for the freeway's faraway hum. Probably the same freeway he'd taken the day before yesterday. The more immediate sounds of the woods he lost in the chaos of his own activity.

He sprained an ankle as he ran, and scratched his face and arms, and tore his filthy shirt on jutting tree branches. He may have run over rocks, rotted wood, abandoned tires. He didn't notice. When he tripped and flew forward and landed on his stomach and skidded across the damp grassy ground, he stayed there because the coolness felt so good. And the earth offered its support.

He knew he should have dragged himself up and on, but he could not override the heaviness of his body. As he lay there he heard the hooting of the forest owls. And something else.

Humans. Two of them. A man and a woman. They passed by him, saw him lying on the ground, slowed and looked down at him, but didn't stop. They spoke to each other in Spanish and separated, disappearing among the trees.

Kali rose and headed in the same direction as before. No one seemed to be following him, so he took a chance and reentered the road. After awhile coming upon an abandoned strip of cheap stucco buildings, home to a short line of boarded-up businesses, except for a laundromat in the center, whose doors were open and whose lights were on, though it looked empty and there were no cars in front.

Inside the machines were idle. "Hombres: don't put your dirty, stinking sleeping bags and other junk in the washing machines," said a handwritten sign tacked to a corkboard on the wall. "This is a family operation."

Kali scanned the place looking for a bathroom, water, a sink to rinse his face, when a movement in the corner startled him. An old woman, lying on a futon near the coke machine, stirred among bags of clothes and a shopping cart brimming with junk. She looked comfortable and unconcerned about Kali's presence. She held a boom box on her lap.

"You surprised me," Kali said, "I hope I didn't do the same to you."

Smiling, she pointed her index finger at her head and spun it around in a circle.

"Crazy? Ah, well. Me, too."

He was desperate for something to drink. He checked his pants pocket—the money from his wallet was still there—and took out a dollar and fed it into the coke machine. When the can hit the slot, the old woman bent over and took it out and handed it to him. Intently she watched him pull the tab and raise it to his lips.

"Here, you take it," he said, and got himself another one. As she savored her drink, smiling brightly at him after every sip, he poured his down his throat. Part of it came up again and he wiped his lips with his tattered sleeve.

Kali thought of what he should do next. Undoubtedly, he was being pursued. Undoubtedly, they were driving, which gave them the advantage of speed. He'd probably see them coming, since there was only one approach they could use. He wondered how many there were: one, two, three, four? Alone or in combination?

The fire marshal, the man in the brown suit, Orville, Shadrack—Kali hadn't figured out whether they were part of some organized entity or whether they'd been thrown together by chance. He had so many questions that needed answering, including whether he was under arrest. Which would make him a fugitive. Which might mean that he could be shot on sight. Or worse. He couldn't, however, think of anything worse.

Meanwhile, he was tired. Too tired to sustain himself on foot for any length of time. In spite of the possibility of imminent discovery, he climbed on to one of the Formica counters and lay on his back and closed his eyes. The old woman turned on her radio.

It played a song he didn't recognize, but that was no surprise, since—as his children enjoyed reminding him—he was old-fashioned, out of date, ignorant of the latest trends. He was thinking of asking the woman, very politely, if she would mind lowering the volume a little, when she stood and began swishing the seven or eight skirts she was wearing back and forth in time to the music. Directing her nearly toothless smile, radiantly, in his direction.

"Well . . . how nice," he said, because it would have been rude to ignore such sincere attention and besides—whether she knew it or not—she could be somebody's grandmother, somebody's *situe*.

The song ended and another began, and the old woman started to dance around the floor. She swooped forward with her arms extended, palms up, and she glided backward. She did twirls and jumps and intricate steps. And flung her arms around with abandonment. Clearly full of joy. Watching Kali for his reaction. And intensely committed to her performance. For it was definitely a performance, and he was her audience.

It was a long song, and at its conclusion, the old woman froze midstep. And she bowed. A deep, slow bow, expectant and hopeful. A child's bow, with one arm at her waist in front and the other in back.

When she stood straight at last, Kali applauded.

"Bravo!" he said softly.

"Bravo!" she said back to him, and returned to the futon to finish her coke.

For the first time in a long time, Kali felt a feeling he loved: equal parts sadness and happiness. A gift from the old woman and for that he was grateful to her. He regretted having to leave her behind uncared for and hoped she wouldn't be lonely, however brief their contact.

"Excuse me, madam, is there a bathroom here I could use?"

The old woman looked at him as though she'd never seen him before. He repeated the question and she pointed without apparent interest to a door marked "No Entry." Through which Kali went and, in the cloudy mirror over the sink, saw his face for the first time since he'd left the Empire Motor Hotel.

It was the face of another being. Not his. Not his. He didn't recognize it. He didn't want to touch it. When he rinsed it off, he saw the water turn reddish-brown and run down the drain. There were no paper towels and he used toilet paper to dry it. He did the best he could do without looking at it again. It amazed him that the old woman hadn't recoiled when she saw him.

When he came out of the bathroom, the old woman took no notice of him as she rested her ear against her radio. Kali had decided to make his way to a busy street, flag down a car, get to the police, and go home. Or, maybe go home first and then call the police. He'd have to see how things worked out. Unless, unless: his interrogators *were* the police, and they had turned the world against him in the short time he was their prisoner.

Time to go. He gave the old woman three one-dollar bills and headed toward the door. He would have given her more, but he didn't know how much he'd need himself and he vowed to return and give her a substantial gift when he was back to his normal life.

Just as he was going to go out the door, a car without lights cruised the street in front of the laundromat, hesitated, and turned into the parking lot. Kali dropped to the floor. Hide. He must find a place to hide in this brilliantly lit room, which had no place to hide. Four car doors slammed and footsteps approached the entrance.

"Any suspicious characters in here this evening?" a familiar voice asked.

Kali didn't see the old woman, animated and smiling, point directly to the industrial-sized dryer into which he had climbed. He didn't see her tilt her head expectantly toward the coke machine. He didn't see her stand and turn on her boom box. He couldn't see her dance, but he imagined she was.

"Fucking nutcase."

The music continued, the old woman danced, and the car doors slammed again. Kali opened the glass door a quarter of an inch for air, but he stayed inside, burying his sore, distorted face in his knees. Limp with relief that he hadn't been discovered. Barely noticing how his stench thickened in the closed-in space or how the metal ridges pushed into his back or that the lint trap bulged with dust and animal fur and the dried shells of small, black beetles.

"How could you be ashamed of your own father?" a voice hissed.

He jumped. "Situe?"

"On your left."

"You scared me half to death."

"Only half?"

"Please, Situe, let me explain . . . I was only a child."

"Then you should have been a better child."

"He never knew, did he?"

"There are things a man doesn't tell his mother."

She struck a match illuminating the inside of the dryer for an instant, then lit her cigarette.

"The four of them," Kali said. "They were here."

"I saw."

"What shall I do?" he whispered.

"Now you ask me for advice? Why not *before* your father exposed himself to humiliation at your hands?"

"I am sorry a thousand times. A million times. But, please, answer the question. What should I do now?"

"Do as you are doing."

"You mean stay in the dryer?"

"I mean, continue your journey."

"And then what?"

"Live your future. Same as everyone else."

"How much more will there be?"

"Some."

"And then?"

"Some more."

"I can't endure any more. I've had more than my share."

"On whose door does the moonlight not shine?"

"That's all you can say to me?"

"I could tell you another story," Situe offered.

"I don't want any more of your stories."

"You're running out of patience?"

"Those people are going to kill me!"

"Maybe, maybe not."

"I've never been so miserable in all my life—"

"Only a poor man knows the meaning of poverty."

"—and I'm sick of your platitudes."

"They may sound trite now, but they were highly original the first time they were said. Besides which, they're convenient when you're running up against a deadline."

"So it's over then?"

"You leap too easily to ultimate reality. Hold steady. You'll surprise yourself."

"I'm trying."

"Good." As she neared the end of her cigarette, its burning tip faded. "Now, Kali, there is something else I must tell you."

"Oh, God. Here it comes."

"I hate to bring it up because you crave such certainty in everything . . . but, for each of the sayings I've told you—my platitudes, as you call them—there is an opposite one."

"What are you talking about?"

"You know, for each 'The early bird catches the worm,' there is an 'Everything comes to him who waits.'"

Kali groaned.

"And just as 'A stitch in time saves nine,' so does "Haste make waste."

"Please, Situ, I'm in pain. My back is killing me."

"I can't think of equal/opposite aphorisms for back pain."

"You're sadistic. I thought you loved me."

"I do love you."

She exhaled, and her smoke rings sought escape through the crack in the dryer door.

"Small comfort."

"It's time for you to be on your way. Courage, dear Kali. And remember to see what's in front of you."

As he climbed out of the dryer, the old woman turned up the volume of the music and, facing Kali, began to dance. Kali saluted her and hobbled across the parking lot and down the road as fast as he could go. Long after he disappeared from sight, the music ended, and the old woman bowed deeply in the direction he had taken. Then she took one of the dollars and got another coke.

18

HE FOUND HIS RHYTHM at the second mile. A battered, scrambling, hobbled man quite pleased with the distance he had covered. Kahlil Gibran Hourani: long-distance runner. In between stabs of pain, he liked the sound of it. As his mind cleared, he thought less about impending death.

But nothing lasts forever, and after a while he slowed like a windup toy and almost fell over into the low grasses that grew along the side of the road. Bent, sucking for air, stopped midstep, Kali longed for a lift the way a starving man longs for food: anything would do—a bike, a truck, a boat, a plane, a car. Anything besides his own power.

That was when he remembered the rental car, the first time he'd thought about it since his kidnapping. Though he couldn't remember its make or model or color. With the foolish hope of a desperate man, he removed the shoe that had delivered his wallet and change to see if somehow he'd overlooked the car key. He hadn't, of course.

No key. No car. What did he expect? His inquisitors probably had both. Or maybe they'd given the key to Jane and she had the car. Not impossible. She had a way of getting what she wanted: Jane with the window down so that her hair—blonde or black, what did it matter now?—flew back from her face; Jane in the driver's seat of that shiny blue car—blue! That was the color: Tyrolean blue, according to Ruchelle.

Kali sighed. Ruchelle: another woman it pained him to remember. Ruchelle, whose offer of economy he'd refused. Choosing instead the financial extravagance of a Tyrolean blue car, an unnecessarily expensive car which, wherever it was and whoever was using it, continued to incur charges at a premium rate. What would Sophie think when she saw the credit card bill? She wouldn't be happy about it. Then he thought: so what? Sophie had long ago concluded that he was careless, foolish, and ineffective.

But here's what he really was: kidnapped and injured, the object of a manhunt. A fugitive avoiding his pursuers. Less ineffective than before; careless no longer; foolish, possibly. If only he'd gone to Cincinnati.

Because they could be closing in. As he stood there, by the side of the road, unprotected and vulnerable, he could be in the scope of their binoculars, or in the scope of something more sinister. He experienced the chill of a hunted man.

And yet he clung to the notion that there was a way out. That through his own efforts or the benevolence of the world or some combination thereof, he would arise and live a long life and die an old man. Most likely with Sophie; most likely, as an optician.

Kali thought of the parking lot attendant, a conscientious young man who'd checked on him when he was sleeping in the car. What if that parking lot attendant noticed how long the blue car had been unclaimed and unmoved and became worried and called the police? And what if he had a vague recollection, something he'd seen out of the corner of his eye, of a drugged man being thrown into the back seat of another car? And what if he put two and two together and realized that the driver of the unclaimed blue car had been taken against his will, against the law, against the protections of the Constitution of the United States of America!

And *that* was the reason the driver of the blue car had not returned and had not paid his parking fee and had not driven that car off the lot. Tyrolean blue, for God's sake, how could the attendant forget Tyrolean blue? Because if Tyrolean blue could be forgotten, perhaps Kali could also be forgotten.

And Kali wanted someone to know what had happened to him. He did not want to suffer in vain, in silence, invisibly. He wanted the authorities to find the culprits, throw them in jail, give him a chance to glare at them in a lineup, identify them, see that justice was done. Unless the fire marshal and the man in the brown suit *were* the authorities. My God, my God, he moaned to himself, they had acted like they were the authorities. They acted like they expected to be backed up and stood behind. These thoughts Kali couldn't shake from his mind. It was not yet dawn. A light rain fell, just enough to release local smells and slick up the ground, not enough to cleanse anything.

Kali walked, head down, along the slightly indented shoulder of the road, thinking. Which is why he didn't hear the growing thunder approaching from behind. And why, when it reached him and passed him in the fullness of its force, it startled him so that his heart leaped in his chest and his body capsized into the dirty dampness of the grass.

A big rig—an eighteen wheeler—had come and gone, dividing the air, shaking the ground. A few minutes later, there were more rumblings, and more trucks of all sizes stampeding down the road, as if a gate had opened unexpectedly and set them free. Free to travel this side road that wasn't made for them and that didn't know how to handle them, while they belched exhaust and spat nuggets of asphalt at each other and at the lone pedestrian who limped along unheeded.

Then there was the hiss and screech of air brakes, and the pulsating presence of a mechanical dragon reined in. Alongside where Kali walked.

"Get in fast," the driver shouted.

Kali did, barely getting the heavy door shut before the truck roared off without causing the others behind it to slow down, without having lost its place in the flow. The whole pickup took about eight seconds.

"You look like you were in a train wreck," said the driver, cheerfully.

"Almost," said Kali.

"Don't smell so good either."

"Sorry."

"Smoke?"

"No thanks."

Oh, the relief. Oh, the sense of refuge. Oh, the unexpected lushness of the overstuffed upholstered seat. Kali's sprained ankle, his sore knee, the injured deposits of skin and muscle, the aching ribs, the burning lungs, the parched mouth, the battered face—his consciousness of these receded in the comforting shelter of the cab as he succumbed to the anesthesia of the driver's surprising compassion.

"Thank you," he whispered, "thank you."

"Don't mention it."

"My name is Kahlil Gibran Hourani," Kali offered for he felt he owed his rescuer at least his full name spoken with dignity.

"Benny."

They drove in silence for a few minutes. A truck roared up from behind and passed too close, taking up the entire left side of the road for a quarter of a mile before pulling over to the right. Benny swore under his breath, reached for the microphone perched on the dashboard in front of him, started to speak into it, let it alone after all.

"I don't suppose you have any water, do you, Benny?" Kali asked, though it pained him to ask his gracious host for something so soon.

"Got it and it's cold."

Benny took a paper cup from a holder on the dashboard and pointed to a spigot that peeked over the back of the seat like the head of a little bird.

"Help yourself."

Kali drank three glasses of water fast. When he was finished, Benny held out his right hand, took the cup and crushed it, then shoved it through a rounded opening on the inside of his door.

"Trash compartment," he said. "Put it in myself."

"Ingenious," Kali answered.

"See that little yellow dial over there?" Benny asked. "Turn it and push it in."

Kali did and the lower part of his seat inflated. Warmth spread over his lower back and down the backs of his legs. He could feel himself becoming aroused and looked down to see if it showed.

"Installed that, too," Benny said. "Look around. There's more."

In plain sight on every surface: buttons and dials, screens, hooks, hangers, holders. Racks holding magazines, tissues, aspirin, and throat lozenges. A container for hand lotion. Overhead a CD rack with a clamp holding each CD in place; a plastic box full of videos and two headsets—no screen that Kali could see, though. For each seat, a button to push to turn on a reading light. An assortment of nuts, chips, cookies, dried fruit.

"Got a kitchen. A bed. A TV. A computer. Better than an airplane, wouldn't you say?" Benny asked.

"Much better," said Kali.

And where there was nothing else, there were photographs. Glued, taped, shellacked. Faces. Kali was sure one of them was Situe's, but when he looked again, it wasn't. He blamed this on hunger.

"Passengers," Benny explained heartily, before Kali could ask. "That way I don't forget. I take a picture of each of my riders."

"That's very interesting."

"You don't talk much, do you?"

"I used to talk quite a bit, actually," Kali answered with effort, for all he could focus on were the snack-sized cellophane bags hard with air like the ones he got in his lunchbox when he was a child. Within arm's reach. He could almost taste the salt.

"Help yourself."

Kali took a bag of peanuts, one of dried apricots. Forced himself to chew slowly; tried, for some absurd reason, to remember how many chews per bite the school nurse recommended. When he was finished he automatically handed Benny the empty bags to dispose of.

"I keep my hands on the wheel and my mind on my driving. I don't pry into why folks are the way they are. Code of the road, you know."

In the background, voices singsonged on the citizen's band radio. Benny fiddled with the microphone, turned the volume down to a buzz.

"So, where you headed?"

"I'm not sure," Kali answered slowly. "What about you?"

"North for a while. Then east, more north, more east. And then back again." He adjusted his rearview mirror and the mirrors on the doors and other mirrors Kali couldn't see. He pulled at the brim of his hat and at the scrawny beard that grew from the bottom of his chin. A tattoo on his right forearm was too blurred to read.

"This isn't my usual route. This is a detour. Two cars going northbound on the freeway ran head-on into each other. Beats me how."

"Strange things happen," said Kali.

"A real incinerator." Benny paused. "Lucky for you."

For the first time since his kidnapping, Kali felt free of imminent danger. He still ached all over, but not as bad as before, although parts of his face, underneath the surface where he couldn't touch, had begun to itch—which he took as a sign of healing.

In front of them, traffic slowed as they came to the end of the detour and approached the curving ramp to the freeway. Benny applied his brakes and they joined the train of trucks, stopped or stopping. And Kali—warmed, cushioned, literally riding high—forgot for a while what was behind and what was ahead. For the elaborate mechanical organisms surging around him—that profusion of mighty machines—intoxicated him. He was part of the intercontinental delivery system. Heady stuff, he thought. On a par, almost, with giving sight to the sightless or bifocals to the aging. Meanwhile, the green lights at the end of the on-ramp blinked and beckoned. One vehicle per light per lane. An orderly procession. It seemed to take forever.

"Weigh station coming up," said Benny. "We'll just ride over the scales to see if we're over limit. Sometimes the inspectors look in." He paused. "Mostly they don't."

"Should be interesting," Kali answered.

"So," Benny continued, "anybody you don't want to see you, you just climb behind the seat."

"What do you mean?" Kali asked.

"They look for illegals. You illegal?"

"I'm not sure."

Benny guided the truck into the renewed flow of traffic. Ahead, the hot, bitter lights of the weigh station drew the trucks in. The scales were open. Two trucks in the line in front of them were directed to the side of the road, but Benny sat behind the wheel like there was nothing to be excited about. He obeyed the swinging flashlights that urged him forward.

"What are you carrying?" Kali asked.

"Paper goods."

"Oh."

"And a few Mexicans. Now smile at the nice men," said Benny as he nodded to the attendants, "we're going through."

Kali froze. He tried to look law-abiding. It seemed that the inspector's gaze lingered long in his direction. They drove over and through.

"Are you serious?" Kali choked.

"Yep," said Benny. "At least I think they're Mexicans."

"Have they been in the truck the whole time?"

"The whole time."

"That's illegal."

"It's inevitable."

The sun had risen, suffusing with light the remaining low-lying clouds. Traffic—mostly long-distance trucks—moved fast and steady. They were far enough from a city to avoid the knots of morning commuters. Kali struggled to say what he thought he had to say.

"Notwithstanding how grateful I am to you for giving me a ride, Benny, I think I'd better get out. I have enough troubles as it is."

"I can't pull over on the freeway just to let you out. That'll bring the highway patrol down on me for sure."

"True," Kali agreed reluctantly.

"And you don't look like an innocent bystander."

"True again," Kali said.

"I have a regular stop in a while. You can get out there. Meanwhile, try to relax. Take a nice, hot shower. You could use one."

"Shower?"

The idea of it, the craving for it, the sheer impossibility of it, dissolved Kali's moral and legal reservations.

"And when you're all spruced up, I'll take your picture so I can hang it up with the others."

Pursuant to Benny's instruction, Kali climbed over the seat and found an aluminum door, half height, through which he crawled, ending up in a room of such density and efficiency that he could have sat on the toilet while making coffee while brushing his teeth while going through a drawer for a clean shirt which when found he could then iron on a pull-down ironing board and hang in a closet on a collapsible hanger that opened to full size.

The shower itself was made of thick, heavy, hanging plastic sheets that didn't stick to him when he got wet. Or when he sobbed as he dislodged the dried blood and filth which ran in small clumps down the drain.

It had been an effort to wash his sorest parts. The nozzle—fierce and pounding—delivered water as a punishment. It hung above Kali's head and lined up with a drain in the floor that opened directly onto the road.

In a drawer stocked with shirts, pants, underwear, and socks in accidental sizes, colors, patterns, Kali found clean clothes. Though nothing matched, they fit well enough. As Benny had directed, he brought his old clothes back to the cab so they could be stuffed into the trash container. Kali had seen no evidence of concealed passengers. He wondered if Benny had been joking.

Up front again, Kali said, "I didn't see anyone else in the truck."

"That's the idea."

"They're really here?"

"They're in back."

"How many?"

"Six, not counting their guide."

"What are their chances?"

"Chances for what?"

"Not getting caught."

"As long as they're in the country, they can get caught."

"And what about you? What if you get caught?"

"So far, so good," Benny said jovially.

Hesitantly, Kali asked, "You sure they're all right back there?"

"No doubt about it. I provide safe, humane transportation. And when I deliver them to their destination, I take their pictures. Look around you."

Kali looked carefully at the photographs scattered about the cab. Each person smiled broadly, directly facing the camera. Most made victory signs with their right hands. They were dark and slight; they gave the impression of being poor. Each one appeared to be, could be, Mexican. Kali wondered how he hadn't noticed before. He admired Benny's foolish courage.

"And when it's time, I'll take your picture, too," said Benny.

"Mine?"

"After I've delivered you safe and sound."

Kali looked around for the camera, assuming it was within easy reach like everything else and located it above the rearview mirror behind a small plastic grate.

"You're not a serial killer, are you?" Kali asked, pretending to be joking. "And these photographs are records of your victims?"

"No," Benny answered seriously, "I'm a serial picture taker."

"Upon reflection," Kali said, "although I'm grateful to you for everything, I'd prefer not to have my picture taken."

"It's the price of the ride."

Benny drove seamlessly through a clover leafed interchange that put them on the road east to the desert cities. He drove like he was riding a favorite horse, like it was an adventure, a pleasure. Like there was no one else around. Like he and the truck were one: two hands, two feet, whole body united in the rhythm of the road.

The terrain on both sides of the freeway flattened and the mountains got farther away. The sky was high and wide.

"I use an old Polaroid. Betty bought it years ago. Every one of my pictures I took with the Polaroid. I like watching the people appear right before my eyes."

Kali looked over the photographs—there were hundreds—wondering at the events that didn't show up on camera: who the people were, why they made the journey, where they were, what they were doing. Face after face smiling. Did Benny order them to smile? Or were they simply happy that the ride was over? Were they settled or did they live life on the run?

Life on the run: who'd have thought that phrase would describe his own existence. Though as the drive went on and time passed without evidence of further danger, he began to think of it more as life on the move. One particular face in one particular picture made him stop and look more intently. Made him twist his head around so he could see better.

"This woman could be your sister."

"Everybody says that."

"No victory sign, though. And she's not smiling like the others."

"Well, not everybody was made to be happy."

Benny looked in his rearview mirror, realigned it, licked his lips, went through the whole procedure again.

"Well, Kali, when are you going to tell me why you were on the side of the road in those filthy, bloody clothes?"

"A reasonable question. But it might be better for you if I don't answer. Knowing about me might get you into trouble."

"Trouble's one thing I'm not afraid of."

"A remarkably brave position."

"Well?"

So Kali told the story of how he left Sophie behind and went to the Palace of Fine Arts to find Jane, and about the fire marshal and the man in the brown suit (leaving out certain painful details) and about Shadrack and Orville, and the woman in the laundromat. And how they came after him and he didn't know who they were and was afraid he wouldn't be able to put things right. And how the truth about what happened didn't seem to matter. And how he had turned into a liar and maybe a criminal or enemy of the state.

Benny listened occasionally nodding, occasionally making small sounds.

Kali mentioned Situe, careful to describe her as the deceased grandparent on whose remembered advice he occasionally relied. What good would it have done to tell Benny that they spoke all the time and that she was probably overhearing their entire conversation and that she appeared to have temporarily entered one of Benny's photographs from which she winked at him during their ride?

When he was finished, Kali laid his head back and closed his eyes and Benny drove. After awhile Kali asked, "What about you? How'd you decide to do what you do?"

Benny stretched his upper body and extended his left leg before answering. "I love it when people ask how I decided this, or how I decided that, as if it was up to me to decide."

"What I meant was . . . "

"I know what you meant and I know you had good intentions. It's just that this deciding business is a sore point."

They were almost to the pass where the mountains came close together again. Here it drizzled and the sky turned dull and gray and the cab filled with melancholy; it took up airspace and settled like dust around them.

"It all started with Betty."

Kali nodded, listening.

"She's the one got me into trucking. It was something I always wanted to do. The freedom, seeing everything. Getting away. We were in business for ourselves and we drove when and where we wanted and stopped when and where we wanted. We did all kinds of things just because we wanted to. Betty was a real adventurer. But she had her troubles."

"Ah."

"You see, after the operation, she never could have any babies. And she wanted them really bad."

"I'm sorry," Kali said. "I know I would feel a great loss without Layla and Philip. My wife, Sophie, would have been desolated if she couldn't have had children."

"So you have a boy and a girl?"

"Yes."

"They say that's a perfect family." Benny passed a trucker in the adjacent lane, muttering mild profanities under his breath.

Kali said, "I can see why a person, a woman especially, would regret not having a family—for all the obvious reasons. But, if it's any consolation, Benny, they bring their share of . . . concerns, too."

"All love is sad," Benny answered.

"A profound statement."

"It's from Betty. She was full of things like that."

Coming up fast was the choice: the freeway forward or a highway back home.

"This is where you get out if you want to. You decide. But you need to decide now. And, no decision is my decision."

Kali thought: if he got out now he could be home at close to the time he'd told Sophie to expect him, thereby sparing her more worry than she already had, for he hadn't contacted her—hadn't been able to, for the most part, he told himself—since she left him at the airport to board a flight that didn't exist. If he got out now, he'd call her on a pay phone, probably sounding desperate, and their son or some other relative would pick him up and he'd be unable to explain what had happened, for he didn't know himself. He hadn't made sense of it yet.

Of course, it was possible to go home without advance notice, simply to appear on the doorstep and spring himself upon them, come what may. Throw himself on Sophie's mercy; count on the fact that he looked so bad he'd get sympathy and not be questioned too carefully.

Either way, once he went back he'd have to explain his disappearance, why he looked like he did, and everything else. He'd have to confess his lies and hope for forgiveness. He'd have to endure the torrent of Sophie's emotions. He was afraid, clearly and ashamedly, and he considered the alternatives.

What if he didn't return when expected? No doubt, he would cause great pain. He could barely contemplate it. Sophie and Layla and Philip at their house, pacing and crying and lamenting and worrying. Sophie's sisters arriving, along with the rest of the relatives. Everyone praying for him: secret prayers—hopeful, condemning.

Not to mention that the Oasis—his beloved store, his sole proprietorship—closed for his weekend trip to Cincinnati, closed for the first time since Philip was born, would stay closed until he was there to run it.

There was more: the inevitable gossip; a newspaper story (unless he overestimated the significance of his presence or absence), hopefully short and buried in the back pages. These consequences, and others he hadn't thought of, would pile up and topple over unless he returned and faced them. Unless he reentered his usual world, followed his usual paths.

But he could not.

He was a man who couldn't describe his place in the world. A man soon to be fifty-three who struggled to identify his role in life—such a man didn't deserve to go back to his loved ones, couldn't go back yet, maybe wouldn't go back at all.

Plus, he told himself, there was the possibility that he was still in danger and that going home would bring that danger to his wife and family and friends and, it was not impossible, to the members of the Hashanian Mutual Aid Society.

The freeway signs came and went.

"I thought so," said Benny.

Kali resettled in his seat. He pushed the button that inflated the cushion that supported his lower back. And felt ashamed. Consumed with his own concerns, he'd ignored the concerns of others. Optician, heal thyself, he thought.

He vowed to be better. He would come down from his cloud (on occasion), and wrestle with, deal with, breathe in and out with, those around him. He would downsize his preoccupations from the cosmic to the immediate (when he could). He would stay on the ground. He looked around him and there was Benny. A perfect place to start anew.

"So, Benny," Kali asked, hoping to convey interest and enthusiasm, "where do you call home?"

"You're in it."

"No, I mean, where are you from?"

"From nowhere, going I don't know where."

"Everybody's from somewhere."

"I'm from here."

"You mean this area?"

"I mean *here*."

Benny continued, though his voice was softer and slower than usual. "You see, folks thought of us as interchangeable. Betty and Benny, Benny and Betty. All across the country, folks thought of us that way."

Kali took in a long, deep breath as he realized that no one had ever thought of him and Sophie as interchangeable. "You must miss her very much," he said.

"I do, although I feel she's always with me."

"A beautiful sentiment. And quite psychologically valid, if I may say so."

"You may say so."

Kali nodded approvingly.

"And Betty loved her slots."

"I see," Kali said gently, though he barely did.

"Before there was a Benny, Betty stopped at every casino on her route and played."

"Slot machines, you mean?"

"And she won. It was more than dumb luck. She had the aura."

"I've only played once," Kali said, "on a trip to Las Vegas with Sophie and her sisters." Involuntarily, he shuddered. "And their husbands, of course."

"And Betty taught Benny how to play. She taught him everything she knew about them."

"I didn't realize there was much to learn," Kali said and Benny's jaw seemed to set and his foot pushed harder on the accelerator, and the truck, huge as it was, made a lurch forward. Kali couldn't think of how to reverse the statement without lying, so he was quiet. For Kali did not lie, usually, except for Cincinnati.

Benny reached over his head to one of the many attached objects and unsnapped a hook and took down what looked like a credit card on a chain.

"Read it."

Kali read one side silently to himself: CHARTER MEMBER—PULL A FAST ONE. He read the other out loud: "'THE SKY'S THE LIMIT. FOR THIRTY MINUTES A DAY.'"

"Betty got it for me for my birthday."

"'THE GALAXY CASINO,'" Kali continued, reading the fine print, "'GOOD IN PERPETUITY. NO EXPIRATION DATE.'"

"Underneath the dashboard," Benny directed. "Take a look."

There they were: two ten-pound dumbbells, rubber-coated, purple, held in place by the kind of metal racks used to attach water bottles to bicycles.

"First time at the slots, my arm killed me afterwards. I must have done a thousand pulls in that thirty minutes. So I got those. Whenever I get the chance, I do a few curls, a few overheads." Ahead a truck, all lights flashing, clogged the lane as it struggled up an incline. "Not while I'm driving, of course." Benny signaled for a lane change, made it smoothly.

"Everything I know, I learned from Betty."

"That's quite a tribute."

"Trucking, too. She got me into it, you know."

"She could manage a vehicle this size?"

"Like a pro. She was an artist."

"Obviously, you loved her very much."

"No question about that."

"It must have killed you when she left."

"In a sense, it did." Benny made a few ritual adjustments, tipped the mirror, pulled at the brim of his hat, checked a few dials, turned off his citizen band—like a baseball coach giving signals. "So I started taking riders. To keep me company."

Which reminded Kali of the others.

"You're sure they're all right back there?" Kali asked.

"I'm sure."

"Shouldn't we go check on them?"

"Feel free to do so when we stop."

"It will make me feel better. And I will, if you don't mind."

"Why should I mind?"

Kali adjusted his position. Despite the customized seat and its available settings, he looked forward to getting out, walking around, having a stretch.

"You see," Benny continued, "the side of the truck first read 'Bouncin' Betty' because she was such a live wire and all. Hell on wheels. You should have seen her arm wrestle." Benny's face, radiant with memories, stared straight ahead at the road.

"And the truck was orange because that was her favorite color. Orange with black trim."

"Sophie likes cranberry with blue trim." Kali's face, too, filled with feeling. "Though I can never tell cranberry from plain red."

Benny guided the truck down the other side of the subtle hill. Downshifting, without brakes.

"One day she erased 'Bouncin' and added 'Benny' and the side of the truck said 'Betty and Benny.' She had the orange painted over. Left the black. So Benny could decide the other color later."

"That was very thoughtful."

"Well, Betty believed strongly in the rights of the individual."

"A fine philosophical position."

"She said we were in a transition period and needed to keep both names."

"Transition to what?"

"To when her name would come off the truck."

"For when she would be gone?"

"Right."

"May I ask what her reason was for leaving?"

"It was because of the operation."

They were on flat land again, and Benny shifted gears. Trucks coming up behind them did the same.

"The side of the truck looked so empty without her name. Everything seemed empty. I was empty, too."

"I'm very sorry, Benny. I really am."

"That's when I added 'Bedroll.' Takes up about the same amount of space as 'Betty.'"

"'Bedroll Benny,'" said Kali, "very poetic."

"Kind of like a cowboy and his horse. I take my bed with me wherever I go. This is my home. There is no other."

"Well, you've made it a very . . . cordial place. Very comfortable."

Benny—hat, tattoos, scraggly mustache—blushed. He moved his dirty hands up and down the sides of the steering wheel, like a cat rubbing himself against a favorite chair leg.

"And I give all my riders the same consideration. Like Betty would have wanted."

"Please accept my sincere sympathy for what must have been a traumatic time in your life."

"'Traumatic.' That's the word, all right."

"Not being able to have children of your own can break a heart. People do unexpected things. I've seen it myself."

"Betty became Benny."

"What?"

"That was the operation. Betty turned into Benny."

19

THEY DROVE THROUGH THE PASS, notorious for its extremes of earth, wind, and fire. This time it was the wind. Signs warned of it for miles in advance, some flapping so wildly it was hard to read the words, and they looked as if they were about to take off into the air, to succumb to what they could announce but not alter, control, or protect against.

The windmills, however, thrived. Taking what they needed from it. Indifferent to the indifference of nature. On both sides of the road they whirled—spinning over gently sloping plains and on the crests of hills. Spaced equally in line after line. Covering every angle of approach like a well-positioned army about to strike. Thousands of them. Some as big as a twenty-story building.

"Damn smart place for windmills, if you ask me," said Benny, requiring no response, which was a good thing, since Kali didn't hear him. For the one sense of his that was operating—sight—focused solely on Benny's visible parts: the cheek and the fine, meager hair on it; the layer of lint over the upper lip; a periodic whisker; the countable strands of beard on the chin; the smooth, freckled arms; the hands, which now seemed girlish in spite of calluses; the narrow waist. Kali's sense of hearing returned for the sole purpose of measuring the depth of Benny's voice.

"Things always change when I tell," Benny said quietly.

"Nothing's changed," Kali lied for the second time since he arrived with Sophie at the airport. What he said to the fire marshal and the man in the brown suit he didn't count as lies: they were survival techniques. What he said to Benny now was a kindness. Though Benny hardly noticed, for his sights were set on what came next.

"Look! Up ahead!" Benny exclaimed suddenly. Beyond the windmills and past the low dunes with bike-scratched paths. To the flat lands. To the center attraction. Where, dominating the landscape, was the tallest figure by far. Visible for miles in all directions. Solitary, massive, glittering like lightning. The one thing to look at whether you were headed there or not. Whether you wanted to or not. Inescapable like Oz. Benny and Kali drove a full fifteen minutes before reaching it.

"There she is!" Benny whooped. "The Galaxy!" He yelled and yelped. He could barely stay in the driver's seat. He picked up the microphone of the CB radio and shouted to no one in particular, "Bedroll Benny has arrived. Come in, come in, please!" and flipped on his turn signal.

"We're stopping?" Kali asked, as Benny swooned up the off-ramp, leaning into the turn like a pilot in a small, open plane. Aiming the truck in the only possible direction.

"From the first minute it opened, it's been like this," Benny announced triumphantly.

Stuffed full. A parking lot packed tight. With motor homes and cars, and small, medium, and large trucks, and motorcycles in cocky lines that dared a passerby to touch. And big rigs, in a vast expanse set apart from the others, with their own entrance and exit. There were no people visible in any part of the lot. As though once they went into the casino they never came out.

Benny guided the truck down the road and turned in, spinning the steering wheel with both hands and, when the truck was straight again, he grabbed his CHARTER MEMBER: PULL A FAST ONE CARD and hung its chain around his neck.

"I stick it in the machine when I want to play and never take it off my neck. That way I don't lose it."

He found a place to park, guided the truck into it with an ease that spoke of years of practice, and turned off the engine.

"Well," Kali said. "I guess this is where I say good-bye."

"Guess so," Benny answered, as he combed his scrawny beard.

"Thank you for everything."

"Don't mention it."

From a pocket attached to the back of his seat, Benny grabbed a clean pressed shirt, and while he changed into it, Kali stole a final fascinated look: at rose-brown nipples as big as silver dollars, at smooth soft skin. A keen and shameful gaze, severed one button at a time from the bottom up, until Benny reached his collar.

"One thing before I go," Kali began, "the people in back."

"Yeah?"

"Do you think they're all right?"

"Everything's under control."

"How can you be so sure?"

"I take care of them same as I did with you. But you can look if you want. Remind 'em not to flush or shower while we're in the parking lot. Mario's the man in charge."

Benny jumped out of the truck and raced away from it only to return a few seconds later.

"I forgot something."

He grabbed the Polaroid and pointed it toward Kali.

"Smile."

Which Kali did as he raised his right hand to give the peace sign like the other people in the other pictures. Benny handed him the camera.

"When it comes out, let it dry. Don't touch the surface."

Then Benny ran through the parking lot toward the double glass doors of the lit and blinking Trucker's Entrance and disappeared inside. Kali imagined him pulling and pulling as fast as he could, with one arm, then the other, then both. He imagined him smothered in winnings, hypnotized by the machines' metallic songs. He imagined Benny's shouts of uncontrolled joy, as other players—less fortunate, less skillful perhaps—surrounded him, got caught up in it, were thrilled, jealous, resentful, let down.

In the picture, Kali's face looked swollen and stained. His smile and his peace sign were crooked. Sophie wouldn't have recognized him. His pursuers, if they still pursued, were the only ones who knew him in his present condition. Pursuers: he sickened at the word. He set the picture on Bennie's seat and went to the back of the truck.

Like Benny said, he carried a flashlight; like Benny said, he opened the double metal doors and climbed inside. He found the entrance to a tunnel that ran almost the length of the truck—a wood-framed and press-boarded secret passage, cutting through and surrounded by a hard-packed cargo of paper towels, napkins, and plates.

What would the people look like? What condition would they be in? Piled on top of each other, desperate, hot, thirsty? Kali was almost afraid to find out. Because what if they weren't all right? What would he have the courage to do? As a man probably running from the law himself, what would he be able to do? Concern, fear, curiosity coexisted, no one predominating over the other, no one diluting the other.

Without the flashlight, it would have been pitch-black. Even with the light, Kali guided himself by touch, floating his left hand along the surface of the inside wall. Getting a few splinters; coming across the sharp side of a few nails. He went slowly.

He came to a door with the same dimensions as the one at the beginning of the tunnel. A door so narrow he'd have to enter sideways. When he opened it, light flooded over him. So strong it almost pushed him back. So bright that it took a few seconds for his eyes to adjust.

The compartment was small and rectangular. The air inside was fresh and cool. The walls, painted a peaceful green. There was a long wooden bench, like a church pew, bolted securely to the floor and wall. With seat belts, though Benny never wore his. And on the bench, sitting still as though required, six passengers—five men and a woman—staring at him without apparent emotion. And within their reach, lightweight blankets, water bottles, and tissue dispensers all neatly packaged and cleverly stored. And the same food as up front in the cab. Leave it to Benny, Kali thought.

"Hello," Kali said, intending to be gracious. The gazes of the six people shifted in unity as the door slammed shut behind him. Kali turned sharply to see a man dressed in fresh khaki pants and a long-sleeved blue shirt. He wore glasses and an unfriendly smile.

"You surprised me," Kali said.

The man walked over to the bench and sat on one of its arms. His smile was gone. Kali couldn't read the new expression on his face. Not interest or fear: something else.

"Benny sent me. He said to ask for Mario."

Still the man didn't answer. The six people on the bench watched the man as if waiting for instructions.

"I mean no harm," Kali said, wondering if he would ever again be free from unusual experiences. Neither the people on the bench nor the other man spoke or moved or looked surprised, and Kali couldn't tell what any of them was thinking. He didn't know what they expected. The woman lowered her head. As if to deny his presence, two of the men closed their eyes. The man with the glasses remained still. He was different from the others.

Kali said, "I apologize for intruding, for alarming you." And he looked from face to face to face along the bench. Noting their eyes. Once in a while at the Oasis, he saw eyes like theirs. Eyes so full of memory and hope that the slightest touch could cause them to overflow.

"I am afraid I have nothing to offer you, nothing to give. Which is not my usual way. We Arabs are famous for our hospitality, you see." He tried again to reach the silent audience. "Friend or enemy, we turn no one away. The hungry, the thirsty, the sick, the weak." He nearly added the nearsighted, the farsighted.

They watched him now with visible interest.

"We're also famous for our stories, for the beauty of our language, which, for various reasons not worth enumerating now, I am ashamed to admit I do not speak."

He retreated to a narrow strip of wall, leaned against it. When he breathed it hurt, though not as bad as before. The borrowed pants he wore hit well above his ankles and they were already soiled—Kali didn't know how. Automatically, he tried to pull them down, to make them look longer.

Outside, the wind had arrived and it wrapped around the truck like a cocoon. No human sounds penetrated; no voices or footfalls or coughs. Only massive engines arriving and departing. The wind grew stronger and its low whistle rose in pitch.

There was little Kali could do for the people on the bench, he knew. He couldn't guarantee their safety or promise them a future. He couldn't deliver their share of happiness or right the wrongs they came from or give them permission to go where they were going. Given the circumstances, he couldn't even improve their vision, although the man with the glasses didn't look like he needed any help. There was but one benevolence he could invoke.

"*In the century before the last century,*" he began self-consciously, since it was the first time he'd tried to enchant, "*a brother and three sisters traveled across the sea from the old world to the new. Their father had died and they were going to join their mother who had gone ahead to try to find a new life.*"

He hoped they would realize from the tone of his voice, at least, that he spoke from his heart. He assumed they didn't understand his words.

"*Their mother married a rich man who agreed to pay for their passage.*"

That wasn't right, Kali thought. That didn't sound elevated the way Situe's stories did.

"Ignore what I just said. I need to start again. I made the mother sound calculating which is not what I intended. I wanted her to sound . . . heroic."

"There are no heroes," snarled the man with the glasses.

"You speak English?"

"I do."

"And the others?"

"Would it bother you if they did?"

"It would make it easier. I'm trying to comfort, after all."

"With a fairy tale? Are you afraid to tell them the truth?"

"Give me a little time. Sometimes truth unfolds slowly. It doesn't explode in your face."

"Not my kind of truth."

Something heavy crashed against the side of the truck. The bodies on the bench jumped; Kali's heart tightened. The man with the glasses froze; he listened the way a hunter or the hunted might listen. The others watched the man as if his response would be theirs. When after several minutes the sound didn't recur and the man's body loosened, the men on the bench—not the woman who seemed caught up her in her own thoughts—following his lead, relaxed in their seats.

"The wind," the man said. *"El viento."*

He pulled a cigarette from a pack in his pocket, smelled it, moistened its tip with his tongue, lodged it in the corner of his mouth. One of the men on the bench started to stand, and the man with the glasses spoke angrily to him in Spanish. The other men watched; the woman sighed deeply.

"They have nothing in their own country," the man said, turning to Kali. "I deliver them to people who give them work. It's a practical system."

"The woman seems very young."

"So?"

"Five men and one woman, I just wondered."

"About what?"

"Where they were going, whether they'll get there."

"They'll get there."

"You're very sure."

"They perform their part of the bargain and I perform mine."

"Which is?"

"You ask a lot of questions."

"I'm interested. What about the woman?"

"Like the others, she does what I tell her to do."

"I see."

"No one cares what you see, old man."

Kali flinched: at most he thought of himself as middle-aged and, possibly, early middle-aged.

The man lit his cigarette. When he spoke again, his voice was soft, but Kali saw that the eyes were hard.

"I attended university in your country as well as my own. After that, I returned to Mexico City. I had an affair with another man's wife. He was enraged and also very powerful. He had me arrested for murdering a man who never existed. A nonperson, a figment of the imagination. They never found a body, of course, because there was no body. Nevertheless, I was convicted."

Kali listened intently, resisting his desire to condemn before hearing the whole story. He did not like this man. He did not trust him. He was wary of tricks and lies. At bottom, he disapproved of infidelity, including his own.

"I was transferred to a prison far from the city where it was planned that I would die trying to escape. The guards had been bribed to make sure my death happened soon after I arrived. My family increased the bribe and the guards let me go. They used all the money they had."

"Love for a son has no limitations."

"And I—now a criminal in adjoining countries, deprived of my profession on both sides of the border, must pay them back—"

"The only honorable position."

"—and the most efficient way to do that—is this." And with a sweep of his arm, he included the people, the compartment and, somehow, Benny up front.

"My name is Mario Trinidad Calderas."

"I am Kahlil Gibran Hourani."

"And you, Señor Hourani? Why are you here?" Mario asked.

"I needed a ride," Kali answered simply. "And Benny gave me one."

"Did he charge you the usual fee?"

"A photograph. That's all he wanted."

"With a smile and a peace sign," Mario said contemptuously.

"Yes."

"*Idiota.*"

"What?"

"Benny's a fool."

"He's a generous man. The rides are free."

"Nothing is free, Señor Hourani." He spoke in Spanish to the others who acknowledged him with a slight movement, a slight sound, then leaned over the woman, took her arm and pulled her up.

"What are you doing?" Kali asked.

"Stay out of the way."

Mario led the woman through the door and into the passageway. She did not resist; she did not acquiesce. Two of the men stood, walked around the compartment speaking in low urgent Spanish. Two watched Kali. The other stared at the floor.

"What's going on here?" Kali asked the men, already knowing the answer. He opened the door and stared into the darkness—"Mario!"—and went down the passageway after them. It was dark and he felt lost, vulnerable to attack. Half expecting Mario to jump him. He came to the end, and Mario and the woman weren't there.

He flung open the back doors of the truck and jumped into the fury of a wilderness reclaiming itself. Sand blasted every surface and penetrated every unprotected crevice of man and machine. It suspended the ability to see and hear and swallow. It took over the air; it became the air.

Kali aimed for the door of the casino. Where there were people, where there was help. For he knew he must act, though likely to fail; act, knowing that one person's rescue might be the ruin of several.

The asphalt came in and out of focus beneath him and for a few seconds disappeared entirely. Kali almost fell. It was like walking blind or drunk or semiconscious. So Kali advanced on faith, trusting that the earth was there though he couldn't see it. He held the bottom of his shirt over his nose and mouth while the sand scratched the surfaces of his eyes. When he reached the revolving door, he stumbled as he went through.

20

"WHERE DO YOU THINK YOU'RE GOING?" the guard in the vestibule asked him, blocking his way. He was huge by anyone's standards. With a shaved head, a uniform, a security badge, and a gun at his side. An impatient smirk tilted his mouth.

"I need help."

"You're beyond help, buddy."

"I need to go inside. To contact the authorities."

"You giving yourself up?" the guard laughed.

A scabbed and swollen face; a jumble of ill-fitting clothes; ardent and agitated; confounded by the lights and noise and fantasy—what had Kali expected? It was a stupid idea: to throw himself on the fire so someone else wouldn't get singed. Because there was no guarantee, no guarantee about anything. The most probable result was that he'd be the only one arrested—maybe returned to the fire marshal and the man in the brown suit, whoever they were—and Mario would get away and Benny would keep driving his truck and have no idea what was going on, and the people—those men and that woman—would be sold to the highest bidder. And then it would happen all over again.

Under the threatening eye of the security guard, Kali reentered the revolving door and went out into the storm. He staggered to a line of semis and took refuge under the cab of a refrigerator truck full of milk. Waiting it out. Expecting no relief.

"No more! No more!" he shouted without fear of being overheard for the wind and sand continued to block messages sent and messages to be received and there was no one out there anyway. "I've had enough. Just let me die."

He closed his eyes and buried his face in the crooks of his arms. And there, within seconds, and with no ready explanation, saw his grandmother's house. And he forgot that he was choking on sand and his own impotence. And he saw the massive, polished mahogany furniture in the dining room; and Situe's crocheted doilies on the back of the sofa and on the backs of chairs, underneath ashtrays, underneath lamps, underneath glass vases; and he smelled the food oh God the food so good hot or cold, so much of it. And Situe saying eat eat eat; pick it up with your fingers, scoop it up with bread, while she brushed it under the nose, against the mouth—tempting. And Jidue by the radio in a white short-sleeved shirt and scratchy wool sweater while he read the Arabic newspaper and nodded stoically over the state of the world. An oasis, a sanctuary. That's what their house was. The world waited outside unless invited in.

Kali may have slept. When he raised his head, the wind had subsided, leaving the air electric and dry and clouds of sand frozen below the skyline. In the soundless aftermath of the storm, Kali crawled out and stiffly headed for Benny's truck. He had decided to stay awhile. Not that he felt better than he had before. He felt worse.

Worse than he'd felt with the fire marshal and the man in the brown suit. Because with them, he had no doubt about his moral position. He was good, they were bad. His only duty was to survive. Crystal clear, uncomplicated with no fallout. That he had fallen into their clutches—partly, indirectly—because he betrayed Sophie, failed to undermine his sense of superiority.

His present situation, on the other hand, demanded measured action. It was more complicated. The fates of many were at stake: five men and one woman, Mario, Benny, and himself of course, in varying degrees of innocence, culpability, legality, morality. Half-heartedly, with part of him moving forward and part of him in retreat, Kali climbed inside Benny's truck and waited for Benny to return. Which Benny did, two hours later, jittery with pleasure and his two shirt pockets bulging.

"You're still here!" Benny exclaimed.

"I am."

"Look! A hundred dollars!"

"Congratulations."

"In ones and fives; makes it look like more."

"An old trick, but a good one," Kali said.

Benny crossed his arms and, with the palms of his hands, caressed the moneyed mounds on his chest, while he gently rocked himself back and forth. "A man needs his wad, you know?"

"A universal requirement." Then: "Benny, if you don't mind, I'll ride a little farther with you."

"Then I'll need a new picture. Otherwise, it's bad luck."

"As you wish."

Benny examined Kali's photograph. "Not a good likeness anyway," he said, and tore it into small pieces, which he dropped into the trash. "Pictures have to be taken at the end of the ride or else they don't count." Then he removed the dollar bills from his pocket and put them behind a false panel in the dashboard and, for the first time since he'd gotten inside the truck, noticed Kali's appearance.

"How'd you get so dirty all over again?"

"I met Mario."

"He's my man."

"Don't be so sure, Benny."

"My amigo from the great city of Tijuana in the great country of Mexico."

"Listen to me."

"Tijuana is where I had my operation. It's where my life began," Benny exclaimed rapturously.

"He mistreats those people, Benny. They're prisoners back there."

"You've got it all wrong. He's my partner."

"He cheats you."

"How can he cheat me? I don't charge for the trip."

"Well, Mario does. And if they can't pay, he sells them to somebody who can."

"Can't be," Benny said.

"The men he sells for work; you can guess what he does with the women. What he's probably doing with that poor young woman back there now."

"I don't believe you."

"I saw with my own eyes."

"I don't want to hear it!"

"He's using you."

"Please, no," Benny wailed. He sounded like he was going to cry.

"Benny," Kali said intensely, "think of those people. Think of that young girl. You were a woman once. You of all people should appreciate what's going on here."

The line. The instant he said it, he knew he had crossed it and he felt himself trip.

"You told!" Benny shrieked.

"I didn't," Kali protested.

"Everyone's going to know now. They'll run me off the road."

"I wouldn't tell anyone, least of all Mario. I only brought it up to you . . . in the interests of basic humanity."

But Benny wouldn't hear him. He forgot there were people in the back of the truck; he forgot Mario; he forgot his hundred-dollar jackpot. He swooped down on Kali and pounced and pummeled, dislocating the water spigot and knocking a few CDs from their overhead racks.

"Get out! Get out of my truck!" he sobbed. "I'm going to kill myself! I'm going to blow myself up!"

Kali didn't go far. He couldn't abandon them. He would not let Mario get away with it. He leaned against an interstate moving van with metal silhouettes of pointy nipples on pointy women stuck to its mud flaps, and collected his thoughts.

He gave Benny some time to calm down and then circled back to the truck to see if there was any chance of further conversation. There was none, not least because, in an effort to escape from a swelling of old, sad memories, Benny had swallowed several of his tiny beige pills. And now drowsily rested his cheek on the steering wheel, while his fingers gripped its leather cover.

Kali took a walk. Hands in pockets, head down, frowning, through the aisles and aisles of parked trucks. Working on a plan. One that would free the mostly innocent, punish the mostly guilty, reward the generous, uphold the spirit of the law, and allow him to retreat into anonymity. It was getting warm. He was getting hungry. The task seemed nearly impossible.

"I never said it would be easy."

"What? Situe? Is that you?"

"Up here."

Her legs hung over the top of a cement truck, over the huge dome where the cement was mixed, one shoe dangling loosely on her toes. "I always wanted to sit on one of these things."

With his hand, Kali shielded his eyes from the sun. "I need to save them, Situe, and I have very little time."

"There's time enough."

"How shall I do it?"

"You don't need me to tell you."

As she swung her feet back and forth and let her heels tap against the side of the huge mixer, the loose shoe fell through the air toward the ground. When Kali bent to where it should have hit the ground, he couldn't find it, and he prepared to crawl under the truck.

"Don't get dirtier on my account."

"I am happy to look for your shoe, Situe-bitue," Kali said.

"Tell me instead about your story."

"You heard it?"

"I did. I was flattered."

"It was actually a very poor story. And only a beginning."

"You were doing fine."

"Thank you. But I shouldn't waste time recounting a failed story. What I'm trying to decide now is what to do about Mario. I'll probably need a weapon."

Around him were weapons enough. Pieces of wood blown into the lot by the wind, tools inside trucks, chains on their backs.

"Why not jump him from behind, grandson?"

"I can do without your sarcasm."

"Is this Mario so much cleverer than you? Must you resort to physical attack?"

"It's one option."

"There are many options," Situe said, and she disappeared from the top of the truck and materialized at ground level, double-shoed.

"He's quite blind without his glasses. You of all people should know that."

"How blind?"

"Blind as a bat."

"In spite of the vileness of Mario's behavior, I find your choice of words disrespectful to all who require corrective lenses."

"No offense intended."

"Although I should have been aware of the weakness of his eyes. Instead, I saw only their hardness."

"A forgivable omission."

It occurred to Kali that he sometimes underestimated the breadth of his grandmother's vision.

"By the way," Situe continued, "the immigration authorities are at the far edge of the parking lot."

"Here?"

"One of their regular stops: so many trucks, so many opportunities to smuggle."

"I need to warn Benny."

"He's barely conscious."

"How much time do I have?"

"Until he wakes up or until immigration knocks at his window?"

"Both."

"The same for each."

"Please, how long is that, dear Situe?"

"The same for each." And, instantly, she was gone.

After a few intense minutes, Kali decided on the solution: he must get rid of Mario. Everything else flowed from that. He ran through the possibilities, all of which, in varying degrees, involved the imposition of physical force.

First, he could give Mario one of Benny's pills and that would solve everything. Then he could just lay him out in the parking lot and Benny could drive away. And the police could arrest Mario when they arrived. Arrest? For what? There would be no evidence of his crimes. And how would he get Mario to take the pills? Hand it to him in a drink? He'd be suspicious. He'd probably suggest trading drinks like they did in the movies and Kali would be the one laying flat on the ground. Not to mention the fact that he knew he couldn't carry it off; he'd give himself away. The opposite of nonchalance, he'd wear his plan on his sleeve.

Second, physical force without possibility of arrest. Maybe all that was required was that Mario be put temporarily out of commission. Why not just knock him out—hit him in the jaw or over the head? But then Kali would have committed a crime and he was in no position to bring himself to the attention of the police. Plus, it was out of character. Him, hit someone? Break a jaw? Smash a head? He was afraid he wouldn't be able to do it unless Mario threatened him or his family in an immediate and dire way, and Mario didn't even know he had a family. He had a hard time premeditating violence. He was a creature of impulse when it came to that. The classic unintentional murderer: at best, a perpetrator of manslaughter, an inflictor of accidental injury.

Third, break Mario's glasses so that he couldn't see and put him at a logistical disadvantage, thereby making him easier to arrest. Kali abhorred the very thought of it. He'd spent his professional life polishing lenses, removing careless scratches from their surfaces. To smash an instrument of vision meant a denial of his professional life. First, do no harm. There must be another way, Situe's probable position on the matter notwithstanding.

Kali kept an eye on Benny's truck from a distance, waiting for another idea. He saw Mario come out the back, light a cigarette, and throw it on the ground. He saw Mario open the passenger door of the truck, then race around to Benny's side: Benny, who had somehow fallen and wedged himself between the steering wheel and his door.

"Benny! You drunken moron!" Mario said. "Wake up! You have to drive." It looked as though he gave Benny a shove before going to the back of the truck. Mario's face was agitated, but not panicked. He didn't know he was running out of time.

But Kali did and, when Mario left, he returned to Benny.

"Benny, can you hear me?"

He lifted Benny to his seat and set him upright. Fastened the seat belt, which Benny usually treated with scorn.

"Benny, Benny," Kali repeated quietly. "Please. Answer."

There was a response. A low gurgle. He was coming to.

Kali went to the back of the truck and climbed in and made his way through the darkness to the entrance of the chamber. Inside, Mario paced back and forth. This time Mario's expression was clearly decipherable: contempt and anger.

"The idiot's drunk," Mario raged. "He can't drive."

"Mario, I need to tell you something," Kali said and he gestured that they should enter the tunnel.

"Don't waste my time."

"Immigration," Kali whispered.

Mario's face hardened.

"Outside."

"How many?"

"Enough."

"When?"

"Soon."

"How do you know?"

"I have it on the best authority."

"Why should I believe you?"

"You can't afford not to."

Mario shoved Kali aside and raced down the passageway to the back of the truck. Impulsively, Kali picked up the flashlight he'd previously left behind and followed him. If necessary, he now had opportunity and the means of taking advantage of it.

"I don't see anything," Mario said. He continued to scan the parking lot.

It was now or never, Kali thought. Hit him and get it over with. The flashlight felt heavy in his hand; heavy enough. He raised it a few inches. Somewhere between a tap and a smash—not enough to injure permanently, just enough to disable him for five minutes. And then Benny could drive away with the others. It was now or probably never.

But Kali couldn't do it.

"If you go now, you'll be ahead of them," Kali urged.

"Why do you care what happens to me?"

"I don't. I care what happens to the others." He relaxed his grip on the flashlight and let it hang by his side.

"How many more chances do you think you have, Mario? How much more money does your family have? If you're caught you'll go to jail. And when your record is discovered, you'll be deported. Framed conviction or not. And when you're sent back to prison in Mexico, the guards will have to beat you unmercifully to show that they had nothing to do with your escape. And if you try to escape, they'll kill you. And if you somehow get away, think of all the people who'll hunt you down. The cuckolded husband, bounty hunters, private detectives, the families of the people you sold, the buyers who blame you when their workers don't work or run away."

They stood on the edge, these two men. Then Mario jumped from the truck, strode across the parking lot, entered the casino, and effortlessly disappeared into its crowds.

Kali, meanwhile, doused Benny with ice water, shook him, slapped his face.

"Can you hear me?"

Benny nodded.

"What's your name?"

"Bedroll Benny," he said groggily.

"Good. Where are you?"

"At The Galaxy. I won a hundred dollars."

"Stay right here."

At the back of the truck, Kali made certain the double doors were closed tight. He fastened the outside chain. And returned to Benny.

"Immigration police will be here any minute. Can you drive?"

"Where's Mario?"

"Mario's gone. He deserted you."

It was sinking in.

"What about the others?"

"They're in back. They're depending on you, Benny." He slammed Benny's door. "Now go! Go!" Kali ordered, pounding on it with his fist. "Go. And don't look back."

Benny fired up the engine and released the air out of the brakes and, as only an experienced eighteen-wheeler driver can do, backed out of his parking space and split cab and trailer into a right angle. He stopped and leaned out the window and yelled, "I need your picture!"

"Later. My ride's not over yet!"

Down the aisles Bedroll Benny rolled. Lurching over the curb, chipping the concrete. Entering the frontage road without signaling or stopping. He cut through four lanes of traffic getting to the on-ramp, then slipped smoothly into the freeway flow. Kali lost sight of the truck as it signaled a lane change and, friskily, rode over a hill.

❧ 21 ❧

FOR THE NEXT TWO NIGHTS, Kali slept outside. His bed, a concrete base that held in place one of four giant legs of a giant windmill. Like others sleeping outside, he turned in as the sun went down and rose when it came up. Whether from exhaustion or fear or both, he slept soundly. The heat that the concrete absorbed during the day radiated out and through him during the cool nights. Altogether he was as comfortable as could be expected, but for the minutes right before he fell asleep and right after he awoke, when he thought about going home: whether he would, when he would, what would happen there if he did. There appeared to be no external obstacles keeping him from Sophie and his children and the Oasis and the Hashanian Mutual Aid Society. It was up to him.

Bunking down among the windmills had not occurred to him at first. As he fled the parking lot of the casino, he assumed he'd hitch a ride or get as far as the fast food drive-thru down the freeway and rest and eat. He still had a little money. And he'd taken water and a few bags of nuts from Benny's truck. But when he hit the sand, he turned away from roads and food and toward the hills. Part of the reason was a desire to remain unseen until he was surer of his safety. But the other was the windmills. For when he looked up and out, they were all he saw and their soft, spinning songs called to him.

There was no freeway. There were no people. There was nothing else but them, spinning at the whim of the wind. They reeled him in like a fish on a line. They looked much bigger closer up.

Kali found it comforting to be in their company. As he walked farther in among them, he saw that every once in awhile, the velocity of the air notwithstanding, some blades did not spin like the others, but stayed still or lazed in slow, casual circles. A cause for rejoicing, he thought—these machines, which retained their individuality and self-direction—and he mused contentedly on the similarities between their functioning and his. It was getting dark and though he was no longer hungry, he was tired and needed a place to rest.

Which was when he noticed the small cinderblock building nearby, having not noticed several of them previously, having ignored a faraway grouping of slightly larger structures with metal grids, surrounded by a chain link fence. This one was no more than ten by ten. It had a doorless doorway and four jailhouse-sized windows across the top of one side. There was no glass in the windows: something else, something that crackled when he touched it and stuck to his fingers, tough, like barbed wire.

Spiderwebs. Without pattern or apparent reason, as if a drunk or enraged being had spun them. Only one kind of spider made that kind of web. A spider that had no redeeming social value that Kali could think of. It was too dark to see if any—or, rather, how many—were inside, so he took partial shelter under the protective rotation of a nearby windmill and curled up on the warm cement platform and slept and repeated his activities the next day and night. On the second morning before he actually opened his eyes, he felt a familiar presence. There she was, a few feet away, on her stool, smoking, silent. Situe: like before, but different. Something was different.

"What's the matter, Situe? Are you sick?" Kali asked.

She barely looked at him.

"Not sick in body. Not any more. It's my eyes: the older I get, the more I see. That's the way it is now."

"I thought you couldn't get any older once you were . . . up there. I thought that in heaven—if there is a heaven—everything was perfect."

Her small, deep-set black eyes, like onyx stones, hid under half closed lids.

"It's overwhelming. We're hardly prepared for it," she said sadly.

Kali had never seen his grandmother like this. Impenetrable, steady—that's how he knew her; a familiar and reassuring constancy. She rarely varied; she rarely changed expression. Even when tempted to laugh, she turned her head to the side, as though to avoid the loss of equilibrium it might cause. A sphinx, a goddess, the Mother of God—they didn't disclose much either. Neither pain nor praise altered them.

"Please tell me what's bothering you."

"The population explosion," she said weakly. "They're dying everywhere. They're streaming in."

"Can you be more specific?"

"Have I taught you nothing, my boy?" she gathered the force to snap at him. "There are many others who would benefit from our conversations. Don't make me feel like I'm wasting my time."

"You've never been this way before. Not even when you were alive."

"What do you know?" she said, choking back a sob.

"Situe-bitue, how can I help you feel better? Would you like to discuss how good and evil are sometimes mirror images of each other? You always enjoy that. Or maybe you could tell one of your stories?"

Overhead, the blades rotated slowly, creating little noise, barely there, while low lying creosote, hindered by the frequent wind, clung to the ground. Situe paid little attention to the growing ash of her cigarette.

"I ask them why they think they should be in heaven," she said, looking off into the distance. "A preliminary question, one of many."

Kali nodded. His eyes took in his grandmother's sorrow. His breath inhaled it.

"I ask them: 'Did you love or did you hate? Did you cherish or kill?' And do you know what, grandson?"

"No, dear Situe, what?"

"So many killed! So many hated! And they're proud to admit it! They think they did it out of love or for justice. And they all think they've earned a place in heaven."

"I'm sorry."

"They feel entitled; they argue with everything we say. No humility, no insight."

"I'm so sorry."

"It's enough to make me apply for a change of position."

"Can you do that?"

"The system offers some flexibility."

Words of solace, words of truth—Kali struggled for them.

"Maybe you need a vacation."

"There's no place to go."

"That's what you said when you were alive."

He tried again.

"It's seems to me that you're suffering from burnout."

"Ach! Don't use that phrase."

"Forgive me, I only meant—"

"—I know what you meant," Situe said, fading, growing fainter, reducing her presence to an outline, then a shadow.

"Please, come back. Give me another chance."

For a few seconds it was touch and go—would she or wouldn't she?—and then the details of her silhouette reemerged, and she resettled on her stool, and Kali saw that she watched him and waited. Hopeful or hopeless, he couldn't tell. He stepped down from the base of the windmill, collecting his thoughts. Back and forth, slowly, he paced in front of her. The surface beneath his feet, firm or shifting, depending on the proportion of rock to sand.

"Now," he began with as much preliminary confidence as he could summon, "there must be many good things about heaven."

"That's what you come up with?" she asked. "Are you making fun of the entire concept of eternal reward?"

"Not at all, Situe-bitue, though it's not easy to defend something you don't believe in."

"People do it all the time."

He ignored her.

"I'm trying to point out the bright sides of the subject at hand. Didn't you just say, or at least imply, that there's a wide variety of people in heaven?"

"It's an equal-opportunity destination."

"And that's positive, isn't it?"

"Officially, yes."

"Which must mean that those who *don't* get along down here *do* in fact get along up there."

"Not necessarily."

"Let me start again. Is it safe to presume, for example, that there are both Arabs and Jews in heaven?

"It is and there are."

"Muslims and Christians?"

"Naturally."

"And Pakistanis and Indians?"

"Affirmative."

"Blacks, whites?" Kali picked up speed, enjoying this minor logical triumph.

"Of course, of course."

"Hutu and Tutsi? Serb and Croat? Libertarian and socialist? Native and colonial? Conservative and liberal? Northerner and southerner? Believer and nonbeliever?"

"Yes, yes, yes, yes, yes, yes, and yes."

"And they all get along?"

"Within reason."

"Only 'within reason.' Not better than that?"

"Their passionate arguments never end. But at least they go no further. They don't get physical."

"They can still hate each other?" Kali asked.

"Theoretically, yes."

"How can that be?"

"Most are at a very primitive stage of development when they come to us and we must take them as we find them. It's one step at a time. A long, drawn-out process. A kind of spiritual lobotomy. They're cleansed of their desire to do violent acts. But we let them keep their thoughts, their partisan beliefs, their traditions, et cetera, et cetera—it's what makes them—us—human, after all."

"Can't you just teach them to behave better?"

"Apparently not," she sighed.

"That's very disturbing."

"The lobotomy or the tribalism?"

"Both, I guess," Kali admitted.

"If we could modify the latter, we could do without the former."

"Meaning?"

"Whatever you want it to mean: respect differences, accentuate them, assimilate, separate, intermingle, mix and match, embrace ritual, defy convention, look to the ancients, look to the new. It's a matter of balance, harmony, scale. The permutations and combinations offer nearly infinite possibility."

"I don't think I follow you."

"Look at us, you and me. We're a case in point. You and I represent the successful blending of the specifics of a culture and the universals of humanity."

"It's getting clearer, I think."

"Good. Though normally one of *us* isn't assigned to one of *you* if we're from the same family or background. The committee assumes that distance and perspective override the benefits of familiarity."

"The committee?"

"They gave me a dispensation," Situe continued. "They thought it would be beneficial if you worked with someone you already trusted."

"I didn't realize I deserved such consideration."

"Dearest Kali, you don't. *I'm* the one being considered here. I'm only a trainee, you see. You're my first case. Since they expect us to make mistakes the first time around, they thought it would be better if I made them with you. On the assumption that, though greatly in need, you are eminently salvageable."

"Should I be honored or insulted?"

"Both. The committee agrees with me that you have a good heart —"

"—I'm relieved to hear it—"

"—though still moderately self-absorbed and self-indulgent."

"One minute you praise me for being thoughtful, and the next minute you make fun of me."

"The elements are there, grandson. It's your sense of proportion that needs fine-tuning."

Clearly, Situe was feeling better. She lit a fresh cigarette and crossed her thick ankles. She turned her face up and released large, loose circles of smoke toward the sky, then turned with visible fondness turned toward Kali.

"Thank you," she said.

"You're welcome."

For a while, they shared the balmy desert air: like the old country to Situe; like something he yearned for, to Kali.

Then: "Would you mind if I asked you a question, grandmother?"

"Would it matter if I did?"

"Because there's one thing I've always wanted to know."

She looked as though she knew what he had in mind.

"It's this—what about Hitler? Could he have gone to heaven?"

"Somebody always asks about him. Him and Attila the Hun and various serial killers . . . "

"Well?"

"You know the rules. I can't provide information about specific people."

"Ah."

"Besides, the question is far more interesting than the answer."

"Oh?"

"You see, what the questioner is really asking is whether redemption is available to the worst person on earth. Whether being sorry at the end can erase what a person has done before. And the questioner is either angry—thinking, if that's the case, it's not fair. I was good my whole life; I didn't cheat on my wife and I didn't steal from the till, and I look over to this bad guy sitting next to me and he's getting the same infinite rewards I am—or," she paused for effect, "the questioner is relieved, thinking he can live anyway he wants and, at the last moment request forgiveness and get it, unlike the poor suckers who lived by the rules."

"So people really get into heaven that way?"

"You wish."

She stood, and her three-legged stool hovered in the air next to her, and Kali realized he had only a few more seconds.

Quickly he asked, "What about people who commit horrible acts but didn't know what they were doing?"

"I'll leave that one to Sigmund Freud." She started to rise from the concrete platform.

"He's there, then?"

"Now, how did that slip out . . . " she muttered as she rolled up her stockings again in midair.

"What he's like?" Kali called up.

"Glum. Very glum," she responded, losing interest in the conversation. "More attractive then he realizes. But that's all I'm going to say. All these questions; all these answers. I'm tired of the Socratic method—and don't ask me if *he's* there. It's against protocol for me to talk about my colleagues."

Nearly invisible, she continued to talk, more to herself than to Kali, her voice remaining just strong enough for him to hear.

"Nobody has any idea how much time we spend placating these perpetual celebrities who think their privacy was invaded."

"You have all eternity," Kali interrupted, directing his comment to the place above him where he thought she might be.

"Very funny," she said, though he heard in her tone a flicker of approval. And despite the increasing distance between them and

that she may have been a figment of his imagination or a halluci-
nation or a disembodied spirit, he felt peace.

"The child becomes the father of the man," he heard her whisper. "Or the grandmother."

A phrase whose truth washed over him. For Kali had previously experienced just such a reality. It was on the day Situe died.

Situe, rushed from a convalescent home to a hospital to con-
clude a life of nonexpression: seldom demanding, rarely preferring,
facing the inevitable. She didn't speak of her left leg after she lost
it. Battling alone the phantom sensations that told her to scratch
her toes and rub her calves, assuming she was insane or possessed.
Probably the doctors would have explained this common surgi-
cal result, the body's yearning for its missing part, had she asked
them—had it occurred to her to ask them.

At the time of her death, her family gathered around her bed,
discussed her as though she wasn't there.

"She looks good."

"Like she's sleeping."

"Do you think she's in pain?"

"No, thank God."

"How long?"

A son-in-law had braved this question, less unseemly for him to
ask than a blood relation.

When Jiddue died, they'd also flocked around Situe, ordering
the grandchildren, Kali included, to stay outside while they decided what to do. What Situe wanted wasn't asked. There were few
choices for an uneventful life.

And she didn't speak up. Didn't reveal that she had lost her
bearings. That her heart had gone and left her behind. When the
grandchildren came in, Situe looked the same. Kali went to her,
kissed her as required and as he always did, unaware that she had

shifted from alive to dead. For one week—longer, frankly, than anyone expected—Situe lay in that hospital bed, occasionally opening her eyes to witness the vigil. Someone from the next generation remained by her side at all times, or someone from the next-next generation. Which is how Kali, the oldest grandson, came to be with her when the rest of the family retreated to the hospital cafeteria to eat and to plan. The stomach of one uncle rumbled in the elevator all the way down to the lobby.

As Kali sat next to Situe's bed, a nurse peeked in and moved on, knowing there was nothing she could or should do. Kali filled the plastic pitcher with water, poured some into the plastic glass, held the straw to Situe's lips. When she didn't respond, he brushed the end of the straw gently across her mouth to remind her that she could have a drink if she wanted one. She would have nothing else: there would be no feeding tubes, no drips into her veins.

She seemed comfortable. Her brown hands rested, relaxed, outside the covers. Against all advice, she wore on the third finger of her left hand, the black pearl ring Jiddue had given her. She had never taken it off, despite shifts in her marital status and location, despite warnings of theft by staff, or blood poisoning when her finger swelled to twice it size.

Kali thought how good she still smelled. Her usual smell—lightly oiled, lightly musked—learned over years of respectful embrace. And her hair was neat, held back by one comb behind each ear. Who had done that? A daughter, Kali's aunt. The same daughter who would the next evening, after visiting hours, between nurses' rounds, strip her mother of her hospital gown and replace it with her favorite cotton house dress. That Situe wore no underwear didn't matter. Her old woman's body had no need for modesty or additional support.

"She looks like she's just taking a nap."

"She looks like she's dead and laid out," thought one.

They shook their heads and smiled.

Not since Kali was a little boy and spent the night at her house with his two sisters had he seen Situe lying down with her eyes closed. She'd slept on the couch to make room in her mahogany-framed double bed for the three children. Tucked them in tight. Ordered their feet to stay under the covers where they wouldn't get cold, and there they lay obediently, burning from heat, until she left the room.

Kali couldn't sleep in the tiny house. For in the kitchen next to the only bedroom, the black windup clock that stood on its feet on the shelf of the old stove, ticked loudly, and a train ran over the tracks a few miles away, blowing its whistle as it passed. Situe slept through; she was used to them. Kali padded down the hallway to see if he was the only one awake and found her lying on her side on the narrow couch, her sleeping breaths shallow, the only time he ever saw her when he thought she was unaware of his presence.

Except for that last time in the hospital when she wore her favorite dress and rested her well-groomed head straight on the pillow. There was no one else around. He bent over her and revealed to her the contents of his heart. A young man barely formed; neither husband nor father. Had she heard? (One of her doctors had assured all of them that hearing was the last sense to go, saying this in her presence as though she couldn't hear him.)

"Situe," Kali had whispered, "if you can hear me, raise your arm." They were stunned when they returned, those family members with full stomachs and funeral plans. So stunned that they stopped within the frame of the door and began to cry.

"Ma, if you can hear me, wiggle your fingers."

"Stick out your thumb."

"Ma, make a fist."

How they carried on during this last opportunity to say the things that her raised right arm unleashed within them. And it came down—certain proof if more was needed—when they finished. Such exhilaration they felt for that brief time, such awkward fulfillment when they dared look again into each other's faces. There was a move to begin a second round of affirmation and confession, raised arm or not, when Situe, noisily emptying her lungs of air, left the room.

And this was the conclusion they reached: she had heard them. And they took great comfort in it. And at Situe's funeral, one of the family members made reference to the miracle of her raised arm; though others who weren't present for it, at the dinner afterward, argued that it was simply a manifestation of a natural phenomenon and explainable in medical terms. To which Kali shrugged his shoulders, for it made no difference to him. Alive or dead, on earth or in heaven, in time or eternity. Sometimes he found it hard to tell one from the other anyway. It was the beginning of his dreaming period, and he never fully got over it.

22

"DO . . . NOT . . . MOVE."

Kali froze. Behind him, a click and the sound of labored breathing.

"And . . . do . . . not . . . turn . . . around."

An explosion at his left shoulder threw him to the ground, and he lay there, knotted and twisted.

Half a snake—the half with rattles—hung from a man's outstretched hand. The gun in its makeshift holster, kept company with a knife which rested, unsheathed, along the man's thigh. Grinning the whole time, the man lifted the knife, tossed the half-snake in the air, and sliced it pirate-like, then reached down and handed Kali—frozen in position on the ant-ridden sand—the rattles.

"Souvenir."

Kali stayed still.

"Come on," the man said cheerfully. "We'll have it for dinner."

With the snake halves thrown around his neck, the man walked sturdily away, turning back a couple of times, clearly expecting Kali to follow. But Kali stayed where he was: his ability to negotiate the space around him, altered. For he was deaf in his left ear though his shoulder was uninjured. And he didn't know where the one-armed man was taking him.

Dinner was: snake and tomatoes and lettuce and apples and corn with butter, firm and fresh in spite of the heat and their location.

"Everything's homegrown, home caught, or homemade—except the butter."

"I'll take your word for it," Kali answered.

They sat at the edge of a fire pit the man said he'd dug sometime before, one of many scattered over the thousands of acres—among the windmills and beyond—that he claimed as his territory. Out of consideration, he sat on Kali's hearing side and formed his words with exaggerated movement, in case it was necessary for Kali to read his lips. He dangled a piece of snake he intended to put in his mouth.

"Courtesy of John Moses Browning."

Kali bit in, haltingly chewed the meat, waiting for the taste to identify itself, exploring the texture with the inside of his mouth. Both were pleasing—he was relieved and surprised. Surprised also at his sense of being settled, alive, and well.

"The man was a genius."

"Without knowing anything about Mr. Browning, I defer to your judgment," Kali said.

"John Moses Browning invented the gun that shot the snake that we're eating right now."

"The gun that John built," Kali said agreeably.

"Otherwise," the man said heartily, "there'd be nothing for us to eat." Which they did with their hands: Kali, careful not to burn himself; the man, inured to burning, reaching into the fire for more snake, more corn, more apples for both of them.

"This isn't like any meal I've had before," Kali said.

"Like Nam. That's what this is like."

The man offered half an apple, seeds in, dripping its hot juice.

"Not now, thank you. Maybe later."

It was a surprise—this fit, this unexpected harmonious meeting of apparently dissimilar human spirits that comes infrequently in a lifetime and, for some, never comes. It had been nearly instant. An ambush of ease and comfort, and Kali took for granted that whatever they knew of the other would be enough, that what each chose to say would be true.

"My name is Maximilian," the man had said. "After the emperor."

"Kahlil Gibran Hourani. After the poet."

"Call me Max."

"Call me Kali."

They'd settled inside the mouth of the narrow canyon which, before the gunshot, the snake, and the deafness, Kali had been exploring by himself. There were cottonwood trees and full-sized versions of some of the plants, which stayed stunted at lower altitudes. Ribbons of water ran along the surface of the ground, dividing varying widths of rock beds and shrub-dappled sand. Boulders that hadn't yet broken and disintegrated, piled high on both sides. Perfect places for snakes to heat up and coil and strike at what got too close.

"You shouldn't feel bad, Kali. Even if you weren't deaf, you probably wouldn't have heard it. They only rattle sometimes. They're quiet as smoke when they want to be."

"I wasn't deaf until you shot the gun next to my ear," Kali said, intending only to inform, neither angry nor resentful.

"Oh," Max said evenly. "Well, it'll pass, like in Nam."

"You think so?"

"I do."

"By the way, you don't have to speak so slowly. Or so loud. I can hear you fine out of the other ear."

"Good to know."

Friends already, they sat awhile in comfortable silence.

"So, how long have you been out here?" Kali asked.

"Nine years. You?"

"About a week."

When they finished eating, they suffocated the smoldering creosote with sand, and Max stuffed the leftover food in a canvas bag he'd brought to the site after instructing Kali to sit and wait, saying he'd be back shortly with the rest of their meal. Stunned, half-deaf, Kali had done as he was told. And Max returned from somewhere with the bag holding their food, the tomatoes still on their stems as if plucked in a hurry, the apples coated in sand. Kali cleaned his hands as well as he could on the back of his pants; he hadn't explained to Max how he came to be wearing the pants—ill-fitting, ill-matching—nor had he explained how he came to be scraped, scabbed, and swollen, and Max hadn't asked. In return, Kali kept his eyes away from the missing arm, passing and handing and offering without seeming to think or plan around it.

From somewhere around them, a high, shrill animal song swirled through the air: a howling counterpoint. Long, sustained, accelerating, rising. Voices intertwined. It stopped abruptly.

"Couple of coyotes, maybe three," Max said. "They yip until they make the kill. Probably a rabbit."

"How close are they?"

"Don't worry, they don't want to be around us."

"Good."

"Now, the dogs. That's another story."

Max took out a cigarette. "Smoke?"

"No, thanks."

He inhaled deeply and broke into a long, damp cough.

"You should see a doctor about that, Max."

"Already did."

As the late afternoon melted into dusk, Max led the way out of the canyon. He knew where to go without thinking, like a man walking in his own house in the dark. Unlike Kali, who had to watch where he put his feet; even then, misjudging the relationship of stream bank to stream. He blamed this unsteadiness on his newly bad ear. Not his eyes, though; they were fine, he assured himself, because if they weren't, he'd know. Not for nothing, his dedication to his profession, his years of providing lenses and frames. Still, this extra physical effort and his other recent extra efforts to navigate the unforeseen, were wearing him down.

"I'm fifty-three," Kali sighed.

"Sixty-two," said Max.

A gentle breeze came up, teasing a scattering of windmills into motion. Red lights on their trunks warned that they occupied the sky. The darker it got, the brighter the warnings.

"We're here," Max said. He bent and pulled and the surface of the desert seemed to move.

It wasn't much. A supply depot. Underground, Max said, for obvious reasons. Covered by plywood sheets covered by tarps. With reinforced plywood walls. Inside, some tools, barbed wire, ammunition, lighter fluid, dry food, blankets, a duffel bag stuffed full.

"Try these." Max handed Kali a pair of tan work pants, a light brown shirt. "These won't fit either, but you won't make such a colorful target."

"Mothballs," Kali said as he took the clothes and put them on and the smell filled the compartment.

"Keeps the critters out."

"What critters?"

"The usual . . . scorpions, centipedes, tarantulas, vinegaroons."

The clothes felt better than what he was wearing and Kali put their odor out of his mind. They were, after all, cleaner than he was. His last shower had been on Benny's truck, the one before that at the Empire Motor Hotel. When he was with Jane.

"Drink?" Max asked.

"With pleasure."

Max handed Kali a full quart of Scotch, which Kali opened, breaking the paper seal, and it didn't take long for Kali to get used to drinking it straight from the bottle; and they passed it back and forth and each dozed and woke and dozed and woke, while, above ground, the breezes blew and the sand fought its way under the tarp. In general, though, the desert was on its good behavior, delivering the kind of night for which it was prized—a night like velvet or wine—with light, buoyant air that softened other sounds and thoughts.

"I come from a very moderate family when it comes to alcohol," Kali announced from his position on the floor, a motley surface of unmatched tiles, stones, and pavers that Max had scavenged and set in sand as close as their irregular edges allowed. "We drink very little."

"Nothing wrong with that."

"Except for two uncles, two cousins and, during her last years, dear Situe."

Kali remembered finding Situe at home in the tiny side of her tiny duplex, laying on the carpet next to her bed. Snoring gently. Arms folded peacefully on her chest and the half empty bottle of good, red wine—a neighbor had given it to her for her birthday without knowing the concerns of the family—on its side next to her.

"I think it gave her a lot of comfort toward the end."

"Nothing wrong with that."

Kali accepted the bottle from Max, took another drink.

"One short glass of bourbon over ice at Christmas and one at Easter. That's all I usually have."

"A man should know his limit," said Max.

"Although sometimes I have one at a Baptism or birthday party." Kali took another drink and shuddered. "Bourbon is much sweeter than this."

"Never touch it," Max said.

"By the way, *Situe* is the Arabic word for 'grandmother.'"

"You don't say."

"One of the few Arabic words I know, actually."

Kali paused before going on. "What would you think," he began slowly, "if I told you that Situe appears to me . . . now and then?"

"I'd say, 'No problem.'"

"And that I saw her as recently as yesterday?"

"No problem."

Max lay down and set the bottle between them. Kali extended a hand and wrapped it around the neck

"She only had one . . . " Kali stopped.

"One?"

" . . . leg . . . left when she died."

"That's a crying shame."

"And she was nearly blind. All her operations and she still couldn't see."

"A goddam crying shame."

"Once, when I visited her, she asked me to let her die."

"Sad," Max said, "very sad."

"She kept saying, 'Kill me, Kali, kill me.' I begged her to stop saying it."

"John Moses Browning would have known what to do."

"It took me weeks to get her words out of my mind. And after that, I was afraid to visit her. Afraid she'd say it again. Or something worse. Though," Kali turned to look at Max, "what could be worse than that?"

"I'll say it again," Max responded softly, deliberately. "John Moses Browning was a goddam genius."

"I'm sure he was," Kali answered.

Both had closed their eyes by now. Each was warm. Each was aware of the muted voice of the other.

"The finest pistol ever made," Max said softly. He turned his head toward Kali and said, without opening his eyes, "How're you doing over there?"

"Coming right along," Kali answered.

"I'm sorry about your ear, you know."

"Don't mention it."

Kali caressed the neck of the bottle.

"And I'm sorry about your arm."

"John Moses Browning had nothing to do with it, you know. The man was a goddam genius."

"I completely agree."

"He designed that gun in 1911. Or before. I don't remember exactly."

"No problem."

And we used it in Nam, in Korea, during I and II."

"That's a lot of wars."

"Damn right it is. Did I mention Gulf War One?"

"Not that I remember."

"You can count on that gun," Max almost sobbed.

"A good thing when you're shooting at someone."

"Fine bullets: lead core, copper jacket."

"Some bullets are simply better than others," Kali agreed.

"And they don't change shape passing through. I say that's a good thing, but a lot of people don't agree with me."

For a while, wind-sung and nearly drunk, they didn't talk. Kali decided against climbing the ladder to see if anything was going on outside. He decided against moving at all.

"I started telling you about Situe—," Kali began.

"—One leg—" Max interrupted.

"That's right. She was my grandmother."

"I loved my grandmother," said Max. "But I didn't visit her."

"You should have visited."

Kali lay down, turned on his side, letting his cheek rest unsupported on the bare floor, indifferent to the small pieces of rock and smears of fine sand pushing into his skin and scabs.

"On her last day, we were all there. Her doctor came in; I recognized him, of course. He'd been her doctor for years. And he said, 'You've done everything that could be done.' My father was more upset than anyone. And the doctor took my father aside and said, 'You've done everything you could do. It's nobody's fault.' And I swear I heard Situe whisper—but I didn't dare ask if anyone else heard—'Then whose fault is it?'" Those were the last words she ever said."

Last words that never failed to stop Kali in his tracks.

"What do you think of that, Max?"

"Damn fine question."

∽ 23 ∽

THE MORNING AFTER. Stale underground air. Hot, dark.

"I'm sick," Kali said.

Max climbed the ladder. Kali forced himself to lift his head, forced himself to raise his body, and went up.

"Oh, God," he moaned.

"Come on."

As usual, Max led the way; Kali, miserable, keeping up. Through a field of windmills, past three small cinderblock buildings, to a larger installation—POWER PLANT, PRIVATE PROPERTY, NO TRESPASSING—with metal grids and cables and poles strung and connected in straight and orderly tinker toy outlines surrounded by a chain-link and razor-wire fence, and enough lights inside the perimeter to light a prison yard.

"We're here."

Max opened the unlocked gate—

"Should we be doing this?" asked Kali.

—and walked toward a one-story L-shaped building—

"You first," Max said.

—which was clean and cool inside, housing an office sparsely furnished; another room, empty but for a narrow bed and a small refrigerator; and a bathroom with a shower and the basics—soap and thin, but clean, towels.

"You first," Max said.

Within a short time Kali was as clean as his clothes, notwithstanding the minor smudges from sleeping drunk on an underground floor. Max followed and, afterward, they carried two chairs outside and warmed themselves in the early afternoon sun.

"Well," Kali finally asked, "what is this and what are we doing here?" His outside felt better than his inside, though the latter was catching up, his stomach settling down, his appetite stirring.

"Cashing in on my pension." Max leaned his chair on its two back legs. "Wanted: broken down soldier of fortune. Low pay, lousy working conditions, wild dogs. Must have one arm."

"You're very hard on yourself, Max."

"I was the night watchman. And when the job was over, I stayed. They never changed the locks so I figured they wouldn't mind if used the place now and then. And they sure don't miss the extra electricity."

"Which explains the butter," Kali said.

"Mini-mart up the road explains the jerky." Max adjusted his chair to the sun's position, pulled a piece of jerky from his pocket. Offered some to Kali. "More damn jerky than you ever saw."

For the second time since his escape from the fire marshal and the man in the brown suit, Kali had viewed his face in the mirror. After his shower, steeling himself to look. Amazing how a beard grew through scabs. The desert helped dry the scabs out, helped them heal. It also made them itch, on the surface and under. Scratching only made them bleed, assuming he could reach the itch in the first place. He itched like mad as he sat there now.

"So, Kali," Max said quietly, "they still after you?"

"I don't know." It was the first direct question Max had asked and Kali felt obliged to answer.

"They haven't shown themselves in a while. And since I don't know what else to do, I run."

"Like in Nam."

"It's because I'm an Arab. Even though I'm third-generation."

"Never met an Arab before."

"Do I seem different from anybody else?"

"Yep. Not sure if it's because you're an Arab."

Kali shifted position in the chair.

"The last few days have changed me, Max. I'm a new man."

"Never that way for me. I come out same as I go in. Nothing more, nothing less."

"But what about the war? I mean . . . your arm, you know."

"Lost that after Nam. After everything."

"I see," said Kali, but he didn't.

"Lost the arm after, not during," he said matter-of-factly.

He wanted to know more about the arm that wasn't there. Max got up and started walking. Kali followed, and that's how they spent the rest of the afternoon. Both mostly quiet, Kali digesting what Max had said, imagining, reconstructing.

They stayed out of the mountains this time, off the dunes, as too steep, too dirtying, too tiring, confining their unhurried movements to the flatlands, some dotted with windmills, some not. Their shoes crunched over the sand, practically the only noise, except for a breeze that filled their ears if they turned their heads one way and disappeared if they turned them the other. Kali found he heard the wind in both ears, depending on his position. His damaged ear was healing. Max was right about that.

They were on the verge of running out of water when they came upon one of Max's hidden stashes. This time, in addition to the buried water—mild beef jerky. The water and the jerky kept them going until almost sunset. As the hours went by, Kali descended into a soothing melancholy, an absorbed reflection.

But not Max.

For no reason that Kali could discern, Max started and stopped, scanned the horizon, walked, started, and stopped.

"What is it?" Kali whispered.

"Not sure."

"The dogs?"

"Something in the distance."

"Where?" Though straining, Kali saw nothing.

Max hesitated. "Something moving from left to right."

Again Kali tried to see; again he saw nothing.

"Can't get a bead on it."

"Have you seen it before?"

"I have."

"How often?"

"Often."

"Tell me when you see it again."

"Will do."

Max didn't mention it again that day, though Kali registered Max's continued breaks in rhythm and composure. They ended up back at the power plant.

"We'll stay here tonight."

"Sounds fine to me," Kali answered.

Max offered neither food nor conversation. Once inside, he sat on the concrete floor, leaning against a cinderblock wall until he decided to go to sleep. Kali did the same, taking occasional breaks to walk outside for air, staying within the fence. Making sure the gate whose latch was loose, was secured with a large river rock he found half-buried in the sand.

They slept on the floor in the room with the small bed. Both dreamed vigorous, dangerous dreams that marred their sleep and caused them to start and turn and shout an occasional sharp word. In the morning, each seemed embarrassed when he awoke, sensing a vulnerability, a revelation he wished he hadn't made.

❧ 24 ❧

THE NEXT DAY they walked again. Along the canyon path until the boulders closed in and blocked it, across the flatlands close to the freeway, following the lines of the alluvial plains—using Max's hidden sources of water and food as the centers from which they radiated.

Just when it seemed to Kali that he could walk no farther, Max produced jerky. Like magic, from out of the bowels of the earth. Salty, spicy, mild, hot—almost too tough to chew, probably the toughest jerky Kali had ever chewed (though he hadn't chewed much of it before meeting Max), for it had been buried under the scorching sand for a long time, undoubtedly past the expiration dates on the packages which, even if they hadn't faded to illegibility, Kali, out of courtesy, wouldn't have read.

The desert was quiet and seemed mostly empty. But for two jackrabbits and Situe's head—disembodied, like a Cheshire cat, a mischievous smile on her face—in the shade of a gray-green shrub, Kali saw only lizards and insects. He would have been surprised had Situe not made an appearance, and he found her presence comforting, notwithstanding the form it took.

Max timed it so they arrived at one of his underground stashes at nightfall. And from which, no longer to Kali's surprise, Max retrieved what they needed: a flashlight, blankets, cardboard, water, more jerky, canned peaches, and a tube of Boston Brown Bread.

"Always liked the shape of the can," Max said as he dusted it off.

The batteries in the flashlight were dead. So they layered the cardboard and blankets by feel, memory, and early starlight. There was no moon. While Kali opened the jerky and the container of water, Max stabbed his knife into the cans of peaches and bread.

"Can you see well enough to do that?" Kali asked.

"Done it a million times."

They decided against a fire. Too warm. Too much trouble. The air stilled. The sky brightened like a screen in a darkening theater.

"I need to go back tomorrow," Kali said.

"Figured as much."

Max squatted near where they'd eaten. Kali lay flat on the makeshift bedding, his arms folded underneath his head, looking up. There was nothing between him and what was out there—whatever it was, however far it extended. Nothing but inspiration and whatever his imagination could conjure up. He hoped he was up to the task. Some time passed, he wasn't sure how much.

Suddenly he said, "I come from a long line of storytellers."

"Don't say."

"It's part of our tradition."

Kali felt Max turn with interest in his direction.

"I have one in mind, at least the beginnings of one."

"Haven't heard a story in a long time."

"It's about leaving the old country. I told you I was an Arab, didn't I?"

"You mentioned it."

"I see no reason not to tell it, do you?"

"No reason."

So Kali began:

Mansour and his two younger brothers and younger sister boarded a ship in Marseilles for the six week journey over the Atlantic to America. They'd come from Zahle—Situe's village in Lebanon—and were aiming for New York, and then Boston. Mansour was afraid they'd never get off Ellis Island, afraid they'd be sent back because his sister had a cough and one brother had watery eyes.

In Boston, they planned to live in Syria Town. One mile square, bordered on one side by Manchester Avenue. With their mother and her new husband, and the four stepbrothers they had never met. Mansour had been his mother's favorite in the old country. And now he was an orphan.

Max interrupted: "Thought his mother was alive."

"There's more than one way to be an orphan," Kali answered firmly, surprised at the intensity of his response. He breathed deeply and went on.

As they crossed the ocean, the burden of being alone in the world settled on him—

"Alone?" Max asked.

"As a son with a mother can be an orphan, a man with two brothers and a sister can be alone in the world."

"Just asking."

"It's how the story was passed down," Kali explained, although at that moment he couldn't actually remember the specifics—if he was adding or subtracting, emphasizing or overlooking—yet he surrendered to the flow of words and images.

"It's true?" Max asked.

"I think so."

As crossings went, it was all right. Not too cold, not too rough; almost enough food—food they'd brought for themselves. Food they hoped wouldn't spoil, for if it spoiled, they could starve. They knew that this had happened before. And to complicate matters, Mansour's sister had fallen in love with a fellow passenger.

Who wasn't worthy of her, Mansour told her, trying to protect her, but she wouldn't listen and, after all, he couldn't watch her night and day. The ship was crowded and, though each group had staked out a place, people came and went and shifted position according to weather condition or health or whim. Mansour assumed that when they docked, the romance would dissolve and that would be that.

Mansour passed his free time on board ship, reading. In Arabic, of course. He loved to read and write—but at home he had little opportunity to do either. He came from a village so small everyone knew everyone else by his first name and if that first name was repeated in a second or third or fourth family, here's how people kept them straight: besides Mansour the scholar, there was the Mansour who had the patch of white hair on the side of his head from the day he was born; the Mansour who was the son of Sabeh who limped because a camel stepped on his foot when he was a boy; the Mansour who—

"Got it," said Max.

"Of course." Kali cleared his throat.

Yet, in spite of all the obstacles and difficulties, Mansour was glad to be traveling to the New World. He was tired of living in a place where everybody thought the same and if you didn't, somebody called the priest and he came and prayed over you. And if you still didn't, people thought you were crazy or possessed and walked around you without speaking to you. As though you were diseased, as though the mere fact of your original thoughts would contaminate—

"You always yell your stories?" Max said.

"I'm yelling?"

The temperature dropped. Kali took a break and pulled his blankets over him. Max stayed the same. When Kali collected his thoughts again, he continued.

Many from their village and the surrounding villages had heard that in America gold bricks paved the streets of the cities. They were poor people; life was a struggle. So the good things of the old country—the way families took care of each other, the way you didn't always have to think what was coming next—weren't enough to keep them there. Though some planned to take their wealth home and others vowed to follow old country ways even in the New World.

"Did they?" Max asked.

"Some did, some didn't, I guess."

Anyway, they landed and they got through Ellis Island. And they took the train to Boston. The year was 1888.

Their stepfather met them at the station. Holding a sign in Arabic that said simply MANSOUR. *As though there was only one Mansour in the whole city. Not much survives about their first meeting except that he helped no one carry luggage, not even their sister who was small compared to the rest of the family—*

"Not a good sign," muttered Max.

—and who, Mansour found out later, as each passing day made her rosier, tireder and plumper—was going to have the baby of her beloved fellow passenger. They'd married on ship, she assured them. She wrote to the address he gave her—in Cincinnati, Ohio—

Here Kali felt his face redden, his stomach constrict, and his mind flash to Sophie. He was grateful for the cover of night.

—and when they had given up hope, a letter arrived from the father of their sister's child with train fare and a little extra to tide her over. Everyone was relieved, but something gnawed at Mansour. His sister now knew more than he did. He was ashamed. As the oldest son in the family, he felt he should have been the first to experience life's milestones.

"Sex," Max said decisively.

"Exactly," said Kali.

Mansour felt like a child; like he'd done nothing. He had to pretend to be wise in order to advise his younger brothers. Meanwhile, things weren't going well in his mother's house. There wasn't enough room to think or breathe, much less to eat or sleep. And their stepfather exacted the price of their presence in every possible way.

It broke Mansour's heart to see his mother's burdens. Broke it more that she couldn't seem to reach out to him over the chasm of her second family. Broke it further that she blamed him for her daughter's predicament. Still he was determined to stay and work and repay every cent as soon as possible, even though the stepfather's harshness never let up.

Max got up, relieved himself in an audible stream while Kali waited.

Their stepfather hired them out as peddlers. He sent them to Ahmed, who had a warehouse of linen and lace, threads, all types of dry goods, kitchenware, pots and pans. Up and down the East Coast and through the Midwest they traveled, selling, selling, selling—each one on a different route. For the first time in their lives, Mansour and his brothers were separated.

In the middle of his first winter, Mansour found himself lost on the frozen outskirts of a town in the middle of nowhere. Far away from the small, rundown hotel where groups of Arabs—peddlers like him, men and women—rented rooms when the weather was too bad to stay outside and no one offered them a spare room or a barn or shed to sleep in. But Mansour couldn't get to the hotel before dark and snow had begun to fall. In the distance, he saw a farmhouse. And he knocked on the door and asked the farmer's wife for shelter and she invited him in.

"Oldest joke in the world."

"I tell this part of the story merely to illustrate the cordiality of the American people."

They peddled for two years and paid their stepfather back and set some money aside and decided enough was enough. They'd heard that the city of Los Angeles was like the old country. Where they could grow olives and figs and anything else they wanted. Where it could be eighty-five degrees on Christmas Day. So the brothers bought a truck and drove to California and there they settled.

"A fresh start for everyone," said Max.

"Not completely."

One brother was killed by a train when the truck stalled on the tracks.

"Too bad."

And they never saw their mother again. Though they wrote to her occasionally at first. Not the stepfather: his name never appeared on an envelope. And he resented this exclusion. And added to his wife's miseries in countless small ways—reminding her that she was poor and that she needed him more than he needed her; telling her that he'd get along fine after she died, just as he'd gotten along fine enough after his first wife died. Though as it turned out, Mansour's mother outlived their stepfather by half a century. A hundred and three when she died.

"And that's why we talk of Mansour as an orphan," Kali concluded.

"How's that?" Max asked.

"He may as well have been an orphan since he made it all on his own. The story of my grandfather—he was Mansour in the story—became a family legend of Arab success and independence. And there was no room in it for my great grandmother. There was no sympathy for her, no appreciation of her position. No one talked about her. Somehow I knew I had a great grandmother back east who lived to be a hundred and three, but I never put two and two together. I never asked how my grandfather could be an orphan at the same time he had a mother who outlived him."

Kali stopped. Max waited. After a few minutes, he asked, "That's it?"

"So far."

"How does it end?"

Kali sighed. "I don't know."

They lay on their backs looking skyward, as the desert breezes brushed over their faces. As the stars traveled slowly over them in smears and patterns ranging in size and brilliance.

"When I got older I asked some of the older aunts about the inconsistencies in the family history. They looked at me like I was crazy."

For a while, each thought of his own family. Expressing some matters; leaving others inside. They spoke of their current places in the world and what came next. And each refused, in his own way, to let the night go, to let it end. Keeping alive the embers at the bottom of the fire.

And in that subtle glow, for the first time in his life, Kali felt the earth support him. Lying straight out on his back, he understood that he was a recipient of the blessings of gravity, a beneficiary of centrifugal force. And he opened his eyes to embrace the rest of the universe, to take in the stars and all the sky. And felt like he was going to throw up.

"Motion sickness," Max reassured him. "Same thing happened to me at first."

"But nothing's moving."

"The earth is. You finally noticed it, that's all."

Through squinted, guarded eyes, Kali tried again, watching one small, manageable patch of sky for as long as possible. Small, so he wouldn't be overwhelmed. He tried memorizing the positions of the stars in that limited, framed section of the universe so that, when they moved, he'd see.

Which he did. And when he did, he felt the twitch upon the thread—the infinite thread connecting him to all that was up there. The thread that was one filament in the web connecting all to all.

"Used to scare me, too," Max added.

With a little patience Kali found he could see the movements of the stars and think of other things at the same time. His family, for instance. Sophie more than his children, because he figured her thread was about the same length as his.

"Max?"

"Yeah?"

"Did I tell you my wife thinks I'm humorless?"

"What gave her that idea?"

"I usually am."

Max lit a cigarette, inhaled, coughed a preliminary cough, like an engine starting up.

"Did I tell you I have a son and a daughter?"

"Lucky man."

"Both nearsighted. It runs in the family. Sophie's side."

Max laughed to himself, inhaled, coughed.

"Philip and Layla. She's a sculptor. He sells vitamins. Also takes them. He's the picture of health."

Kali hesitated.

"She makes statues of women."

Max listened.

"Ones with breasts, lots of breasts. Sometimes necklaces of breasts. Or belts of them."

"Don't say."

"We haven't seen her in a while. She says she's coming home for Christmas. She says that every year."

"Sorry."

"She lives in a forest in a cabin. No running water, no electricity, no telephone."

"Like in Nam." Max hesitated. "So I hear."

"I wish I'd paid more attention to them. Not that I wasn't around—I was—but I was usually . . . preoccupied. Eternal questions and all that. A favoring of the general over the specific. It's been a lifelong problem."

A sound like a sigh slid through the crack of Max's opened lips.

"About my arm . . . "

"Something wrong with it?"

"The other one."

"Ah."

Max stood as a coyote howled, as the windmills stirred, as desert critters scurried along the desert floor.

"The truth hurts," Max finally said.

"Maybe. Not always."

"I wasn't in Nam."

There followed a period of not talking, not moving, not looking in the other's direction. Each trying to decide what to do or say next.

"Well, in all fairness to you, you never said you were. You simply talked about it a lot—the way we all talk about things."

"I led you to believe."

"I was a willing follower."

"Somebody asked if I lost it in Nam and I said yes."

"He probably had no right to ask in the first place."

"And I just left it at that."

"It's understandable that you wouldn't want to talk about what was undoubtedly a painful incident to remember."

"Lost it by accident, plain and simple."

"However you lost it, it's a very sad thing."

"My fault."

"It does no good to assign fault."

"I was drunk."

"Car accident?"

"Windmill."

"Oh, God."

Kali winced. He cleared his throat, as if to speak, but he could think of nothing to say. Absurdly he wondered how Max got up the pole with one arm. Max offered no further details; he lay still and quiet, breathing regularly.

To avoid the bloody images that flooded his mind, Kali focused on the sky, inspecting various constellations as they traveled over him. He had slipped into a light sleep when a rustling on the nearby ground roused him.

Whatever it was sounded relatively small and close. Hopefully, not a snake. A rabbit was all right. So was a lizard.

"Max, I forgot to ask. What's a vinegaroon?"

But Max didn't answer. For, invoking a skill he had developed during his time in the desert and before, he had willed himself to sleep. Max's snoring and other noises kept Kali awake for much of the night, giving him time to ponder his return to Sophie and his son and daughter and everything else. A few times he thought he saw a shooting star, but then he decided it was just Situe fooling around.

∞ 25 ∞

KALI SAW THEM COMING and he saw them going. So small in the distances, they looked like toys. And when they met, they sidled up like coupling snakes, only this time it was for the purpose of uncoupling. A few cars from one, a few from the other. And then a switch of track and off they went to their respective destinations. Leaving the empties behind to be picked up later.

Kali planned to take the next one going west.

"Twice a day," Max said. "About six A.M. About four P.M."

There was a romance to them. Their cars labeled with flashy letters and places they'd been and were going to or aimed for or hoped to evoke: Atlantic and Pacific, intermountain, skylight, expressway, bullet, the Great Muddy. And their few passengers perpetuated the romance: they sneaked on, sneaked off, travelers in boundless freedom. Kali brought the process back to earth: he just needed to get back to his part of Los Angeles.

He'd try to board the four o'clock. If that didn't work, he'd stay by the tracks until he got on. On the other side he could hide in the border of tamarisk trees that separated the freeway—twelve lanes total—from the tracks. The trees ran for miles, giving Kali the cover he'd need to run the entire length of the stopped trains, if necessary, looking for an open car—for he'd probably have to run, and there wouldn't be much time.

Max accompanied him as far as the last line of windmills.

"Well, I guess this is it," Kali said.

"Guess so."

"This may be inappropriate, given the circumstances," Kali fumbled, "but I'd like to leave my address with you . . . just in case you get to town again."

"Nothing to write it on."

"Of course. What was I thinking."

Max handed Kali the pack he'd put together, and Kali swung it over his back.

"Will you be staying here?"

"Not sure."

That tidal wave of feeling. Unwelcome, unfamiliar. As dangerous as trying to breathe underwater. Kali waited for it to subside before he spoke again. He had time. The train wouldn't be there for hours. Max stood by, steady, quiet.

"One last thing I wanted to tell you," Kali started tentatively as though he didn't know how to bring it up.

Max: stepping away, hard to read.

"Those darting figures that seem to come from the left and move by too fast for you to see them? The ones you can't catch up with?"

"Yeah?"

"Floaters." Shifting the weight of the pack from one side to the other, Kali continued, warming up to the subject. "I'm quite confident that's what they are."

Max listened, did not move.

"Small bits of debris—maybe cells, maybe pigment—trapped inside the eye."

"Don't like the sound of it."

"It happens when we get older, Max."

"'We'?"

"Mine look like cobwebs."

"Floaters," Max said as though committing the word to memory.

"They drift around in the jelly behind your eyeball and when they pass across your field of vision, they cast shadows. So we think we see something outside, but, actually, it's inside."

Max said nothing, though Kali waited for a response.

"And they always seem to dart away, just out of sight, when we look for them. They're always ahead."

"Floaters," Max repeated.

"But the good news is that the brain adjusts. It compensates somehow. And pretty soon you won't notice that they're there—"

Max wrapped his arm around his waist.

"—until there's another one to adjust to."

Each looked in the distance, straining to see, darting his eyes back and forth—identifying floaters, old and new.

Kali sighed. "Well, it's time."

They shook hands, left hand to left hand, the first time they'd touched. Then Max turned away and started walking and did not look back. Probably toward the canyon, Kali thought. To check on his hidden crops: to see how his little patch of corn was doing, pick the last of the tomatoes from that one fertile plant that had spawned a whole race of tomatoes, or gather the remaining fruit from his apple tree. The Sinai Apple. The only apple tree, Max had explained, that could grow in the desert.

When he came to the freeway, Kali stopped. Calculated the speed and density of the cars. Fast and infrequent. He sighed. Another first: running across a freeway in broad daylight. How had he gotten to the point in life that he stood at the edge of the slow lane of the Interstate trying to decide when to dart out? This did not fit him. Or his age. Or his profession. Or citizenship. Or nationality. Or physical condition.

He plunged into the westbound lanes. He hurled himself over the divider. He raced across those bound east. Traffic was light, but the few drivers who saw him looked in amazement or cursed at him. The pack Max had given him bounced on his back, throwing him a little off balance. It contained two half-gallons of water and three selections of jerky. Enough to get Kali on the train and through the four or five hours of his trip.

The trains had stopped, and there was an open car in front of him going in the right direction. Kali climbed in. He never thought it would be this easy. He was unexpectedly excited, like a child beginning a trip. The car was dirty, of course, but with clean dirt. And with a large sandbag in a corner, which Kali sat on. After an interval of five minutes or so, the train started moving again with a rumble, soon establishing a clicking rhythm over the tracks.

At full speed, the car swayed and the ride got rough, so Kali braced himself, pushing his back against one side of the car and his feet against the sandbag whose presence he now understood. And watched the outside rush by: desert, windmills, billboards, and little else.

But, oh those billboards: one of Situe selling coffee, one of Situe urging citizens to vote, another of Situe exhorting passengers to believe in the Lord Jesus Christ. Kali marveled at her apparent inability to resist playing jokes—the stoic, silent grandmother of his childhood, transformed. She had a much better sense of humor dead than she'd had when alive. He was glad she was there; her presence in any form was better than none and it gave him comfort and confidence.

The terrain changed.

From brown grassy hills to scorched ones with blackened oak trees that looked like they'd died an instant fiery death. From an occasional low-lying, tilt-up concrete warehouse to clusters of identical houses dropped in gullies, on hillsides, in open fields.

Kali smelled the stockyards, got a glimpse of cattle, horses, sheep. Saw the high mountains, real mountains, far back from the hills. Three times they stopped. They stayed still for ten minutes or so and headed out. Each time, Kali's heart leaped. The one time he heard a man's voice close by, he squashed himself against the inside corner of the car. But it wasn't necessary; the man came no closer, to Kali's great relief. For it occurred to him that he was not merely an illegal passenger, trespasser, hobo—which could seem bad enough—but an *Arabic* illegal passenger, trespasser, hobo. A detail of increased significance, given the fire marshal and the man in the brown suit. When he got home and had time to reflect, he'd have to rethink his mixture: how many parts Arab, how many parts husband; how many parts father; how many parts optician, church member, nonbeliever, neighbor, Chamber of Commerce member, voter (not down party lines, usually). Man?

The train seemed to go faster than before and the ride became bumpier and noisier. Kali spilled water down his front when he tried to take a drink, the whole time keeping his legs straight and his feet hard against the bag. Concerned that if he didn't, he might just bounce around the floor and toward the door and fall outside on the tracks. And be cut to bits under the wheels and no one would know what happened to him.

As the ride roughened and the rugged rhythm of the wheels clicked over the rails, and Kali's anxious thoughts approached gigantic proportions, Situe appeared. She sat on the sandbag facing Kali, impervious to anything but herself and Kali, whom she drew in to her noiseless, bumpless cocoon. She allowed him to enjoy the peace, gave him the opportunity to surrender to the calm, before speaking.

"There is something I would like to say to you."

"Of course, Situe-bitue."

"I don't think you meant to do it. You're not malicious, dear Kali, whatever else you may be."

"What are you saying? What have I done?"

"You told your new friend about your 'poor drunken grandmother, passed out on the floor.' It was humiliating."

"Max?"

"You revealed secrets. Leaving me no privacy, no pride."

"It just came out. It made sense at the time."

"Sense?"

"Part of a loving . . . tribute. . . . A recollection."

"I want to be remembered with dignity."

"But you are—"

"You see, in my lifetime, I accomplished very little."

"That's not true. Your children . . . your grandchildren."

"Mere biology."

"Your wonderful food. Your gracious hospitality. Anyone could come over at any time and you had a feast cooking on the stove."

"I was an average cook as cooks go."

"You were the center of the family. We talk about you all the time—'Situe this and Situe that.'"

"I was the sphinx on the porch. The silent woman who sat and smoked. Who did what was necessary to preserve the illusion."

"I didn't know," Kali said solemnly.

"That's because you need to remember me in a certain way: wise, steady, strong—as opposed to slow, trapped, dull—"

"Please, stop."

"Ah, well. I shouldn't get bogged down in my legacy. I left be-hind what I left behind."

"You were—and are—loved and revered."

"History will be what we need it to be."

Half of him struggled to accept her self-revelation; the other half, stuck in a railroad car hurling him back to face people who would probably believe nothing that he said, worried. About who might be waiting to drag him off to jail. Or worse.

"Time to move on," she said crisply. "Time for the Theory of Ten."

She patted him on the shoulder—he couldn't feel it, of course, and since he wasn't looking at her when she did it, he didn't know. Nevertheless, he was aware of a certain lightness of spirit, a lifting of woe.

"To assist you in your reentry into domestic life."

"I have larger things to think about than my domestic life."

"Nevertheless."

As the car rumbled along through outlying towns, through air turned sour and yellow, Situe began.

"For every trait in a couple—and sometimes in larger social units—there are ten points to go around."

Not another esoteric theory, Kali thought.

"A total of ten points for anger, for example; ten points for be-ing organized; ten points for openly expressing affection—"

"Or ten points for being torn apart with worry."

"Try not to personalize. One's focus should not always be one's self." She continued. "And every couple divides up the ten points according to their particular characteristics. Or, they wouldn't have gotten together in the first place."

Kali thought: Situe's trying to tell him that Sophie has already abandoned him.

The New Belly Dancer of the Galaxy | 245

"Take speaking your mind, for example. Suppose you have a husband and wife who give their opinion to each other all day long. Both talk all the time. Nobody lets anything go by, which means they fight all the time or say nothing of importance to each other."

"Sophie and I don't fight all the time."

"Kali, Kali, Kali: distance—psychological and intellectual—is required for this conversation to succeed. Please expand your point of view."

He would try if she said to.

"As I was saying, if they're both talking ten points worth, they'll never have time for anything else."

He nodded.

"Their house could fall apart. The children could run away and they wouldn't notice."

He said he understood.

"Just as, if one of them is quiet, closes up, never talks at all, it destroys the other one. Tears him apart. Makes him face life alone." She had left eternity and traveled back into time. Her face showed it. Her voice had trailed off.

Kali saw and asked, "Jidue?"

"Ah," said Situe, "a good man. He spoiled me. I was fifteen when I married him; he was thirty. I took whatever points I wanted."

The train entered the far-flung city limits. Maintaining its speed through the increasing density. A small forest of buildings, miles away, marked downtown.

"Well," Situe said as the engines slowed while pulling the cars up the final incline before the geography flattened and rolled itself out, "Now from the general to the specific."

"I don't think I like the sound of that."

"Take you and Sophie."

He grimaced.

"Sophie's got her feet on the ground. You've got your head in the clouds. On imagination, Sophie, one; Kali, nine. Or, to put it another way: on keeping things running on a daily basis, Sophie, nine: Kali, one."

"I disagree! What about the Oasis? I manage that by myself."

"The Theory of Ten doesn't apply—at least not yet—to matters of commerce."

"That isn't fair."

"It's not a matter of fairness. It's simply as far as I've got. It may surprise you to know that I formulated the theory. That I came up with the idea, the numbers, their allocation, et cetera, et cetera, et cetera. It's my one original contribution."

"Nothing you do or say surprises me anymore, Situe-bitue."

"My colleagues are intrigued. It has to go through a peer review process, but I think it will survive."

"I have no doubt."

"And you, dear grandson, are part of the research. Now. I shall make my concluding points, combining theory and practice, and then we can go on to other things."

"Situe," Kali said, sounding more urgent, "We're getting closer."

"I can hardly leave the theory without addressing the issue of relative sex drives."

"I'm afraid you'll have to."

"Don't you want to know how many points you have, how many Sophie has?"

"You said you didn't look."

She paused. "I didn't."

"Then how would you be in a position to know?"

"Observation of other behaviors. Deconstruction of certain conversations."

The train whistle blew. The train began to slow.

"There's no time," Kali said. "Besides, this is one area where I must tell you . . . to mind your own business."

It took ten minutes to come to a full stop. Kali filled his lungs. He stood, bracing himself this time with his legs planted firm. Situe had disappeared.

26

HIS LEGS CONTINUED to vibrate after his feet hit the ground. Which made his first steps uncertain. Which necessitated his leaning against the pole of a nearby platform. He took in his surroundings. Only once before had he been in the freight yards. Years ago when he took Sophie, and Layla and Philip as children, to buy a Christmas tree fresh off a boxcar. Straight from the forest. Not a pine needle on the floor until after New Year's Day.

He started slowly down a channel lined by trains on both sides. Came to another one and walked down it with increasing speed. Then another. And another. It was a maze. Turn right: there were trains. Turn left, there were more. He lost his sense of direction, but was encouraged by his belief, however hard to sustain, that the train yards were finite. That they had limits and that he would encounter them. He was spotted by a couple of uniformed men who didn't bother to chase him.

When he came to a concrete wall, he scaled it with relief and without interference or hesitation. On the other side was a channel—also concrete—and he jumped in. The L.A. River. Which he negotiated with relative ease. For it contained little more than an occasional shopping cart, a few marsh grasses, and a kaleidoscope of graffiti.

In a short time he was hitchhiking on Sunset Boulevard. He hardly noticed the drivers who unwisely picked him up. He was thinking of home and whether he'd actually get there. Of what would happen if he did. Of what he would say or not say. Whether he should lie or not lie. Whether he should hurt with the truth or protect (himself as well as Sophie) with a lie. And what if Sophie wouldn't let him come back? He guessed he could live at the Oasis; maybe put a cot in the back office next to the filing cabinet. He hoped Sophie's sisters wouldn't be there to watch his banishment. They'd never stop talking about it; it might be the only thing they'd ever talk about again.

By the time he reached his neighborhood, it was dark. Which was good. Because that way he could see Sophie before she saw him. He entered his yard and went to the side of his house to a window whose blinds Sophie never closed because there were shrubs—the hated oleanders he planted fifteen years before to please her—blocking the views in and out. He was dirty and sweaty and itchy, but not tired. He was much too excited to be tired.

Through this window, he saw her. Looking much more serene than he thought she would. Sitting in his armchair—not exactly *his* armchair, but the one he usually sat in—reading a book. With the light of the floor lamp falling on the pages. That wasn't where the floor lamp used to be. Was she rearranging the furniture already? Less than two weeks gone and Sophie was changing things?

And what was more, she was smiling. There was no doubt about it. And possibly laughing. Maybe laughter through tears? That would be understandable. She took a tissue from the side table and blew her nose. Well, that's better, thought Kali. The light from the floor lamp was the only light visible from the outside. None coming from the bedrooms Layla and Philip occupied when they were home. Sophie seemed alone. Where was the family when she needed them? Where were Father Gregory and representatives of the Hashanian Mutual Aid Society in the wake of his dramatic and unexpected disappearance?

Sophie switched on the evening news, watching halfheartedly as she turned the pages of her book. After a few minutes she left the room. When she returned, she was wearing her nightgown and robe, and she came to the window through which he peered and closed the blinds. Kali dropped to the ground unseen, and that's where he spent the night, going over, among other things, the Theory of Ten.

If he understood it right, Sophie, when she saw him, would be overcome with emotion while he would remain calm. For self-possession: Kali, ten; Sophie, zero. Then after she recovered and became more rational, he would tell her . . . what exactly would he tell her? There were no good choices: Cincinnati, Jane, the Empire Motor Hotel, the New Belly Dancer of the Galaxy Contest, the fire marshal, the man in the brown suit, Orville and Shadrack, the woman in the laundry, Betty and Benny and Mario, Max. And Situe's appearances. Kali cringed with shame (Kali: ten; Sophie, zero) as he anticipated Sophie's shock and hurt and disappointment and anger. No more points. He couldn't face them.

Sophie's sisters got to Sophie first. They arrived the next morning, barely dawn, before Kali awoke in the dirt below the window and had the chance to announce his return. From what he could hear through the closed, blinded window, the four sisters were taking a day trip up the coast. For Sophie's good. To get her mind off things. It was the first time Kali had been glad that the sisters' voices—expressive, unrestrained—carried through stucco.

There would be no time for Kali to accomplish gradual reentry. No possibility of a subtle broaching of delicate subjects. Or privacy. Yet, in spite of the disadvantages, Kali knew that he must contact Sophie at that instant, must not wait for further, additional developments beyond his control—like his discovery and apprehension, for example. He could be a fugitive in the eyes of the law. They could be watching him as he prepared to walk to the front of his house and step on to his front porch.

He knocked, would have done so out of respect for his wife, even if he did have his house keys. There was muffled movement from inside. Voices wondering who it could be at that hour of the morning. Anguish that seeped through the cracks around the door.

Which Sophie, flanked by her sisters, opened.

Two neighbors called 911 upon hearing the screams. For when Sophie and her sisters saw Kali—disheveled, filthy, scabby, bruised—though Sophie stared silent and stunned, her sisters, with their power-packed voices, screamed again and again:

"My God! He's here!"

"His head!"

"It's here!"

"God help us!"

"He's here!"

"Oh, God! Oh, God! Oh, God! Oh, God!"

"Kali's head!"

27

FOUR BODIES. THREE HEADS.

From the spectacular collision of two cars on the same side of a northbound freeway two weeks before, which caused the traffic to snarl and stop, which resulted in the detour that Benny and his truck took down the road on which Kali ran, desperate to escape: from that collision, the shells of two burned-out vehicles, the ashy remains of four bodies, and three heads. Accident reconstruction experts offered several possible answers to the frequently posed question, "So, where the hell is it?"

One. The force of the impact sent it flying like a batted ball— into the back of an open truck, down a well, or into the surrounding countryside. Two. Somebody stole it. Three. The guy never had a head.

Which raised all sorts of further questions like why somebody didn't turn it in if he found it; and if somebody had taken it, what did he do with it; and if it lay undiscovered in the bed of somebody's pickup, what a surprise that guy was going to get.

The identities of the three bodies with heads were determined conclusively by the fillings in their teeth and the sizes of their bicuspids, the coming together of uppers and lowers, slight malformations in a jaw. Then these identities—duly established, duly recorded—disappeared. And were never seen again by local law enforcement personnel, or discussed by them, or, it was hoped, remembered. Because of orders from higher up. For security reasons, it was rumored, and to protect certain reputations.

The one name publicly announced was Kahlil Gibran Hourani. It had been assumed, it had been concluded, that the body without the head was his. And since there was no reason not to, police gave out his name, and it was printed in the newspaper and mispronounced on the radio and the local nightly television news. And since a headless body is more interesting than one with a head, readers and watchers forgot about the others. The erroneous conclusion about the demise of Kahlil Gibran Hourani was reached because of Shadrack's greed.

For at the moment of impact Shadrack was going through Kali's wallet, hoping for a few remaining stashed bills. And when the cars—one of which was a Tyrolean blue rental sedan—careened into each other, the wallet flew from Shadrack's hands out the window—he sat on the passenger side in the front seat—and landed safe and sound, with Kali's driver's license and credit cards and membership card in the American Optician's Association intact.

The police notified the wife.

The wife contacted her children, her sisters, Father Gregory, and The Hashanian Mutual Aid Society. The mystery of their missing husband, father, brother-in-law, parishioner, and member—dissolving into tragedy. Leaving a widow, two fatherless young adults, and a burial society without a corresponding or recording secretary.

So it wasn't surprising that Sophie's powers of speech left her when Kali appeared at their front door. And that her sisters screamed, one of them also fainting. "Sophie? It's me."

A tableau in the doorway on the steps: each person astonished, staying in place.

"I don't blame you if you're upset, but can I come in? Please?"

Still no words other than Kali's.

"I know my shoes are filthy. I'll take them off. I'll leave them out here on the porch."

He bent and untied his laces, removed the shoes and, seeing the condition of his socks, removed them, too. Exposing the wide feet with the hairy toes and the high insteps that Sophie knew so well. A wave of recognition and relief engulfed her and she extended her hand, which he took, and she led him inside. And she asked her sisters to leave.

"You missed your funeral."

"Oh, Sophie," Kali said, and a tear ran down his face, stinging the one or two new open scratches.

"It was very nice. The Hashanian Mutual Aid Society took care of everything."

"Well, they're good for something then."

Standing in the middle of the den by the armchair and the side table and the relocated floor lamp, they held each other's hands. Then pressed together their shuddering bodies, Kali recognizing her touch and smell and breath; beginning to realize how little he knew about the rest of her. Situe, relaxing with a cigarette on the couch, invisible to both, left the room.

The police were notified of Kali's return, of course. And within a remarkably short time they appeared and took him to the station. They had questions. About his battered, but healing face and how it got that way. About where he was and what he did and who he did it with.

Their orders were to find out what Kali knew and then put a lid on it. No further publicity, no arrests, no nothing: that was how it came down. Find out if he could be relied on to keep quiet. Determine if he would spill the beans.

Since the exact nature of the beans had been revealed on a need to know basis, and it was deemed that the local police didn't need to know, they were somewhat hindered in their investigation. Nevertheless, they noted his wariness—the kind of circumspection that was usually a cover-up for criminal behavior. No problem. They could handle that.

So, Mr. Kahlil Gibran Hourani—can you pronounce your name for us again—why was your wallet at the scene of the accident? Why was the car you rented one of the cars destroyed in the collision? Who was in the cars when they crashed? And, of course, do you know where the head is and who it belongs to?

To each question, Kali responded that he had no idea. When they asked him who'd he'd been with during his absence, he answered, "My grandmother."

"Where does your grandmother live, Mr. Hourani?"

"Technically, she's dead. Although she came back to earth to help me." Kali looked around the room. "But I don't see her in here now. She must have someone else to take care of."

Was he crazy or was it an act?

Partly an act. Kali knew what he knew, but he also knew not to tell it. So, when asked, why Cincinnati? he said he didn't remember. When asked why *not* Cincinnati (for they knew he hadn't gone there), he said he didn't remember. When confronted with fingernail scrapings, credit card receipts, residues on his clothes, tapes from video cameras, he didn't remember.

Why the Empire Motor Hotel in Santa Vista, California? Why the Palace of Fine Arts? Why the New Belly Dancer of the Galaxy Contest? Why the Galaxy Casino? Why the desert? Why the train?

I don't remember, I don't remember; I don't remember, I don't remember. To the detectives, the district attorney, the forensic psychiatrists, and the criminal profilers.

"Tell us about Jane."

So they knew about her.

"I don't remember."

There was a break in the questioning. Kali waited for them to ask about the others. But they didn't. And the more he thought about it, the more he understood that the reason they didn't ask about the woman in the laundromat, Benny and Mario and their passengers, or Max was because they didn't know about them.

And he also concluded that the reason they didn't ask about the man in the brown suit, the fire marshal, and Orville and Shadrack was because they *did* know about them. And they didn't want him to know they knew. Or jog his memory by bringing them up.

In fact, they didn't want him to remember a thing about the last two weeks. Because there was secret business afoot, and if Kali knew, something might have to be done. And though no one there was sure what that was, no one wanted to do it.

As Kali put two and two together he began to think of himself as the luckiest man in the world. For it finally dawned on him that the four people in the two cars must have been the man in the brown suit, the fire marshal, Orville, and Shadrack. And the fireball that consumed them all also consumed their operation against him—whatever that was.

Not that he would have wished such a death on Orville and Shadrack, for whom he sustained some positive feeling. But their misfortune was Kali's good fortune. And he hadn't caused their deaths, had nothing to do with them. So he could acknowledge this unintended benefit without guilt. However it happened, the flames that tore across the freeway, blocking traffic for miles in both directions, offered him salvation. A jubilant salvation that made him want to stand and sing and shake the hands of everyone around the table.

But he restrained himself. He didn't give himself away. And neither did they. For although they indicated that they intended to press forward, what they really wanted was a way out. Kali was next in line for a lie detector test, to be followed by a Rorschach test, when Sophie made an appointment to see the chief detective.

"How much has he told you about Situe?" she asked.

"Who?"

"His dead grandmother."

"He mentioned her."

"Did he tell you that a huge white eagle appeared to him in our bedroom and offered to take him to heaven to see her; that he prepared a list of questions about the meaning of life, which he and Situe discussed after sneaking onto the porch of her old house in East Los Angeles; that she appeared to him at a meeting of the Hashanian Mutual Aid Society and he got lost while giving the secretary's report; that she smokes smokeless cigarettes that no one else can see or smell and that she blows the largest smoke rings he had ever seen?"

In case that wasn't enough, she added that Kali worried day and night about tsunamis and locust invasions and California's breaking off from the continent and sinking into the ocean. And finally, she said that, as a man of a certain age, he was having trouble in . . . that department. All of which gave the chief detective a more accurate picture of the mental state of the subject.

Kali's interrogations stopped as suddenly as they had started.

"You can go home, Mr. Hourani."

"I can?"

"The case is closed."

"What about the missing head?"

"What about it?"

A reporter doing a follow-up story on the four bodies and three heads was told the same thing.

Sophie waited for him in the lobby.

"I'm free to go."

"Good."

"Where to?"

"Home, where else?"

The party was in full swing when they arrived. It happened the way all their parties did: someone called someone and that someone called someone else and pretty soon everyone had been called. They knew what to bring and that they would stay as long as they wanted.

Kali groaned as Sophie pulled into their garage.

"Courage," said Sophie.

"Your sisters did this."

"I'm afraid so."

This is who came: Joseph and Leena Maksoud; Emmeline and Nicholas Maksoud; Salma Maksoud; Lenore and Philip Shammas; Basil and Diane Shammas; Alexander and Ellen Shammas; Mai and Thomas Kaady; Annie and Georgie Kaady; Phillis and Edward Chahine; Victoria and Saba Malouf; Nabieh and Lilllian Hourani; the uncles Joseph, Andrew, and Mark Hourani, all widowed; Joseph Saleeby and Kenny Buttras representing the Hashanian Mutual Aid Society; and Father Gregory.

They left the children at home. Who knew what Kali would do? Or say? Or look like?

This is what they brought: *tabbouleh, laban, sfeeha, fatayir bi sabaanikh; malfouf mihshi bil lahme ou riz; malfouf mihshi siyeme; kousa mihshi; waraq 'inab; riz bit feen; lubihey miqliyeh bi zeit; hummus bi tahini; tilme bi zeit; tilme bi zaa'tar; caak bi simson; nus qamar; baklawa.*

And strong, strong coffee.

At the appropriate time, Father Gregory stood in the middle of Kali and Sophie's overflowing living room and offered the following prayer:

> Your Martyrs, O Lord our God, by their struggle, have received from you the imperishable crown; because, in obtaining your strength, they destroyed the devil's tyranny, and crushed his powerless audacity.

(Oh, no, thought Kali. Not this one again. He'd heard it at two funerals of members of the Hashanian Mutual Aid Society. He wondered if Father Gregory had said it at *his* funeral.)

> Just as Kahlil, your willing servant, in his recent—ah—struggles—fought his earthly and spiritual fires, literally and figuratively, crushing those evil forces with his—ah—physical and devotional strengths, aided by the instrumentalities provided by Our Lord God, including modern devices such as the telephone, railway, automobile, et cetera, et cetera, et cetera.
>
> Accordingly, we welcome home dear Kahlil, prodigal son, to the womb of his loving family. In particular to his loving wife, Sophie; his daughter, Layla; and his son, Philip.

In response to which Philip, tan, robust, muscular, smiled a gleaming, white smile, while Layla, dark and less morose than usual, stood beside him. Would they forgive him, Kali wondered?

Could they continue to think of him as their father? Would they believe he risked his life to save them?

Kali's eyes sought Sophie's. He could barely breathe as a reception line formed and in ones and twos his family and friends passed by him. Trying not to stare; wondering what to say. He looked around for Situe, careful not to step back, since she often positioned herself behind him and he didn't want to crush her toes.

Long after the party was over, long after the leftover food had been divided and the kitchen sink and counters scoured by a few devoted friends, long after Layla and Michel had gone to sleep in their old rooms, in the dark of the house, Sophie and Kali lay awake in bed. The first time in two weeks they had been together that way.

"It's a good thing our parents aren't alive to see this," Kali said.

"In some ways," Sophie responded, unusually calm, Kali thought. So far, there'd been not a word of recrimination or anger. No probing, no cross-examination. For which he was grateful as well as surprised.

"I look at you, this woman I've been married to for thirty years. And you seem different."

"You finally opened your eyes."

"Forgive me, Sophie. I didn't mean to be so blind."

Sophie turned her head and looked directly at him. "What did you tell Situe about me?"

"I didn't think you believed she was here."

"I don't. But I want to know what you said."

"I really didn't have to say much. She knew about you already. . . . she's in heaven, you see."

"I thought you didn't believe in heaven."

"I don't."

"If you had said something, what would it have been?"

"Not what I would say now."

"One more question."

"Yes?"

"Did she see us . . . together?"

"She said she didn't."

"And you believe her?"

He paused.

"I think so."

28

AFTER ALL THAT HAD HAPPENED, Kali found that he knew things. And he knew that he knew things. Though exactly what, he couldn't say. For in its present state, this fledgling knowledge didn't lend itself to words. But in the initial days after his return and for some time thereafter, when he awoke in the morning, he felt it coating his skin. His mind. His heart.

He thought of it as an invisible cloak. And he hoped that, as time passed, he would absorb it into himself. He wished he'd weighed himself the first day he felt it to see if he was heavier, like people are weighed before and after death to see if there's a difference. To see if there's a soul.

Knowing that something extra, Kali resumed most of his ordinary activities. He reopened the Oasis, taking down the "Closed for Vacation Sign" Sophie had taped to the inside of the door. It hadn't fooled anybody. When he walked through the small parking lot, eyes from the small neighboring shops followed him. For a while, he was an object of curiosity. But the world kept spinning and there was more news, good and bad, and Kali again slipped into the background.

Giving him time to reflect upon what it was that he knew. For the world around him didn't look the same as before. He saw the familiar objects and events of his everyday life through a different lens. Adjustments in tone, in intensity, in duration, in significance—these are what he experienced. Though sometimes he was blindsided by the unfamiliar like when, out of the corner of his eye, he thought he saw the man in the brown suit or maybe Shadrack or the fire marshal. Kali would spin around, but no one was ever there.

His world inside was different, too. Yet still he couldn't say how; he could only acknowledge there was a difference. The one person most likely to help clear the matter up, he couldn't find.

"Situe's gone."

"It's about time," Sophie answered. She sat on the end of the couch in the den, her feet curled under her, reading.

"I'll miss her."

"You still have a lot to do here."

"I have a terrible ache where she used to be."

"You'll get through it."

She reopened her book, read a page, smiled.

"I won't survive if I can't float away sometimes."

"Then by all means, Kali, float."

He sat in the armchair, his feet up on the stool, watching her.

"What are you reading?"

"Jokes," she said, muffling her rising laugh, which was the way she always laughed. "I've been reading them for quite some time."

"Really?"

"Long before you lost your memory and disappeared. I kept the books on my nightstand. Sometimes four or five. They made quite a pile."

"I never noticed."

"I know."

And she knew something else, too: laughing people have fewer rashes. On the advice of her dermatologist, who'd taken a special interest in her condition, she got joke books. And when Kali was gone, while she waited—thinking he'd run off with another woman, for she discovered almost immediately there was no conference in Cincinnati for the American Optician's Association—she devoured volume after volume: jokes for all occasions; patriotic jokes; religious jokes; jokes about money, celebrities, growing up, city jokes, country jokes. Usually several books a day. Though, given the unfortunate circumstances, it was hard for her to laugh without restraint and she missed punch lines and developed rashes under both arms and between the toes of one foot. She carried a slim paperback of military jokes in her purse when she went to the police station to discuss her husband's future.

"You know, Kali, when the bottom dropped out—I didn't fall the whole way."

"I'm glad," Kali said simply.

"I fell about halfway. That was all. My sisters were with me, of course."

"Of course."

"They're still furious with you, in case you didn't know."

"I'm not surprised."

For against the silent curses of his sisters-in-law, he had alleged, asserted, defended nothing, which seemed to enrage them further. They came over less frequently now and Sophie didn't seem to miss them.

She set the book in her lap. "Kali, I have to ask you one question. Was there another woman?"

"Sophie, I can tell you in all honesty, no." Because, as he sat there then, in his current condition, knowing things he now knew, there had been no one else.

"You're sure?"

"I'm sure."

"The police say they know everything from the time we got to the airport to when you left some abandoned building down south. After that, they lost your trail."

"My trail?"

"Your psychiatrist thinks you were having some sort of delusion connected to your obsession with Situe."

"He's not my psychiatrist. I only saw him once."

From his first moment home, Kali had said very little and Sophie hadn't pressed him. Now he wanted very much to talk about what he'd done, where he'd been, and what it meant—in metaphorical and not literal terms, of course—but he felt tied up, blocked.

Sophie resumed reading. She sat very still, turning pages, nonsmiling, nonlaughing. Kali sensed that more was needed.

"Sophie, my dear, let me tell you about the Theory of Ten," he began in a deliberative voice hoping to overcome her resistance, "according to which there could never have been anyone but you . . . or someone exactly like you."

He explained the theory, enthusiastically illustrating it with incidents from their married life. Showing what a perfect fit they were.

"You mean," Sophie asked, "when it comes to being philosophical, you're a nine and I'm a one?"

"I think that's accurate."

"How about when it comes to being impractical and unrealistic?"

"Point well taken. Which, I think, necessitates an adjustment in one of our other scores: oral argument. Kali, five; Sophie, five."

She looked pleased.

"How about the ability to be happy?" she asked.

"Neither of us has done very well on that one."

"How about the ability to relax?"

"An essential trait, of course."

"How about trying to heal thyself?"

"'Thyself'?"

"My dermatologist said, 'Patient, heal thyself.' I like that word."

"It sounds as though your dermatologist is—"

"—a *very* remarkable man."

It was the third Sunday after his return. Kali, who couldn't yet face Saints Peter and Paul, stayed home. And Sophie with him.

"Thank you," he'd said to her.

"You're welcome. Besides, I don't enjoy being stared at either."

"Of course not."

"And people are still talking—"

"True."

"You know, Kali," Sophie said slowly, "I think it's significant that you got your mind back when Situe went away. Or when you thought she went away. She's been dead for years, you know that now, don't you, Kali?"

"I never said she hadn't died."

"And she didn't come back. She was never here."

Kali turned his head aside—a gesture much used by Situe to avoid a situation or a feeling she didn't desire. It was too much to ask—this disavowal. He must sidestep; he said nothing.

"It's over now, Kali. You're back with your family. With me. You're back at the Oasis. Father Gregory told me he blesses you in his silent prayers. That's good of him, isn't it?"

"Well, it *is* his job."

Looking squarely into his face, Sophie said, "You need to get your tooth fixed."

Later, upstairs in bed, while Sophie slept with the second edition of *Tasteful Ethnic Humor* open on her chest, and the outside breezes rode through the window, cooling the silky surface of the covers, Kali thought again of the Theory of Ten.

Could it be expanded to apply to the world at large? Could states or tribes or countries be rated on the presence or absence of various characteristics? On the ability to maintain peace? The ability to take care of its people? He imagined Situe presenting the theory to a committee of her peers and hoped she'd let him know the outcome.

29

IT TOOK SEVERAL TRIES to find the laundromat. And when Kali went in, the old woman and her things were gone. Gone without a trace. The five hundred dollars he carried inside a plastic bag inside a paper bag—to give to her—back to the bank, he guessed.

He'd solved the question of denomination after some thought. Not hundreds—too easy to lose, too easy to steal. Ones were too bulky, though they made a wad Benny would have loved. A combination of tens and twenties would have been best, but she might confuse the values of the bills, and she was already confused enough.

Most coke machines took five-dollar bills, so Kali settled on fives. He redeposited them the next day in the same bank at the same window with the same teller eyeing him for an explanation which he did not give.

He never tried to contact the others: Jane, Benny, Max. As to Jane and Benny, what could he say? What could he expect? Why would they want to see him?

And Max? A good man. To be esteemed. But he wouldn't see him either. Max and the desert had done what they were supposed to do. No need for more.

He took a perverse pleasure in knowing that there was no possibility of seeing the fire marshal and the man in the brown suit.

The thought of them shrunk his stomach to the size of an ice cube—and burned hard and hot inside. For Orville and Shadrack, he would have offered a prayer, if he believed. He wondered which one of them didn't have a head.

Not all Kali's scars faded away. Not all his inner aches disappeared. But what he knew became clearer in a pattern of two steps forward and one step back.

He reserved the right to dream. Publicly or privately, as the spirit moved him. And became a dreamer who strove to see the world clearly.

A dreamer who took his best shot, regardless of what he saw.

A dreamer who knew there were no guarantees.

Which meant, among other things, that he cherished each foot hitting the pavement and the sun rising in the east. And that he put money in other people's parking meters in front of his store, once he got the business up and running again.

He continued to acknowledge—no, be alarmed by—the tsunamis, earthquakes, famines, and holocausts of the world. And nearly stopped breathing when he thought of them. But since it did no good to faint dead away, he started again before he turned blue.

He embraced the changing seasons and the beginnings and ends of life in them.

And he worked on his sense of humor, which Sophie bolstered by reading him jokes. Of which she became a well-known collector and deliverer, knocking them dead at the Annual Talent Show Fund-raiser at Saints Peter and Paul.

One matter did not fit into Kali's new scheme of things and that was the Hashanian Mutual Aid Society. He resigned.

His sources of joy? Like many, his children. Or what he thought they were. Special dispensations for them. One area where blindness was acceptable: a salve, an unguent, a spiritual necessity. An honorable retreat.

Sophie? There was an accommodation on both sides, brought about by the recognition of love under threat of permanent mutual loss.

"What if . . . " Kali started to say to her, stumbling over choked fear.

"If we both . . . " she said in return, stopped by the same choking.

And often they discussed the Theory of Ten, measuring their progress and lack of it.

Adventures, excitement, exploration continued. Kali went around the world: to Botswana, Lima, San Francisco, Maine—in person or by dream, depending on his finances.

He achieved ebb and flow. He got a sense of rhythm. And when the sadness of the world washed over him, he reminded himself that moonlight shines on all doors. When carried away by euphoria, he sought the poor, because only a poor man knows the meaning of poverty. Though sometimes he couldn't tell what was sorrow and what was joy, what was pleasure and what was pain—so profound were his feelings.

Which is why he wasn't bothered at first by the growing pressure in his chest, pushing its way out like there wasn't enough room for it inside, like it was too large for the container trying to hold it. He thought it another of the many passionate, intense experiences that had informed his life.

The drop to his knees did not alter this perception.

He caught the asphalt open handed, palms down. He lowered himself gently and lay on his side with a cheek borne firmly by the ground. He did not struggle. Not for breath, not to get up, not to readjust his place in the world. He felt no fear. Surprise?

Yes, there was that. For in the accomplishment of Situe's first two directives—seeing, taking his best shot—he occasionally forgot about the third: no guarantees. As to the aims themselves or, if achieved, the time allotted to enjoy them.

As he lost his focus and strength, allowing the earth to enfold him for a second time, he enjoyed an immersion in the moment so complete it defied reflection. He *was* his body; he *was* his spirit. He *was* what was happening then and there.

He saw Sophie, Layla, and Philip; he heard their voices. They were behind him on the same path. Looking ahead in his direction.

If only he had had more time: ah, but he didn't. That was the point, after all. No going back; no stopping. So for his family, his beloved family, a good-bye. Greetings and salutations he reserved for Situe who, ahead of him, had turned around and waited with outstretched hand. And this time, instead of the plump hand of a small boy, the hand of a man, albeit imperfect, accepted her welcome.

She pulled him up and he, assuming they would go together down the same path, attempted to walk by her side.

"Not so fast."

Some kind of final test, he wondered? Some kind of entry ceremony or rite of passage?

"Collect yourself, grandson. Pull yourself together."

Which he did, obedient to the end. Reining in the wandering senses which itched to explore the other side; putting the parts of himself back together such that the reintegrated, reoriented Kahlil Gibran Hourani stood tall and looked around.

"Is there a problem?" he asked.

"Nothing fatal."

"Bad news?"

"There's news. It's neither bad nor good."

"Please don't keep me in suspense, Situe-bitue."

"You're staying awhile."

"How long?"

"That's where we began, dear Kali."

"Something I did?"

"No, no. A mistake in the timing. Sometimes our clocks are off. What can I say?"

"Did I have a brush with death?"

"Call it what you will."

"So I have a second chance?"

"And a third and a fourth—as many as you decide you have."

"I'll take them," Kali said and his fingers and hands and feet and lungs and heart and everything else filled with life. And he looked behind him on the path and saw that it was full of possibilities and sorrows; and he looked at Situe who, for the first time since the dream, looked exactly like she used to look when she was his flesh and blood grandmother on earth. And she gazed at him with what could only be called infinite love as she moved away.

"It's a cruel world, Kali. Enjoy."

FRANCES KHIRALLAH NOBLE, a lawyer, lives in southern California. She is the author of *The Situe Stories*, which
is also published by Syracuse University Press.